DATE DUE

FEB 2 3 2004	11-16 6:10
AUS. 500	11-17 4:59
11-8-05 5:23	11-18 2:43
11-8-05 3:09	6-27 - 4:14
11-8-05 9:00	JUL 1 0 2008
11-9-05 8:00	AUG 1 3 2009
11-9-05 9:00	
11-10-05 10:50	
11-10-05 7:48	
11-10-05 7:53	
11-10-05 8:41	
11-13 - 12:17	
11-14 11:48	
11-14 4:00	
11-15 5:04	
11-15 5:37	

BRODART, CO.   Cat. No. 23-221-003

Literary Lives

General Editor: **Richard Dutton**, Professor of English, Lancaster University

This series offers stimulating accounts of the literary careers of the most admired and influential English-language authors. Volumes follow the outline of the writers' working lives, not in the spirit of traditional biography, but aiming to trace the professional, publishing and social contexts which shaped their writing.

Published titles include:

Literary Lives
Series Standing Order ISBN 0–333–71486–5 hardcover
Series Standing Order ISBN 0–333–80334–5 paperback
(*outside North America only*)

You can receive future titles in this series as they are published by placing a standing order. Please contact your bookseller or, in case of difficulty, write to us at the address below with your name and address, the title of the series and one of the ISBNs quoted above.

Customer Services Department, Macmillan Distribution Ltd, Houndmills, Basingstoke, Hampshire RG21 6XS, England

Kate Chopin

A Literary Life

Nancy A. Walker
Professor of English
Vanderbilt University

First published 2001 by
PALGRAVE
Houndmills, Basingstoke, Hampshire RG21 6XS and
175 Fifth Avenue, New York, N.Y. 10010
Companies and representatives throughout the world

PALGRAVE is the new global academic imprint of
St. Martin's Press LLC Scholarly and Reference Division and
Palgrave Publishers Ltd (formerly Macmillan Press Ltd).

ISBN 0–333–73788–1 hardback
ISBN 0–333–73789–X paperback

This book is printed on paper suitable for recycling and
made from fully managed and sustained forest sources.

A catalogue record for this book is available
from the British Library.

Library of Congress Cataloging-in-Publication Data
Walker, Nancy A., 1942–
    Kate Chopin: a literary life / Nancy A. Walker.
        p. cm. — (Literary lives)
    Includes bibliographical references (p.) and index.
    ISBN 0–333–73788–1
    1. Chopin, Kate, 1851–1904. 2. Women and literature–
–Louisiana—History—19th century. 3. Authors, American–
–19th century—Biography. 4. Louisiana—Biography. I. Title.
II. Literary lives (Palgrave (Firm))

PS1294.C63 Z94 2001
813'.4—dc21
[B]
                                                            2001021747

10   9   8   7   6   5   4   3   2
10   09 08 07 06 05 04 03 02

Printed and bound in Great Britain by
Antony Rowe Ltd, Chippenham, Wiltshire

Contents

List of Abbreviations

CEKC Alice Hall Petry (ed.), *Critical Essays on Kate Chopin*. New York: G. K. Hall, 1996.

CW Per Seyersted (ed.), *The Complete Works of Kate Chopin*. Baton Rouge: Louisiana State University Press, 1969.

KCC Thomas Bonner, Jr (ed.), *The Kate Chopin Companion*. New York: Greenwood Press, 1988.

KCM Per Seyersted and Emily Toth (eds), *A Kate Chopin Miscellany*. Natchitoches: Northwestern State University Press, 1979.

KCPP Emily Toth, Per Seyersted and Cheyenne Bonnell (eds), *Kate Chopin's Private Papers*. Bloomington: Indiana University Press, 1998.

Rankin Daniel S. Rankin, *Kate Chopin and Her Creole Stories*. Philadelphia: University of Pennsylvania Press, 1932.

Seyersted Per Seyersted, *Kate Chopin: a Critical Biography*. Baton Rouge: Louisiana State University Press, 1969.

Toth Emily Toth, *Kate Chopin*. New York: William Morrow, 1990.

VV Emily Toth (ed.), *A Vocation and a Voice*. New York: Penguin Books, 1991.

Chronology of Chopin's Life

1850 Born Katherine O'Flaherty in St Louis, Missouri, 8 February.

1855 Enrolls in Academy of the Sacred Heart. Father killed in railway accident.

1863 Half-brother George dies while a Confederate soldier in the Civil War.

1868 Graduates from Academy of the Sacred Heart.

1869 Writes first known short story, 'Emancipation: A Life Fable' (unpublished).

1870 Marries Oscar Chopin. Honeymoon in Europe, June–September. Chopins settle in New Orleans.

1871 Son Jean Baptiste born.

1873 Son Oscar Charles born. Brother Thomas killed in buggy accident.

1874 Son George Francis born.

1876 Son Frederick born.

1878 Son Felix Andrew born.

1879 Chopins move to Cloutierville, Louisiana. Daughter Lélia born.

1882 Oscar Chopin dies.

1884 Returns to St Louis with her children.

1885 Mother, Eliza O'Flaherty, dies.

1888 Begins writing seriously.

1889 Publishes first work, 'If It Might Be' (poem). Publishes first story, 'A Point at Issue!'.

1890 Publishes first novel, *At Fault*, at her own expense.

1891 Completes novel, *Young Dr. Gosse and Théo*; later destroys manuscript.

1891–93 Stories published in *Youth's Companion*, *Vogue*, *Harper's Young People*, *Century*

1894 Publishes *Bayou Folk* (stories).

1897 Publishes *A Night in Acadie* (stories).

1899 Publishes *The Awakening*.

1900 Appears in first edition of *Who's Who in America*. Publisher declines to issue *A Vocation and a Voice*.

1902 Last story, 'Polly,' published in *Youth's Companion.*
1904 Dies in St Louis, 22 August.

1
The Context of a Literary Life

A glance at the chronology of Kate Chopin's life suggests a personal history that divides neatly into two parts: the first consisting of the Catholic-school education appropriate to her upper-middle-class Irish and French family, marriage to a young businessman with a promising future, and the birth of six children between 1871 and 1879; and the second devoted to professional authorship. Indeed, one scholar has written, 'Chopin in her twenties and thirties, married and bearing six children, was living one sort of life but quite another through her forties and early fifties, writing, publishing, and involved in literary society until her death in 1904.'[1] And Chopin herself, in her diary, seemed to differentiate her life as wife and daughter from her life as a writer. In 1895, she mused about the changes in her life following the deaths of her husband (1882) and her mother (1885):

> If it were possible for my husband and my mother to come back to earth, I feel that I would unhesitatingly give up every thing that has come into my life since they left it and join my existence again with theirs. To do that, I would have to forget the past ten years of my growth – my real growth. But I would take back a little wisdom with me; it would be the spirit of perfect acquiescence.
>
> (Seyersted, 58–59)

For a critic more than a century later to take seriously such a sharp division, however, would be both incorrect and misleading. Much in Chopin's life before she moved back from Louisiana to her native

1

city of St Louis, Missouri, in 1884 had prepared her to become the published writer she was in the 1890s, and most of the fiction that she wrote drew, in turn, on her experience in and observation of Louisiana – both the cosmopolitan Creole life of New Orleans and the rural, largely Cajun (Acadian) culture of Cloutierville, in Natchitoches Parish, where her only daughter was born and where she lived for a year and a half after her husband's death. Further, to separate completely Chopin's life as a wife and mother from her life as a writer is to suggest that writing was for her a compensatory activity, something she turned to in widowhood, or that following the death of Oscar Chopin she was forced to find a socially sanctioned means of supporting herself and her children. Neither assumption is borne out by the facts of Chopin's life. While it is true that her return to St Louis gave her access to intellectual circles that encouraged her art, these associations merely fostered talents that Chopin had been exercising in less public ways for many years.

This is not to suggest, however, that American women in the nineteenth century were routinely encouraged to be professional writers, or professional artists of any sort. Chopin herself reflected the cultural ambivalence about women's artistic production in her best-known work, *The Awakening* (1899). Her central character, Edna Pontellier, has talent as a painter, but her family and friends assume this to be an avocation, a pleasant adjunct to her real role as wife, mother, and hostess. Only Mlle Reisz recognizes that Edna may have more serious aspirations, and warns her that 'the artist must possess the courageous soul'.[2] Mlle Reisz, a highly skilled pianist, is portrayed in such a way as to suggest the social costs of that courage. Upon her first appearance in the novel, the narrator describes her as 'a disagreeable little woman, no longer young, who had quarreled with almost every one, owing to a temper which was self-assertive and a disposition to trample upon the rights of others.... She was a homely woman ... [who] had absolutely no taste in dress, and wore a batch of rusty black lace with a bunch of artificial violets pinned to the side of her hair" (*CW*, 905). Such a description echoes the many unflattering portraits of the nineteenth-century 'bluestocking', so devoted to her writing that she neglects both her femininity and her proper female role. Although by the end of *The Awakening* Mlle Reisz has become Edna's trusted confidante, and her music a source of joy and solace,

Chopin's depiction of her betrays cultural anxieties about the woman wholeheartedly devoted to her art.

Since the early 1970s, during the period when the work of Kate Chopin achieved the prominence it had been denied following her death in 1904, scholars have reassessed the part that women writers played in the development of nineteenth-century American literature, the constraints under which they wrote, and their motivations for becoming authors. While there had never been any doubt that many women actively published poetry and fiction during the century, and that their work was quite popular – Susan Warner's 1850 novel *The Wide, Wide World* defined the category of 'best seller' – comments such as Nathaniel Hawthorne's 1855 dismissal of the 'd——d mob of scribbling women', the exclusion of widely read literature from the realm of 'real' art, and the creation of the academically defined canon of nineteenth-century literature had obscured this fact by the middle of the twentieth century. In 1971, Ann Douglas Wood, one of the first scholars to investigate the circumstances of women's literary production in the nineteenth century, published an article titled 'The "Scribbling Women" and Fanny Fern: Why Women Wrote'. Wood argued that a male critical establishment had dictated that women were not to represent themselves as deliberate, conscious artists, but rather to write 'naturally', without pretense to artifice, and preferably out of moral or economic necessity. In Wood's view, this presented women with a paradox: 'On the one hand, economic necessity was a better excuse for writing than a sheer burning unladylike desire for self-expression. On the other hand, it was ... taboo for the lady writers to be what Hawthorne realized they were: shrewd competitors in the literary market.'[3] In other words, women were constrained to hide their true motivations behind a mask of innocence.

Fanny Fern (pseudonym of Sara Willis Parton), who serves as one of Wood's central examples, is a complex figure whose career has parallels with the later one of Kate Chopin. If we are to believe the outline of her life provided by her autobiographical novel *Ruth Hall* (1854), Fern did begin to write out of economic necessity and with moral purpose. As a young widow with two small children, she attempted the few approved ways for a white, middle-class woman to earn a living before she found that she had talent for writing short columns on motherhood, marriage, and religious faith for

Boston newspapers. Whether her tone was sentimental or sarcastic – she was equally skilled in both modes – Fern wrote with a clear sense of right and wrong, thus fulfilling woman's 'natural' role as moral exemplar. Fanny Fern further seems to fit Wood's thesis when, in her preface to the first collection of her columns, *Fern Leaves* (1853), she professes not to have really written a book at all:

> I never had the slightest intention of writing a book. Had such a thought entered my mind, I should not long have entertained it. It would have seemed presumptuous. What! *I*, Fanny Fern, write a book? I never could have believed it possible. How, then, came the book to be written? some one may ask. Well, that's just what puzzles me. I can only answer in the dialect of the immortal "Topsy," "I 'spect it growed!" And, such as it is, it must go forth.

No such disclaimer, however, prefaced *Ruth Hall* when it was published the following year, and it is doubtful that such a distancing of the writer from the text would have stemmed the flood of negative criticism that greeted the novel. Like Chopin several decades later, Fanny Fern had overstepped the bounds of what a woman should write. Whereas Chopin's *Awakening* offended taste by allowing its heroine social and sexual freedom, *Ruth Hall* demonstrated the author's lack of filial piety by including scathing portraits of her father and brother, both of them well-known in the publishing world (her pseudonym was quickly penetrated). After *The Awakening* was denounced as immoral, Chopin issued a statement similar in tone to Fern's *Fern Leaves* preface:

> Having a group of people at my disposal, I thought it might be entertaining (to myself) to throw them together and see what would happen. I never dreamed of Mrs. Pontellier making such a mess of things and working out her own damnation as she did. If I had had the slightest intimation of such a thing I would have excluded her from the company. But when I found out what she was up to, the play was half over and it was too late.

While it is difficult to know precisely how Fern's and Chopin's statements would have been understood by nineteenth-century readers, their facetiousness seems obvious to contemporary readers, and suggests that such denials of responsibility for their work were far more playful than serious. Further, Fanny Fern was as audacious in her writing as was Chopin. Both authors questioned the conventional view of marriage as the ideal state for women, and condemned religious hypocrisy. Although the sexual freedom that Chopin gave some of her female characters in the 1890s would have been unthinkable at mid-century, Fern openly advocated women's economic independence, and favored clothing reform. Neither writer allowed gender to prevent her from expressing deeply held views, and neither was sincerely apologetic for what she wrote.

When Judith Fetterley edited *Provisions: A Reader from 19th-Century American Women* in 1985, she took issue with Wood's interpretation of women's relationship to the writing process, arguing that a number of nineteenth-century writers neither disavowed artistic intention nor professed to be writing exclusively for economic or moral reasons. In the introduction to *Provisions*, Fetterley stresses the variety of relationships to authorship that women express in their work, finding, in contrast to Wood, that many women 'manifest a considerable degree of comfort with the act of writing and with the presentation of themselves as writers', and going so far as to posit that 'mid-nineteenth-century American women writers were more comfortable with the idea of writing than were their male counterparts'.[4] Fetterley acknowledges that the writers whose work she includes in *Provisions* tended to work in short forms rather than the novel, 'the more traditional, conventional, and "big" form for nineteenth-century fiction, ... the most literary and artistic'. Writing 'an essay, a sketch, or a letter' instead of a novel could have altered the writer's relationship with the work, Fetterley suggests: 'aiming at less than art and lower than immortality,' the writer of short fiction 'may have avoided some of the psychic trauma that afflicted those who aimed higher' (6). Although Kate Chopin once commented about the short story and the novel, 'I do not consider one form of more value than the other', she also stated that 'the novel does not seem to me now my natural form of expression,' and remarked about her never-published novel *Young Dr. Gosse and Théo* that 'it was written ... before I had found my way to the short story' (Toth, 245). It is certainly the case that during Chopin's lifetime she was far more successful with short stories than with novels; of the three novels she completed, one was published at her own expense and a second was destroyed after she failed to find a publisher for it.

Yet the century that culminated in the publication of Chopin's *The Awakening* was one in which many women wrote and published novels, stories, and sketches, often enjoying long careers as professional writers, and because Kate Chopin both benefitted and suffered from the experiences of those who had gone before her, it is worth establishing a context for her brief late-century career. As literacy and literary markets expanded during the century, debate increased about who should be included in the intellectual life of the nation. The growth of cities, such as Chopin's St Louis, played a role in the development of sharp social-class divisions, and accompanied the spread of middle-class gentility and propriety, which, paradoxically, attempted to dictate a private, domestic role for white women. At the same time, the establishment of nationally distributed journals, most notably *Atlantic* (1857), *Century* (1869), and *Scribner's* (1870), helped to define literary standards; as magazine historian Frank Luther Mott has written: 'for a large section of the American public, whatever the *Atlantic* printed was literature'.[5] Thus, even as women's access to intellectual and artistic circles expanded, the codification of both literary standards and women's cultural role made women's relationship to literary production more complicated. Fortunately for Kate Chopin, the regional sketches with which she began her publishing career were in great demand in the final decades of the century; on the other hand, late-century Victorian notions of feminine propriety had a devastating effect on the novel that should have been the capstone of her career.

When the history of nineteenth-century American literature began to be revised in the 1970s and 1980s, especially as feminist and new historicist scholarship focused on works and authors not canonized – or even completely forgotten – in the preceding decades, many scholars assumed that authorship for virtually all nineteenth-century women was fraught with difficulty and self-doubt or, as Wood had suggested, with deception. The examples of the few well-known women writers of the period, in fact, lent credence to such concepts. Emily Dickinson was perhaps the most extreme case, seldom acknowledging to the world beyond Amherst, Massachusetts, that she was a poet, and refusing most social interaction once she was an adult.

Harriet Beecher Stowe claimed that her 1852 anti-slavery novel, *Uncle Tom's Cabin*, was divinely inspired, and Louisa May Alcott, known to most readers for her novel *Little Women* (1868–69), was the economic mainstay of her family. Also contributing to the stereotyping of women writers of the period was the common characterization of their work as 'sentimental' and 'domestic', the former because of style and plot elements that highlighted the emotional or the sensational, and the latter based on the propensity of women's fiction to follow a plot line that ends with the heroine's marriage, and to emphasize the values associated with home and family. Such generalizations suggested that women indeed shied from intentional authorship, and that when they did write they bowed to convention by writing about subjects appropriate to their gender in properly feminine terms.

Several factors have allowed us to break through these generalizations to a more accurate and nuanced assessment of Chopin's predecessors. One of these is a recognition of the complexity of the concept of the woman writer in the nineteenth century. Women, like men, were for much of the century not self-identified as just poets and/or fiction writers; hard and fast distinctions between forms of writing that counted as 'art' and those that did not were not developed until late in the century. American writers wrote history, political and philosophical treatises, newspaper columns, and literary criticism. Some genres, such as stories for children and homemaking manuals, were dominated by female writers, and there is every reason to believe that most of these writers regarded such forms as every bit as important as that 'most literary and artistic form' – the novel – at least until after the Civil War. Further, many writers – both women and men – produced work in several genres rather than being committed to a single form (although it should be said that poetry occupied a pre-eminent position in the minds of most). Lydia Maria Child, for example, in the 1820s alone – the first decade of her career – published two historical novels, a number of short stories, several collections of stories for children, and her well-known homemaking manual, *The American Frugal Housewife*. In the following decade, Caroline Kirkland began her career with *A New Home*, a fictionalized account of frontier settlement; she went on to write short stories and sketches for such periodicals as *Godey's Lady's Book*, and later became a journalist and magazine editor. Fanny Fern wrote newspaper columns throughout the 1850s and 1860s, but also published two novels and several books of stories for children. And although Louisa May Alcott was known for many years solely as the author of juvenile fiction such as *Little Women*, she was at least as committed to writing sensational thrillers, and she published poetry, essays, and two novels for adults. Such multi-genre careers were the rule rather than the exception; it was not until the latter part of the nineteenth century that status in the literary world was more readily accorded to those who published novels than to those who published travel writing, such as Margaret Fuller's *Summer on the Lakes* (1848), or religious treatises, such as Catharine Beecher's *Letters on the Difficulties of Religion* (1836).

Further, readers have begun to regard the language that women used to speak in and about their writing as rhetorically manipulated to serve a purpose rather than taking it at face value. Just as the 'apologetic' comments by Fern and Chopin cited earlier can be read as facetious rather than sincere, so other statements about women's work and careers can be understood as linguistic poses to satisfy convention instead of candid expressions. In *Doing Literary Business*, Susan Coultrap-McQuin analyzes the relationship between women writers and their editors and publishers, showing that they were frequently shrewd about the advancement of their careers, but pointing also to the way in which their public rhetoric was frequently designed to disguise this fact. For example, Grace Greenwood (pseudonym of Sara Jane Lippincott), whose long career included travel narratives, stories for children, and journalism, and who was an outspoken proponent of the abolition of slavery and of prison reform, wrote that 'true feminine genius is ever timid, doubtful, and clingingly dependent, ... A true woman shrinks instinctively from greatness'. And of the poet Louisa Chandler Moulton, her contemporary Harriet Prescott Spofford wrote that she '[cared] nothing for place or power, for social rank and position, or for wealth; of childlike nature throughout life, a triumphant woman, but always a child'.[6] Such public professions of 'true womanhood' could deflect attention from ambition and self-satisfaction, positing instead demure women who bore no responsibility for their success. Yet even during the nineteenth century, it seems likely that most readers would have understood these descriptions as the conventions they in fact were – ritualized statements for public consumption, not revelations of reality.

Just as these statements employ certain terms that would have signaled to a nineteenth-century reader the qualities associated with conservative notions of true womanhood – terms such as 'timid', 'dependent', 'instinct', and 'childlike' – so women writers used plotting and language in their own works in such a way as to tell more than one story at the same time. What Susan K. Harris terms the 'cover plot' of many novels was more or less deliberately designed to meet the expectations of some readers, while a more subversive story unfolded, conveying a radically different sense of women's abilities and priorities. In Susan Warner's *Queechy* (1852), for example, the cover plot resembles that of a fairy tale as the orphaned heroine, Fleda, having endured a poverty which serves to make her even more saintly than had her grandfather's teachings, eventually marries an English aristocrat. Much of the novel, however, details Fleda's development as the efficient manager of her deceased grandfather's farm, overseeing several male workers and effectively becoming the head of the household. Simultaneously, she becomes a published poet. Yet Warner is careful to associate Fleda with flowers, which she is skilled at growing, and with the preparation of food, providing codes that allowed readers who wished to to see her as properly feminine and domestic even while she instructs farm laborers on how to tap sugar maple trees. 'Rather like modern professional women,' Harris writes, 'Fleda learns to excel in both male and female spheres of endeavor',[7] but Warner's nineteenth-century readers were free to select the emphasis which fit their own desires. Plot and linguistic codes work somewhat differently in Fanny Fern's *Ruth Hall*, but Ruth, like Fleda, inhabits both conventionally masculine and feminine arenas. The plot of *Ruth Hall* takes Ruth away from rather than toward marriage; she is widowed early in the novel, and pursues a career rather than remarriage. Yet even as she becomes increasingly successful and adept at managing her own career, Fern continually emphasizes her dedication to her children, for whose sake she has turned to writing, and in the final two chapters associates her with images that show her inhabiting both 'male' and 'female' worlds: in the next-to-last chapter she is presented with a certificate for one hundred shares of bank stock, representing her business acumen, and in the last she visits her husband's grave, which signals her continuing fidelity to her marriage vows.

By the middle of the nineteenth century, such codes were familiar to most readers, and allowed authors to achieve a range of purposes. While the most common of these was to place the heroine in a conventional plot that led to inevitable marriage while at the same time expressing possibilities beyond the familial and domestic, coding could also serve political ends. One of the most overt examples is Stowe's *Uncle Tom's Cabin*, in which the cabin of the title is depicted in terms that make it the moral equivalent of a white middle-class home; by describing the slave cabin of Uncle Tom and Aunt Chloe as surrounded by flowers and featuring white linens inside, Stowe implicitly makes the point that the slave couple are as genteel and as deserving of freedom as are their white owners. Conventions of plot and language, then, were not merely formulae upon which an unimaginative author could rely, but instead deliberate forms of shorthand used to convey sometimes subversive messages. Further, the fact that they required active interpretation on the part of readers belies the common nineteenth-century assumption that women readers were easily swayed by their reading into foolish or dangerous thinking or behavior. As Kate Flint notes in *The Woman Reader*, accounts that nineteenth-century women wrote about their reading suggest rational, thoughtful consideration: 'the activity of reading was often the vehicle through which an individual's sense of identity was achieved or confirmed. This frequently involved the assertion of practices or preferences which opposed that which was conventionally expected of the young woman within the family circle'.[8] Given this background, it seems unlikely that the responses of women readers would have caused Chopin's *The Awakening* to virtually disappear by the time of her death in 1904 – indeed, one would expect the reverse to have occurred, as Edna's search for self resonated with women readers' desires. The novel's fate seems instead the result of the historical moment, which was in turn the result of the previous century of changes in women's relationship to authorship and shifts in literary taste.

Just as Kate Chopin's literary reputation underwent extreme swings, from national recognition at the end of the nineteenth century to relative obscurity during the first half of the twentieth and finally to the wide acclaim it enjoys today, so the literary culture – and women's place within it – of the nineteenth century changed dramatically between the early part of the century and the 1890s. For much of the twentieth century, critical attention to women's writing tended to focus on the middle of the nineteenth century, in part because such widely read works as Warner's *The Wide, Wide World* and Stowe's *Uncle Tom's Cabin* were published in the 1850s, and in part because two of the earliest critical studies of nineteenth-century women writers – Fred Lewis Pattee's *The Feminine Fifties* (1936) and Helen Waite Papashvily's *All the Happy Endings* (1956) – focused on this decade. One result was a tendency to generalize from the 1850s to the rest of the century – to assume that the ways in which women wrote, their attitudes toward writing and publication, and the regard with which they were held was constant throughout most of the century. More recent scholarship, however, suggests that in the earlier part of the century, women writers participated with men in defining American literature and the American experience, and that only later in the century were their interests and responsibilities presumed to belong to a special 'woman's sphere' which could be construed as secondary to that of men. By the end of the century, these changes in literary culture ironically helped to account for Kate Chopin's success as a writer and also created a climate in which *The Awakening* could be dismissed instead of acclaimed.

In the decades following the Revolutionary War, educated Americans repeatedly expressed concern about the need to create a uniquely American culture, by which they meant manners, customs, values, and above all art forms that did not imitate English or European models. Perhaps the most ringing – and certainly one of the best-known – of such calls for indigenous creation was contained in Ralph Waldo Emerson's 1837 address to the Phi Beta Kappa Society at Harvard University. In the speech now known as 'The American Scholar', Emerson announced that 'Our day of dependence, our long apprenticeship to the learning of other lands, draws to a close', and he concluded by predicting that 'we will walk on our own feet; we will work with our own hands; we will speak our own minds'. In the same year that Emerson spoke to his audience of Harvard men, Thomas Chandler Haliburton published the first volume of *The Sayings and Doings of Samuel Slick, of Slickville*; in creating the Yankee peddler named in his title, Haliburton participated in the first wave of the regional literature that was to be popular with American readers throughout the century – including Chopin's Louisiana stories. Before Emerson spoke, however, American authors had already begun to take a different approach to creating 'American' literature, which was to mine the nation's colonial past for settings and stories, as Nathaniel Hawthorne would most famously do in *The Scarlet Letter* (1850). Lydia Maria Child's *Hobomok* (1824) and Catherine Maria Sedgwick's *Hope Leslie* (1827) were both historical novels set in the Massachusetts Puritan colonies; both novels were acclaimed by the influential *North American Review* as important contributions to an indigenous literature. The *Review* described *Hope Leslie* as a 'beautiful book', and encouraged Sedgwick to continue writing 'for the public's sake, and for the honor of our youthful literature'[9]; of Child, the *Review* noted in 1833, 'few female writers, if any, have done more or better things for our literature'.[10]

Despite the fact that the writer for the *North American Review* felt compelled to call attention to Child's gender, it is clear that both she and Sedgwick were regarded as helping to form an American literary tradition. This is not to suggest that gender was not an issue in the intellectual life of the young nation. Child's father saw no reason why she should receive a formal education as did her brother Convers, and Sedgwick felt the need to qualify her success as a published author; although she acknowledged that she felt 'pleasure in being able to command a high station wherever I go', she immediately added, 'I am conscious that what distinction I have attained is greatly owing to the paucity of our literature' (quoted in Kelley, p. ix). Nevertheless, by the 1840s, women writers were widely regarded as major players in the drive for an independent literature. As Elaine Showalter has written, 'rather than contesting the myth of the American spirit, American women saw their own writing as its true incarnation'.[11] When Rufus Griswold edited *The Female Poets of America* in 1849, he called attention to gender in a way he would not have in an anthology of male poets, but he also expressed pride that so many American women were involved in the production of literature, and threw down the gauntlet to British readers by announcing that 'the proportion of female writers at this moment in America far exceeds that which the present or any other age in England exhibits'.[12] Indeed, by the time Griswold published his collection, he could claim a tradition of women writers that went back to 1650, to the publication of Anne Bradstreet's *The Tenth Muse Lately Sprung Up in America.*

There was little unanimity of opinion in the first decades of the nineteenth century about what would chiefly constitute a truly indigenous American literature. Should it celebrate the nation's history, as did the novels of Sedgwick, Child, and others? Should it depict the vast landscape of the continent, so open and expansive in comparison with the English countryside? Did it require entirely new forms? Could it represent the egalitarian ideals embodied in a democratic form of government and fostered by a largely frontier environment? To focus on the last could evidence national pride, but it could also seem overly defensive, especially after the British visitor Francis Trollope published *Domestic Manners of the Americans* (1832), which criticized Americans precisely for their *lack* of manners. For Caroline Kirkland, writing in the *North American Review* in 1853, the most distinctively American literature was being created by women writers such as Sedgwick, Warner, and Stowe, who, by writing about the people and places they knew best, used themes that were, in Showalter's terms, 'domestic, local, and vernacular' (12) – characteristics which would be used to describe regional literature later in the century. In Kirkland's view, women writers were able to capture the essence of the American experience precisely because they were not attempting to impress anyone or prove anything with their work: 'we gave up trying to write to please or instruct anybody but ourselves; and lo and behold', an American literature!'.[13] But Kirkland was well aware of the growing, substantial cultural prejudice against the woman writer, and also knew the arguments against educating women. In her 1850 essay 'Literary Women', Kirkland facetiously defends the 'bluestocking' against 'the prejudice entertained against this class',[14] first by pointing out that they are not sufficiently numerous to be a threat:

No fear of usurpation; no danger that the pen will be snatched from strong hands and wielded in defiance, or even in self-defence [sic]. A handful of chimney swallows might as well be suspected of erecting their quills against the eagles – or owls. Swallows! literary ladies are hardly more abundant than dodos.

(195)

At the end of her essay, Kirkland proposes in the same facetious tone that if intellectual pursuits are a threat to women's femininity, then their education could be delayed until the age of 40, beyond which 'none but very robust beauty lasts', so that 'the remains of a lovely woman might have an opportunity of some education suited to the 30 years which may be supposed still to lie before her' (200).

Thus, at mid-century, in the year that Kate Chopin was born, the position of the woman writer was a paradox. On the one hand, women's writing – especially novels – was extremely popular, particularly but by no means exclusively with women readers. By 1855, Fanny Fern was the highest-paid newspaper columnist in America, earning $100 for her weekly *New York Ledger* columns, Harriet Beecher Stowe was internationally acclaimed for *Uncle Tom's Cabin*, and E.D.E.N. Southworth and Susan Warner were best-selling authors. At the same time – and perhaps partly as a result of such visibility – depictions of the 'bluestocking' became increasingly negative, and critics were alert for any evidence that a female author had overstepped the bounds of decorum. A number of commentators pronounced women talented within a carefully limited scope that precluded true literary greatness. British journalist R.H. Hutton provided a clear sense of these limitations in 1858. Women's imagination, Hutton wrote, 'can observe, it can recombine, it can delineate', but women lack the ability to invent:

> [Women's imagination] cannot leave the world of characteristic traits and expressive manner, so as to imagine and paint successfully the distinguishable, but not so easily distinguished, world out of which these characteristics grow. Women's fancy deals directly with *expression*, with the actual visible effects of mental and moral qualities, and seems unequal to go apart, as it were, with their conception, and work it out firmly in fields of experience somewhat different from those from which they have directly gathered it.[15]

Women, in other words, could depict what they had directly seen and experienced, but were incapable of imagining and depicting anything beyond the actual and concrete. Thus, as another critic explained two years later, women would not 'produce a fiction of the highest order', but by sticking to 'the region within which

[they] acquire [their] knowledge', could instead 'produce the best fiction of the class in which [they are] most likely to excel'.[16] Thus, what most women writers *chose* to write about – the 'domestic, local, and vernacular' – was conflated with what they were *able* to write, and that, in turn, was reduced to a lower form of art.

When women were praised for their literary productions, the terms used similarly marked out a special status for their work. Even Sarah Josepha Hale, who, as editor of the influential *Godey's Lady's Book* championed women's intellectual development and achievements, used decidedly different language in reviewing books by men and women. In the 'Editors' Table' section of *Godey's* in January of 1865, for example, Hale describes a novel by T. Adolphus Trollope as having a 'pleasing novelty and originality', and calls the plot 'dramatic and ingenious'. In the same column, however, a novel by 'Mrs. Hubback' is praised for being 'of the purest and healthiest tone', and rather than being 'ingenious', the plot succeeds because it teaches a valuable lesson: 'To the youthful romance reader its denouement may seem sad; but its lessons of duty and sacrifice should be well studied, as necessary preparation for the great struggle of life, in which it will be found that love cannot always reign supreme without the neglect of some essential duty.'[17] In July of the same year, praising a collection of stories by Marion Harland, editor Hale uses language that expresses Hutton's analysis of women's talents. Harland, Hale writes, 'attempts no high flights of fancy, but descends at once to the most practical affairs, and writes of the people and occurrences of everyday life'. Readers admire Harland, Hale states, because she writes 'of human nature as she sees it from a standpoint gained by experience and careful study'. Once again, Hale stresses the positive moral influence of women's fiction: 'The lessons [these stories] teach, if carefully treasured, may save many a woman from a shipwreck of her happiness.'[18] When Harriet Beecher Stowe felt compelled, in the early 1850s, to write what was essentially a political novel, she could justify it by her sense of moral outrage at the passage of the Fugitive Slave Law. Even then, as her title suggests, she foregrounded the familial and domestic aspects of slavery; and those (primarily Southerners) who criticized *Uncle Tom's Cabin* did so largely on the grounds that Stowe could not claim authenticity for her book because she had no firsthand experience with slavery.

In both their fiction and their lives, middle-class American women had developed what cultural historians have termed a 'women's culture' by mid-century. Prohibitions against too much familiarity between the sexes before marriage encouraged strong friendship bonds between young women. In fiction, the mother–daughter relationship was presented as particularly important; even when – as was frequently the case – the heroine has been orphaned as a young girl, the teachings of the mother or other maternal figure sustain her. Women wrote each other letters about their lives and their reading; those who kept diaries often gave them female names, effectively turning them into friends and confidantes. It is just such a women's culture that Chopin recreates on Grand Isle in *The Awakening*. With their husbands in the city during the week, the female vacationers sew together, watch each others' children, exchange confidences, and share reading material. As Showalter and others have argued, the social culture of women spawned literary and political subcultures. The values of domesticity, broadly defined, informed the fiction women wrote; at the same time, however, female unity made possible political action for women's rights, especially after the Seneca Falls Convention of 1848. While overt support for women's greater personal freedom and political rights would not enter women's fiction until later in the century – most notably in the work of Marietta Holley and in what came to be called 'new woman' novels – by the time of the Civil War women were responsible for nearly half of all novels published in America, and many of them had developed supportive networks of other writers. When, in 1855, the New York Association of Book Publishers held an elaborate dinner as a public relations event, a toast to the female writers invited referred to the best-known of them only by the titles of their most popular works; the 600 guests could easily supply the authors' names.

But for a number of reasons, both literary culture and women's culture changed significantly after about 1870. The expansion of the railroad both unified the country symbolically and moved family members and friends away from one another; in 1855, when Kate Chopin was five years old, the completion of a railway bridge across the Mississippi River earned St Louis the title 'Gateway to the West'. In values as well as geography, women were pulled apart. As Showalter notes, 'relationships between mothers and daughters became strained as daughters pressed for education, work, mobility, sexual autonomy, and power outside the female sphere' (15). Exemplifying this trend is the protagonist Christie Devon, in Louisa May Alcott's 1873 novel *Work*, who proclaims 'a new Declaration of Independence' as she leaves home to find a meaningful job. At the same time, American literary culture was becoming more businesslike and professionalized. As Coultrap-McQuin shows in *Doing Literary Business*, the 1870s marked a shift from the 'Gentleman Publisher', characterized by a true love of literature, a sense of fairness and honor, and supportive relationships with authors, to the 'Businessman Publisher', more interested in profit margins and aggressive competition. As the literary norm became more 'masculine' than 'feminine' toward the end of the century, women writers were conscious that rather than being judged on their own terms – which could also be used to demean their efforts – they would be judged by different standards. As Mary Abigail Dodge wrote in 1872, 'the products of her toil, the value of her labor, must be brought into direct comparison with those of men, and be judged solely by their worth' (quoted in Coultrap-McQuin, 1990: 116). When American literature had matured sufficiently to warrant having its history written, such volumes as Moses Coit Tyler's *History of American Literature* (1878) sought to discover not a diversity of literary voices, but instead a unifying concept, a 'development toward uniformity'.[19] For many women writers, the crowning blow in this transformation was the dinner party given in December of 1877 to celebrate the twentieth anniversary of the *Atlantic Monthly* and the seventieth birthday of John Greenleaf Whittier. Despite the fact that a number of well-known women, including Louisa May Alcott, Rose Terry Cooke, and Rebecca Harding Davis, had published in the *Atlantic*, not a single woman was invited to the celebration.

Coincidentally, at the very time that American literature was beginning to be defined in such a way as to denigrate women's contributions to it, writers in various parts of the country were developing a genre of which women – including Chopin – would be major practitioners. First called 'local color' literature because of its representations of the language, customs, geography, and manners of specific regions, this genre consisted primarily of short stories and sketches that captured the flavor of ordinary lives in New

England, the West, the South, and to a lesser extent the Midwest While the appeal of such stories to a national audience no doubt had much to do with its presentation of colorful – even exotic, to some readers – details of life in Maine or Georgia or California, the term 'local color' suggests a superficiality that is far from character- istic of the best of these stories, and scholars in recent years have preferred the term 'regional literature'. No matter which term is employed, this popular genre made use of the very talents that had been identified with women writers: observation of everyday life, faithful delineation of real human experience, and sympathy for ordinary individuals. More than one irony attends women's signif- icant involvement in writing regional fiction in the second half of the nineteenth century. One is that when such literature fell out of favor after the turn of the twentieth century, when the rise of modernism and the professionalization of the academy made such elements as dialect seem nostalgic and old-fashioned, many of the women who created it were reduced to literary footnotes or virtu- ally forgotten. A second irony, better recognized in hindsight than it was at the time, is that precisely in preserving in print the pecu- liarities of specific regions of this country, these writers were working – perhaps unwittingly – against the very nationalizing tendencies that had effectively moved their writing to a secondary status by insisting that only a certain kind of literature was truly 'American'. Sarah Orne Jewett's story 'A White Heron' (1896) is a frequently cited case in point. In the story, which is set in Maine, an ornithologist, representing the urban world of scientific inquiry, wants a young rural girl to disclose the habitat of a white heron so that he may add it to his collection, but she, understanding the danger the scientist poses to the beauty she admires, refuses to cooperate. As Josephine Donovan notes, such a story represents resistance on two levels. Such regionalist writers writers as Jewett were 'identifying with their region against homogenizing, federal- izing tendencies', but 'it was also and perhaps principally a matter of defending their own life-world against the encroachments of modern normalizing disciplines that would relegate it to the status of deviant'.[20]

Although the flowering of American regional literature occurred in the 1870s and 1880s, it has its origins in the 1830s. Two publi- cations of that decade helped to establish the deep South and New

England as prime locations for such fiction: Augustus Baldwin Longstreet's *Georgia Scenes, Characters, Incidents, &c. In the First Half Century of the Republic* (1835), and Harriet Beecher Stowe's story 'Uncle Lot', published in the *Western Monthly Magazine* in 1834. The latter is significant for several reasons. It announces women's long association with regional literature, and the magazine in which it appeared was published in Cincinnati, Ohio, so that Stowe was speaking about her native New England to many readers who had no firsthand experience of the region. Further, early in the story Stowe is candid about her regional chauvinism. In trying to decide what to write about, she has rejected 'the sky of Italy', 'the beau ideal of Greece', and 'vigor from England' in favor of 'My own New England; the land of bright fires and strong hearts; the land of deeds, and not of words; the land of fruits, and not of flowers'. Put another way, Stowe intends to write an *American* story. Lest readers feel she should not be bragging about her own region, she asks them to consider how they feel about '"Old Kentuck", Old England, or any other corner of the world in which they happened to be born and they will find it quite rational.' By the 1870s and 1880s, such writers as Jewett, Rose Terry Cooke, and Mary E. Wilkins Freeman were writing stories about New England, Mary Noialles Murfree was introducing readers to the hill country of Tennessee, and Grace King was exploring the culture of Louisiana, especially New Orleans. As part of the development of literary realism in the second half of the nineteenth century, this fiction features particularly strong delineations of characters, especially women. As Judith Fetterley and Marjorie Pryse have noted, 'a fictional form that takes its energy from character creates an opening for storytelling that makes plot a lesser concern; women writers could – and did – readily appropriate this form, the sketch, to portray their culture'.[21] As a writer of regional short fiction, Chopin was particularly adept at portraying strong, complex female characters.

This skill also accounts in large measure for the popularity of Chopin's *The Awakening* a century after it was published. At the time the novel was written, another literary subgenre with which it had important affinities had emerged in England and the United States: the 'new woman' novel. The 'new woman' herself was the product of several decades of agitation for women's political rights, increased educational opportunities, and the admission of women into intellectual circles such as the one that nourished Chopin in St Louis in the 1890s. The term is normally applied to privileged white women born after 1850, many of whom had mothers who were active in abolition and other social causes (decidedly not the case for the Southern Chopin), and who were determined to make choices about the conduct of their own lives. The novel that arose to depict this 'new woman' was controversial because it challenged cherished assumptions about woman's role and relationships between the sexes. In *The Woman Reader 1837–1914*, Kate Flint identifies the major challenges these novels embodied:

> protests against the restrictive upbringing of girls and the inade-quacies of their education; the challenging of the assumption that woman's best possible future lay in marriage, that the only place to bear and bring up children was within such a marriage, and that, indeed all women possessed a "maternal instinct"; the importance placed on women's struggles and achievements in their working lives, whether as journalist or doctor, teacher, or musician; and the questioning of double sexual standards.[22]

On the level of plot, these novels frequently emphasize women's struggles to overcome obstacles to their freedom, rather than their success in doing so. As Flint notes, these novels are not 'dramas of wish-fulfilment [sic]'. The heroine experiences a 'resigned or compromised fate', and the reader is left with the wish that 'either ... she could internally have been stronger and have stuck more bravely to her principles; or that social pressures did not render principled stances almost impossible to maintain' (297).

Although there is little evidence to suggest that Kate Chopin considered herself a 'new woman', and *The Awakening* is usually not placed in the same category with novels by Sarah Grand, Mona Caird, Mary Austin, and Frances Newman, it is clear that Chopin departed significantly from the domestic novel of many of her predecessors. In the person of Edna Pontellier, *The Awakening* ques-tions both the fulfillment of marriage and the universality of women's maternal instinct. Perhaps even more importantly, much of the current debate about the novel focuses on its ending, in which Edna drowns in the Gulf of Mexico. Not only does such a conclusion not constitute 'wish-fulfilment', but so artfully has

Chopin written the novel that there is no critical agreement about whether the cause of this denouement is that Edna was not sufficiently 'strong' or that social pressures render such strength ineffective. Indeed, some readers see the ending of the novel as triumphant, with Edna freed from such pressures to join with her natural element, the sea. Furthermore, *The Awakening* is in some ways a pivotal novel, making use of some of the conventions of the nineteenth-century woman's novel but altering them to convey radically different messages. Like many of her predecessors, Chopin uses codes to identify some of her characters. Just as Mlle. Reisz wears 'artificial violets' that signify society's view of the unmarried musician as unnatural, so Madame Ratignolle is coded as the conventional female ideal. On Grand Isle, she always has her sewing with her, whereas Edna is 'idle' (28); she dresses in 'pure white' as befits her feminine nature, while Edna is described as having a 'graceful severity' (33); most importantly, Madame Ratignolle is a 'mother-woman' (26), while Edna is 'fond of her children in an uneven, impulsive way' (37). The conventional codes thus establish Madame Ratignolle as the cultural ideal while Chopin's protagonist is clearly different. Similarly, Chopin creates the women's culture on Grand Isle to show that Edna is not really a part of it. She is embarrassed by both the conversations about childbirth and a book that is shared reading; she likes to spend time alone, and fails to understand the nature of Robert Lebrun's flirtation. As Madame Ratignolle says early in the novel, 'she is not one of us' (*CW*, 900).

By creating a character who thus stands apart from the culture that her time period, her region, and her social class deemed appropriate for her, Chopin was poised at the close of the nineteenth century to influence the course of subsequent women's fiction. But the novel's overwhelmingly negative critical reception caused it to lay dormant for half a century, while what remained of Chopin's literary reputation rested on her stories of Creole life. The most obvious reason why many readers rejected *The Awakening* is Edna's frank sexuality; not only does she have an extra-marital affair with a man to whom she feels little emotional connection, but throughout the novel she increasingly delights in the sensuality of the Gulf waters, in food and drink, and in the solitary pleasures of music, walking, and sleeping. While it is this aspect of the novel that led the reviewers to consider it 'not healthy', 'morbid', and 'poison', and prompted Chopin's mock apology for Edna, there were other, less remarked upon reasons for its fall from critical favor. Neither the Kentucky Presbyterianism in which Edna was raised nor the Louisiana Catholicism into which she has married is presented in a positive light; the former, represented by Edna's father with his 'ponderous oaths' (91), is rigorous and punitive, and Edna finds the Catholic mass 'stifling' (54). Stylistically, *The Awakening* departs from the prevailing realism of its era. The novel is impressionistic, lyrical, devoted to internal instead of external reality. Elaine Showalter describes its structure clearly: the 'thirty-nine numbered sections of uneven lengths, ranging from [a] single paragraph to [a] sustained narrative ... are unified less by their style than by their focus on Edna's consciousness, and by the repetition of key motifs and images: music, the sea, shadows, swimming, eating, sleeping, gambling, the lovers, birth' (72). Even readers who were not shocked by Edna's sexual freedom would have had different expectations of a novel written about and by a woman – especially a woman known for colorful depictions of Creole life.

The only sustained study of Chopin and her work during the 50 years following her death is tellingly titled *Kate Chopin and Her Creole Stories*. Daniel S. Rankin's (1932) critical biography of Chopin has been superceded in most respects by later biographies and critical studies, but it is valuable as an index of critical regard for her work in the 1930s, when *The Awakening* could be seen more as an unfortunate incident than a literary event. To Rankin's credit, he does try to correct the mistaken impression that Chopin was so devastated by the reception given her novel that she gave up writing altogether (a story that nonetheless persisted for decades), but he is at best equivocal in the brief chapter he devotes to *The Awakening*, spending much of his discussion trying to point out what in Chopin's life, attitudes, and reading would have caused her to write such a novel. He finally decides that Chopin's reading of Russian and French authors and her exposure to the music of Wagner and the drama of Maeterlinck induced her to participate in 'the current of erotic morbidity that flowed strongly through the literature of the last two decades of the nineteenth century'. Such pernicious European influences, Rankin suggests, prompted Chopin to momentarily depart from a career that he otherwise admires greatly: 'The end of the century became a momentary dizziness over an abyss of voluptuousness, and Kate Chopin in St Louis experienced a partial attack of the prevailing artistic vertigo' (Rankin, 175). Like critics of women's writing before him, Rankin admires most the work that can be seen to emerge directly from the author's own experience. Of Chopin's story 'A Pair of Silk Stockings', for example, originally published in the 16 September 1897 issue of *Vogue*, Rankin states that the story's protagonist 'is in a situation and a mood that had been reality to the author'. The story, Rankin observes approvingly, is 'distinctly feminine and real, with quiet touches of humor to free it from sentimental pathos' (107). But *The Awakening*, clearly not patterned after Chopin's life history, he finds less explicable, and although he admires the skill with which Chopin created the novel, he echoes a number of 1899 critics of the novel when he asks rhetorically, 'But was the theme deserving of the exquisite care given it?' (177). The implicit answer is no.

Thus matters rested until 1956, when Kenneth Eble drew renewed attention to Chopin's novel in an article in the *Western Humanities Review*. Calling *The Awakening* a 'first-rate novel', Eble wrote of its 'general excellence', describing the work as 'amazingly honest, perceptive and moving'. Immersed as he was in the New Critical methodology then in vogue, Eble cares less about any social message the novel embodies than with Chopin's skill in creating patterns of image and symbol, but gone is the moralistic assessment of either Edna or Kate Chopin that had characterized previous critical studies.[23] To be sure, Eble's was not the first twentieth-century voice to defend the novel, although his article was positioned to draw more attention to it than were previous statements in reference books and literary histories. In the 1930 edition of the *Dictionary of American Biography*, Dorothy Anne Dondore remarked that 'one of the tragedies of recent American literature' was that 'Mrs. Chopin should have written this book two decades in advance of its time',[24] and in 1952, in *The Confident Years, 1885–1915*, Van Wyck Brooks gave *The Awakening* high praise indeed: 'But there was one novel of the nineties in the South that should have been remembered, one small perfect book that mattered more than the whole life-work of many a prolific writer.'[25]

Ironically, but perhaps not unexpectedly, the most significant rediscoveries of Chopin's work at mid-century were the efforts of

European-born rather than American scholars. In 1953, French critic Cyrille Arnavon compared *The Awakening* to Gustav Flaubert's 1856 novel *Madame Bovary* (he would not be the last to do so), and translated the novel into French. Arnavon placed Chopin not in the company of other regionalist writers, but instead in the group of late-nineteenth-century realists that included Theodore Dreiser and Frank Norris. When, in 1961, Arnavon suggested Chopin as a topic for study to a Norwegian student in his class at Harvard, the reclamation of Chopin's work for a wide audience was assured: Per Seyersted wrote his doctoral dissertation on Chopin, and in 1969 published both *Kate Chopin: a Critical Biography* and a two-volume set of *The Complete Works of Kate Chopin*, which included the texts of her novels *At Fault* and *The Awakening*, ninety-six stories, twenty poems, and more than a dozen essays. The influential literary critic Edmund Wilson, writing the foreward to the *Complete Works*, called Chopin a 'daring and accomplished woman'. While Seyersted was at least as enthusiastic about Chopin as were Arnavon and Wilson, he was cautious about the future of her reputation, well aware of the criticism of *The Awakening* seventy years earlier. In the chapter of his biography titled 'The Long-Neglected Pioneer', Seyersted calls Chopin 'a rare, transitional figure in modern literature ... [who was] too much of a pioneer to be accepted in her time and place', and he predicted that readers of the late 1960s would respond to her more daring work along gendered lines: 'Mrs. Pontellier will for a long time to come be faced with male condescension and prejudice.... Most female readers, however, are likely to take to their heart this deeply moving portrait of a woman's growth into self-awareness' (Seyersted, 199).

Fortunately, Seyersted's caution was unnecessary. While some critics continued to regard Chopin primarily in the context of what was still called 'local color' writing, interest in her work grew rapidly, and in the mid-1970s Marlene Springer compiled an annotated bibiography of commentary on her work published between 1890 and 1973. *The Awakening* was clearly becoming the centerpiece of her work; during the 1970s, three separate editions of the novel were issued, each volume including a selection of Chopin's short fiction as well. The short stories merited renewed attention as deft studies of character as well as of locale; a collection of 29 of her stories published in England in 1979 is titled *Portraits*. But scholars also mined the stories for echoes of the themes and characters of her best-known novel, seeing in such stories as 'The Story of an Hour' a glimpse of a woman's feeling of entrapment in marriage. Increasingly, Chopin was compared favorably to other major authors in the American literary tradition. In an essay in his 1971 book *Southern Excursions: Essays on Mark Twain and Others*, Lewis Leary likened Chopin's use of the sea as a dominant motif to the sea as an image in Walt Whitman's poetry, and wrote of Edna Pontellier that she was 'worthy of place beside other fictional heroines who have tested emancipation and failed – Nathaniel Hawthorne's Hester Prynne, Gustav Flaubert's Madame Bovary, or Henry James's Isabel Archer'.[26] By the end of the decade, readers and scholars had access to more primary material when Per Seyersted and Emily Toth co-edited *A Kate Chopin Miscellany*, a volume that includes, in addition to several of her stories, two of her diaries and assorted letters and poems. An additional facet of Chopin's career became available to readers in 1988 with the publication of Thomas Bonner's *The Kate Chopin Companion* (1988), which includes her translations from the French of a story by Adrian Vely and eight stories by Guy de Maupassant, five of them previously unpublished.

By the time Emily Toth published a major biography of Chopin in 1990, the author's position in the first rank of American authors seemed secure, especially as measured by its appearance on college students' reading lists. In 1976, *The Awakening*, accompanied by cultural contexts, contemporary reviews, and excerpts from critical studies, became part of the Critical Editions series published by W. W. Norton, and the volume was revised and enlarged in 1994. By 1988 the novel was the subject of the sixteenth volume of the Approaches to Teaching World Literature series published by the Modern Language Association, joining such acknowledged classics as Chaucer's *Canterbury Tales*, Milton's *Paradise Lost*, and Melville's *Moby-Dick*. Testimony to the utility of such volumes was provided in a 1980s study by Paul Lauter of the Feminist Press that found Chopin to be the thirty-seventh most frequently taught American author in the nation's colleges and universities. By 1993, the novel had been the subject of so many critical approaches that it was a logical choice for inclusion in the Case Studies in Contemporary Criticism series published by Bedford Books. In addition to having become a staple in college literature courses, Chopin's novel has become widely familiar as a cultural icon. Robert Stone's 1986 novel *Children of Light*, for example, not only deals with a Hollywood filming of *The Awakening*, but its plot parallels that of Chopin's novel as the actress playing Edna Pontellier replicates Edna's fateful final swim in the ocean. And in her 1992 book *Kate Chopin's* The Awakening: *Screenplay as Interpretation*, Marilyn Hoder-Salmon uses film not as a backdrop, but as a way to engage with the meaning of the novel; writing a three-act screenplay becomes a means of rewriting the text in a different form in order to sort out its motifs and messages. As Hoder-Salmon puts it, 'Chopin told what she had seen, and through my adaptation of her witnessing I seek to tell what I have seen.'[27]

All of this is not to suggest that Kate Chopin is regarded as a one-book author, although it does seem appropriate that the novel that once seemed to foreclose forever her reputation as a writer should have been the catalyst for her rediscovery and current critical acclaim. Chopin's short fiction, once regarded as charming renderings of Creole culture, are now appreciated for their range of themes, sensitive study of characters in a variety of social settings, and stylistic versatility. The very titles of her three published collections of short stories is evidence of movement from stories that connote place to those with more abstract and universal concerns. *Bayou Folk*, published in 1894, was followed by *A Night in Acadie* (1897). The publisher's notice in *Publisher's Weekly* advertising the former collection describes it as a group of 'picturesque' tales of the 'semi-alien' Creoles and Acadians (quoted in Toth, 223), and the title of the second uses the name given to the French-settled part of Louisiana. The quite differently titled *A Vocation and a Voice*, which was accepted for publication in 1898, was never issued by the publisher which had accepted it, presumably because of a reduction in its publication list; the collection was finally published in 1991. *A Vocation and a Voice* contains stories that differ markedly from the fiction that Chopin published during her lifetime. As one scholar has noted, 'from 1893 to 1900, *Vocation* became Chopin's repository of troublesome pieces, the majority difficult to place, five [of twenty-three stories] not accepted anywhere during her lifetime'.[28] While a few of the stories have a Louisiana setting, many are not localized at all, and most of them deal with characters who become removed in some way from the ordinary realities of their lives.

'Elizabeth Stock's One Story', which appears in *A Vocation and a Voice*, concerns a young woman's thwarted ambition to be a writer. While the story is in no sense autobiographical – the title character is postmistress in a small Missouri town – it does show Kate Chopin's sensitivity to the particular dilemmas confronting women with artistic aspirations. Significantly, language leads to Elizabeth Stock's demise – specifically, the writing on a postcard addressed to one of her postal patrons that sends her out into a cold rain which precipates her illness and death. Although the critical reception of *The Awakening* did not cause Chopin's death, or even end her work as a writer, it delayed by at least half a century the wide readership that now attends her work. In the Foreword to *Kate Chopin Reconsidered*, Cathy N. Davidson describes the experience of a generation of scholars when she writes, 'Kate Chopin did not exist when I was in graduate school, at least not in any institutional sense.'[29] Kate Chopin now 'exists' institutionally, and it will be the task of this study to trace her existence as a writer in the context of the second half of the nineteenth century.

Notes

1. Victoria Boynton, 'Kate Chopin', *Nineteenth-Century American Women Writers: a Bio-Bibliographical Critical Sourcebook*, ed. Denise D. Knight. Westport, CT: Greenwood Press, 1997, p. 50.
2. Unless otherwise indicated, all page references to Chopin's fiction will be to the 1969 *Collected Works*, identified as *CW*.
3. Ann Douglas Wood, 'The "Scribbling Women" and Fanny Fern: Why Women Wrote', *American Quarterly*, 23, no. 1 (Spring 1971): 9.
4. Judith Fetterley, (ed.) *Provisions: a Reader from 19th-Century American Women*. Bloomington: Indiana University Press, 1985, p. 5. Subsequent references will be page numbers in the text.
5. Frank Luther Mott, *A History of American Magazines 1850–1865*. Cambridge: Harvard University Press, 1938, pp. 493–4.
6. Susan Coultrap-McQuin, *Doing Literary Business: American Women Writers in the Nineteenth Century*. Chapel Hill: University of North Carolina Press, 1990, p. 10. Subsequent references will be page numbers in the text.
7. Susan K. Harris, *19th-Century American Women's Novels: Interpretive Strategies*. Cambridge: Cambridge University Press, 1990, p. 84.
8. Kate Flint, *The Woman Reader 1837–1914*. New York: Oxford University Press, 1993, p. 14.
9. Quoted in Mary Kelley, 'Introduction', *Hope Leslie*. New Brunswick, NJ: Rutgers University Press, 1987, p. x.

10. Quoted in Carolyn L. Karcher, 'Introduction', *Hobomok and Other Writings on Indians*. New Brunswick, NJ: Rutgers University Press, 1986, p. xi.
11. Elaine Showalter, *Sister's Choice: Tradition and Change in American Women's Writing*. New York: Oxford University Press, 1991, p. 11. Subsequent references will be page numbers in the text.
12. Ibid, p.11.
13. Caroline Kirkland, 'Novels and Novelists', *North American Review*, 86 (1853): 111–12.
14. Caroline Kirkland, 'Literary Women' (1850); reprinted in *A New Home, Who'll Follow?*, ed. Sandra A. Zagarell. New Brunswick, NJ: Rutgers University Press, 1990, p. 193. Subsequent references will be page numbers in the text.
15. R. H. Hutton, 'Novels by the Authoress of John Halifax', *North British Review*, 29 (1858): 474.
16. 'Female Novelists', *London Review*, 1 (1860): 137.
17. [Sarah Josepha Hale], 'Editors' Table', *Godey's Lady's Book*, LXX, [no.1] (January 1865): 97.
18. [Sarah Josepha Hale], 'Editors' Table', *Godey's Lady's Book*, LXXI, [no. 1] (July 1865): 86.
19. Moses Coit Tyler, *A History of American Literature, 1607–1765*. 1878. Williamstown, MA: Corner House Publishers, 1973, Vol. II, p. 319.
20. Josephine Donovan, 'Breaking the Sentence: Local-Color Literature and Subjugated Knowledges', *The (Other) American Tradition: Nineteenth-Century Women Writers*, ed. Joyce W. Warren. New Brunswick, NJ: Rutgers University Press, 1993, p. 231.
21. Judith Fetterley and Marjorie Pryse, (eds), *American Women Regionalists 1850–1910*. New York: W. W. Norton, 1992, p. xv.
22. Kate Flint, *The Woman Reader 1837–1914*. New York: Oxford University Press, 1993, p. 294. Subsequent references will be page numbers in the text.
23. Kenneth Eble, 'A Forgotten Novel: Kate Chopin's *The Awakening*', *Western Humanities Review*, X (Summer 1956): 261–9.
24. Dorothy Anne Dondore, 'Kate Chopin', *Dictionary of American Biography*, Vol. IV. New York: Scribner's, 1930, p. 91.
25. Van Wyck Brooks, *The Confident Years, 1885–1915*. New York: Dutton, 1952, p. 341.
26. Lewis Leary, *Southern Excursions: Essays on Mark Twain and Others*. Baton Rouge: Louisiana State University Press, 1971, p. 174.
27. Marilyn Hoder-Salmon, *Kate Chopin's* The Awakening: *Screenplay as Interpretation*. Gainesville: University Press of Florida, 1992, p. 25.
28. Sara deSaussure Davis, 'Chopin's Movement Toward Universal Myth', *Kate Chopin Reconsidered: Beyond the Bayou*, eds Lynda S. Boren and Sara deSaussure Davis. Baton Rouge: Louisiana State University Press, 1992, p. 199.
29. Cathy N. Davidson, 'Foreword', *Kate Chopin Reconsidered: Beyond the Bayou*, eds Lynda S. Boren and Sara deSaussure Davis. Baton Rouge: Louisiana State University Press, 1992, p. ix.

2
St Louis to Louisiana and Back

> Chopin's creative moments were inspired by the place in
> which she lived and worked. A journey to this region opens
> yet another door to the artist's psyche.
>
> Lynda S. Boren, *Beyond the Bayou*

The place to which Lynda Boren refers in this statement is the
bayou country of Louisiana, and specifically Natchitoches, the
oldest town in the Louisiana Purchase, founded in 1714, near which
Kate Chopin lived at the time of her husband's death in 1882. A
journey to St Louis, Missouri, in the middle of the nineteenth
century takes us to the place where Kate Chopin spent the first 20
and the last 20 years of her life – 40 of her 54 years. While the intervening 14 years in Louisiana supplied the settings and characters of
most of her fiction, it was in St Louis that she prepared – no doubt
unwittingly – for the career that she would pursue when she was
again a resident there. St Louis and New Orleans – the city where
Chopin spent nine of her Louisiana years – shared some important
characteristics. Both were river towns, established to take advantage
of the transportation afforded by the Mississippi River; both were
therefore meeting places for people from various parts of the
country and even the world. Because the Mississippi and its
surrounding land had been owned by France until the Louisiana
Purchase in 1803, both cities had strong traditions of French
language and culture, and those who could claim lineage to inhabitants of the French colonial period tended to regard their
'American' neighbors as uncultured upstarts. Katherine O'Flaherty –

later Kate Chopin – was the product of an interaction between old and new St Louis. Her father, Thomas O'Flaherty, was born in Ireland in 1805 and settled in St Louis in 1825, becoming a merchant. Her mother, Eliza Faris, 16 years old at the time of her marriage, was Thomas' second wife; both of his marriages enhanced his social standing by allying him with the city's old French families. As a businessman, engaged in selling goods, Thomas O'Flaherty represented the entrepreneurial spirit that characterized frontier America; Eliza Faris' family, in contrast, was rich in distinguished ancestry and some land holdings, but not in money. The couple were married in 1844, and their first child, also named Thomas, was born in 1848.

By the time Kate O'Flaherty was born on 8 February 1850, the second child of Thomas' second marriage, St Louis looked to the newly opening West as much as it did to the South. Thomas O'Flaherty sold supplies to those people for whom the city was the staging area for western settlement, and he prospered sufficiently to settle his new family in a large two-story house. Tragically, his very success contributed to his early death: when the Gasconade Bridge was opened in November of 1855, making possible railway travel across the Mississippi, Thomas O'Flaherty was one of the prominent citizens invited to ride the first train to cross the river; but the trestle collapsed, and 30 people, including Kate's father, were killed. While such a public accident on a day of celebration was unusual, St Louis, as a frontier city, had its share of violence and lawlessness, particularly with its partly transient population – the aspect of St Louis that most impressed Francis Parkman as he traveled to do research for *The California and Oregon Trail* (1849):

> Last spring, 1846, was a busy season in the city of St Louis. The hotels were crowded, and the gunsmiths and saddlers were kept constantly at work providing arms and equipment for the different parties of travelers. Steamboats were leaving the levee and passing up the Missouri crowded with passengers on their way to the frontier.
>
> (Rankin, 10)

After she had begun writing and publishing stories, Kate Chopin was inspired by Western as well as by New England and Southern regional writers, especially Hamlin Garland, whose *Main-Travelled Roads* (1891) she admired. She had less admiration for Garland's collection of essays, *Crumbling Idols*, which she reviewed for *St Louis Life* in 1894, but she called Garland a 'representative Western man of letters', 'vigorous and sincere, and ... one of us' (*CW*, 694).

In the 1850s, however, St Louis also had strong ties to the South. Houses such as the one the O'Flaherty family lived in had wide front porches with columns in the popular southern style, and the city's strong French heritage was evident in the prevalence of Catholic churches and schools, including the venerable St Louis University, founded in 1818. Perhaps most importantly, many St Louis families, including the O'Flahertys, owned slaves, and were to be ardent defenders of the Confederacy during the Civil War. The Mississippi River was an important avenue in the slave trade; it is down this river that Uncle Tom is sold in Stowe's *Uncle Tom's Cabin*, and it is the Mississippi that Huck and Jim try unsuccessfully to avoid in Twain's *Huck Finn*. Slave auctions were as much a feature of St Louis as were westering pioneers during Kate O'Flaherty's childhood, and as a young girl some of her everyday needs were met by black and mulatto servants. Given this background, the mature Kate Chopin was remarkably open-minded about racial issues, at least in her fiction. While she depicted – accurately, for her day – African-Americans primarily as servants occupying the lowest rung on the southern social ladder, a story such as 'Désirée's Baby' reveals the tragedy caused by suspicion that a young mother may have Negro ancestry, and in 'For Marse Chouchoute', a young black boy nearly gives up his life to see that a small-town mailbag is delivered to the train on time.

Kate O'Flaherty's earliest education brought her in touch with her Southern French heritage. Her maternal great-grandmother, Madame Victoire Verdon Charleville, taught her to speak and read French, and to play the piano – at both of which endeavors Kate showed great skill. Madame Charleville was also a noted storyteller, whose tales of family history introduced Kate to some strong and unconventional female ancestors, including Madame Charleville's own mother, who in 1785 had obtained a legal separation from her second husband (the first such separation in St Louis history; divorce was impossible for Roman Catholics), and subsequently became a highly successful businesswoman engaged in trading goods up and down the river between St Louis and New Orleans. At the age of five, then, Kate began to learn of a 'women's culture' that featured independence and self-determination. More conventional values informed the more formal education she began receiving at the same age at the Sacred Heart Academy, first as a boarding student and later as a day student. The nuns who ran the Academy belonged to an order established in France around the turn of the nineteenth century; the school drew its students from middle- and upper-middle-class Catholic St Louis families, and its mission was both religious and educational – to prepare young Catholic girls eventually to become good Catholic wives and mothers. Following her father's death, Kate O'Flaherty was removed from Sacred Heart for nearly two years and educated solely by Madame Charleville, but she returned to the Academy in 1857 and remained until she graduated from its secondary school in 1868.

Discipline was strict at Sacred Heart, and students adhered to a rigid routine that included mass and prayers as well as lessons. Younger students were taught spelling, arithmetic, penmanship, and Catechism, and later moved on to history (including Church history), geography, and science. The goal of the educational curriculum was to produce young women who could think clearly and converse intelligently, and it included some skills deemed appropriate for proper young women, such as needlework, which was required at all levels of the curriculum. Although Kate O'Flaherty no doubt learned to sew well, her attitude toward years of required training in this craft can be surmised from the identification of it with Madame Ratignolle rather than Edna Pontellier in *The Awakening*; indeed, as Madame Ratignolle busies herself making children's clothes, '[Edna] could not see the use of ... making winter night garments the subject of her summer meditations' (27). Another constant in the Sacred Heart curriculum bore more directly upon Kate's future life: writing. The Plan of Studies for 1852 is clear on the centrality of writing for those past the primary level: 'The mistresses of the higher classes will assign each week two themes, or essays; one of these will always be a letter, the other alternately an essay, narrative or descriptive, and a literary analysis' (Toth, 46).

Like many young women of her day – particularly those who were later to become writers – Kate O'Flaherty was an avid reader, both in and out of school, and reading was a shared as well as a solitary activity. Kate's close friend from her Sacred Heart days, Kitty Garesché (who became a nun), recalled for Kate Chopin's first biographer some of the books the two girls read in common. Some, such as Grimm's *Fairy Tales*, *Blind Agnese* (a Catholic cautionary tale), and *Dickens for Little Folks*, were intended for children; some, such as *Pilgrim's Progress* and the romances of Sir Walter Scott, were staples of the mid-nineteenth-century middle-class home. In a reminiscence written in the 1880s, Chopin recalled the childhood pleasures that she and Kitty shared – including reading: 'We divided our "picayunes" worth of candy – climbed together the highest cherry trees; wept in company over the "Days of Bruce", and later, exchanged our heart secrets' (*KCM*, 104). But Kate and Kitty also read the popular women's novels of the 1850s, including Susan Warner's *The Wide, Wide World* (1850) and *Queechy* (1852). Much later, Kate Chopin wrote an essay opposing the prohibition of certain books to young people. In addition to the fact that the forbidden book is more attractive to most children than are those that are sanctioned, Chopin articulates her belief that a young person learns best from that which she finds for herself rather than from formal education:

> As a rule the youthful, untrained nature is left to gather wisdom as it comes along in a thousand-and-one ways and in whatever form it may present itself to the intelligent, the susceptible, the observant. In this respect experience is perhaps an abler instructor than direct enlightenment from man or woman; for it works by suggestion. There are many phases and features of life which cannot, or rather should not be expounded, demonstrated, presented to the youthful imagination as cold facts, for it is safe to assert they are not going to be accepted as such. It is moreover robbing youth of its privilege to gather wisdom as the bee gathers honey.
>
> (*CW*, 713)

Eclectic reading, the adult Kate Chopin argues, is more convincing to the young mind than 'facts' presented by adults; and it seems likely that the stories of her great-grandmother were closer to the former category than to the latter. What is certain is that the discipline of the Sacred Heart Academy had the effect of making her resist most forms of discipline in later life. There is evidence also, however, that Chopin retained some fondness for her Sacred Heart years. Her short story 'Lilacs' (published in the New Orleans *Times Democrat* in 1896 and later collected in *A Vocation and a Voice*) features a protagonist who revisits her convent school for periods of rest and renewal; Kitty Garesché remained a lifelong friend; and Chopin never formally renounced the Catholicism into which she was confirmed in May of 1861, when she was 11 years old.

Although the Sacred Heart nuns assumed that their students were destined for adult lives as wives and mothers (or alternatively, as in the case of Kitty Garesché, members of religious orders), they fostered whatever emerging talents they discerned, and Kate showed herself to be a skilled writer in her required compositions. She was a sufficiently able student to be selected for the school honor society, the Children of Mary, and she read an original essay during her graduation ceremonies. Like other young women of her era – although perhaps with more dedication than most – Kate kept a 'commonplace book', a journal in which she recorded her reading and into which she copied passages from it that had particular meaning for her. The entries, many of them from assigned school readings, show Kate O'Flaherty at the age of 16 and 17 absorbed in the work of primarily male European and English writers, including Charles Lamb, Chateaubriand, Goethe, Victor Hugo, and Hans Christian Anderson. An exception is Longfellow, one of the few American poets considered standard academic fare in the 1860s, whom she called 'a poet and a true one' (*KCPP*, 37). Kate's training in European literature, however, drew her admiration to Longfellow's celebration of the Rhine Valley in 'Hyperion', about which she wrote, 'I read and reread with the keenest enjoyment his exquisite descriptions of German scenes and scenery; for my passion has always been to travel in that land[,] that cradle and repository of genius' (*KCPP*, 37) – a passion that would be fulfilled during her honeymoon journey in the summer of 1870. In her travel diary on July 14, she noted ecstatically, '"The Rhine! the Rhine! a blessing on the Rhine" so says Longfellow & so say I ... Shall I ever forget the beauties of the beautiful Rhine?' (*KCM*, 75). Interestingly, in light of her future translations of de Maupassant's stories, she writes in response to an English translation of the *Life and Letters of Madame Swetchine*, 'translations from the French or

German rarely interest me; because French and German notions and ideas are so different from the English – that they loose [sic] all their naive zest by being translated into that most practical of tongues' (*KCPP*, 17). Her own original writings during the last years of her formal education tended to the conventional and senti-mental, as when she memorialized a deceased classmate: 'Alas why should this spring flower, so favored with graces, so dowered with loveliness, in preference to the faded and drooping be snatched from our midst?' (*KCPP*, 18). More sprightly and amusing is a long poem, written as a class assignment, describing a 'Congé', a school party, but even this is composed in iambic pentameter rhymed couplets. As Daniel Rankin notes with some understatement, 'No indication of her future skill is evident in these outpourings' (48).

About a year after her graduation from Sacred Heart Academy in 1868, however, a short story – the earliest of Kate Chopin's stories that has survived – comes closer to displaying that skill. Titled simply, 'Emancipation. A Life Fable', this story of scarcely a page in length describes an unspecified animal escaping from the cage in which it had been born, and in which its physical needs for food, water, and warmth have been well-supplied, to an uncertain but far preferable world outside it. 'So does he live', and the description concludes, 'seeking, finding, joying and suffering' (*CW*, 38), suggesting that the hardships of freedom are more fulfilling than the comforts of con-finement. While this youthful story – more allegory than realistic fic-tion – is certainly no blueprint for *The Awakening* 30 years later, it does sound a note that was to be amplified in many ways in Chopin's mature fiction: the joy of personal freedom is worth its attendant risks. In Chopin's 1894 story 'The Story of an Hour', Mrs Mallard, believing herself newly widowed, whispers, 'Free! Body and soul free!' (*CW*, 354). In the 1896 'Athénaïse', the title character runs away from a marriage that has begun to oppress her; reaching New Orleans, she is 'a good deal flustered, a little frightened, and altogether excited and interested by her unusual experiences' (*CW*, 440). And in the final chapter of *The Awakening*, Edna stands naked on the beach 'like some new-born creature, opening its eyes in a familiar world that it had never known' (136).

The title and the brief plot of 'Emancipation' also suggest the influence of the Civil War and the Emancipation Proclamation issued by President Lincoln in 1863. The war was very much a presence in St Louis during the early 1860s. Missouri was a border state, deeply divided on the issues of slavery and secession; Calloway County, west of St Louis, went so far as to declare its secession from both the Union and the Confederacy, and still refers to itself as the 'Kingdom of Calloway'. Sympathies in St Louis were divided in part along ethnic lines, with the older French families supporting the rights of slaveowners, and the large German immigrant population favoring abolition and the Union. The state of Missouri did not become part of the Confederacy, but militia groups representing Union and Confederate sentiments skirmished in and around the city, and when the Union troops occupied St Louis during part of the war, they spent much of their time searching out and punishing active Confederate supporters. The father of Kate's friend Kitty Garesché moved his family to South Carolina rather than signing a Union loyalty oath. The war affected the O'Flaherty family in very direct ways. Sacred Heart Academy was forced to close for a time in 1861; Kate's half-brother, George, died of typhoid fever while a soldier in the Confederate Army; and Kate herself became a minor celebrity when she tore down and hid a Union flag that someone had attached to the front porch of her house – at the age of 13, she was threatened with arrest. In a letter to her relative Frederick Alexander Charleville, in California, written about 1864, Kate's mother, Eliza, mentions this incident along with other disruptions caused by the war:

> These are strange times we are living in. My Negroes are leaving me[;] old Louise ran off a few days ago, I suppose the rest will follow soon. *God*'s will be done[.] … It is a mistake about the Charleville Boys [sic][;] they have been wounded, but are now well, the poor fellows, they have fought like *heros* [sic] for their freedom, & I hope they will be rewarded[. O]n the 11th of July last I was forced by a compy [sic] of dutch devils at the point of the bayonet to illuminate my house & to hoist a flag, it was to celebrat [sic] the taking of Vicksburg, they threatened to burn the house over our heads –

> (*KCM*, 104)

The most immediate impetus for Chopin's 1869 story of 'emancipation', however, may have been the requirements of the social life that increasingly occupied her time following her graduation from Sacred Heart in 1868. Like other young women of her social class, she was presented to society as a 'belle', which essentially meant that she was eligible to receive proposals of marriage. The round of luncheons, teas, and dances that constituted the debutante 'season' had its moments of gaiety and fun, but the demands of the social regimen encroached dismayingly on the intellectual life that had become important to 19-year-old Kate O'Flaherty. On New Year's Eve, 1868, she wrote in the diary she had begun to keep:

> What a nuisance all this is – I wish it were over. I write in my book for the first time for months; parties, operas, concerts, skating and amusements *ad infinitum* have so taken up my time that my dear reading and writing that I love so well have suffered much neglect.
>
> (*KCM*, 60)

In late March of 1869, as the end of Lent and the resumption of the social season approached, Kate wrote that she 'should like to run away and hide myself; but there is no escaping'. She describes herself as a person who loves amusements: 'I love brightness and gaiety and life and sunshine.' But the forced interaction and fatigue are taking their toll:

> I am invited to a ball and I go. I dance with people I despise; amuse myself with men whose only talent lies in their feet; gain the disapprobation of people I honor and respect; return home at day break with my brain in a state which was never intended for it; and arise in the middle of the next day feeling infinitely more, in spirit and flesh like a Lilliputian, than a woman with body and soul. – I am diametrically opposed to parties and balls; and yet when I broach the subject – they either laugh at me – imagining that I wish to perpetrate a joke; or look very serious, shake their heads and tell me not to encourage such silly notions.
>
> (*KCM*, 62)

The word 'soul' in this passage resonates not only with her Catholic training but also with the original title she gave *The Awakening*, 'A Solitary Soul', in which 'soul' has more to do with essential selfhood than with religious doctrine. In May of the same year, Kate may have simply been recording her frustration with serialized fiction, but her comment is similar to the resentment she concurrently expressed at the time her social obligations took from her reading. 'What a bore it is to begin a story, become interested in it and have to wait a week before you can resume it.' The story in question was 'The Man Who Laughs', by Victor Hugo, which she was reading in *Appleton's Journal* to satisfy her 'ravenous appetite' for reading (*KCM*, 64). Meanwhile, Kate reports, she has mastered the art of being 'agreeable' in social settings: 'It is not necessary to possess the faculty of speech.... All required of you is to have control over the muscles of your face – to look pleased and chagrined, surprised, indignant, and under every circumstance – interested and entertained' (*KCM*, 63).

However artificial the social interactions of the debutante season may have seemed to Kate O'Flaherty, they produced the intended outcome: in May of 1870 she became engaged to Oscar Chopin, the 25-year-old son of plantation owners in Natchitoches Parish, Louisiana, who had come to St Louis in 1866 to study banking at a firm owned by relatives of his mother. Thanks to the Civil War, Oscar had been partly educated in France; his French-born father had moved the family there in 1861 so that his son would not have to fight in what seemed to him a conflict to which a Frenchman owed no allegiance. (Dr J. B. Chopin, despite his land holdings in Louisiana, remained staunchly French; he resented the fact that following their marriage Oscar and Kate settled in the newer 'American' section of New Orleans rather than the French Quarter.) There is every indication that Kate O'Flaherty entered into her marriage with happiness and assurance. Announcing her engagement to her diary, she wrote that 'in two weeks I am going to be married; married to the right man.... I feel perfectly calm, perfectly collected' (*KCM*, 67). The couple were married on 9 June 1870, at Holy Angels Church in St Louis, and embarked on a three-month honeymoon in Europe.

By 1870, the genre of travel writing was well established; in the preceding year, in fact, Mark Twain had published his spoof of both the genre and the ignorance of American tourists in Europe, *The Innocents Abroad*. Many travelers kept journals of extended European travel with no other motive than to record the experience for themselves and perhaps members of their families, and such was the case with the newly married Kate Chopin. Nevertheless, her written account of the couple's journey through Germany, Switzerland, and France testifies to the powers of observation and skill in capturing colorful detail that would later characterize her fiction. Emily Toth's title for the section of her biography of Chopin that deals with the trip – 'A Writer's Honeymoon' – is somewhat misleading in its implication that Chopin already regarded herself as having a vocation, but it is true that her travel journal is rich in its depictions of people and places, and not a mere recounting of miles traveled and sites dutifully visited. Kate and Oscar Chopin were better prepared for the experience by their educational backgrounds and linguistic abilities (though neither had mastered German) than were many American tourists; they bought books and music as well as linens and other souvenirs, visited Goethe's house in Frankfurt, and appreciated regional foods and wines. Visiting a gambling house in Germany, Kate noted 'the sang froid of the croupier – the eager, greedy, and in some instances fiendish look upon the faces of the players' (*KCM*, 75). In Frankfurt, she is 'struck by the familiarity of an otherwise very refined German lady, with her maid. They seemed more like sisters, than mistress and maid' (*KCM*, 76); and in Switzerland she described in some detail the inhabitants of a peasant hut where she and Oscar sought refuge from a rainstorm. The start of the Franco-Prussian War in July of 1870 required refuge of a different kind; their journey to France was delayed and shortened, and the Paris they finally reached at the end of August was under siege. Perhaps because she had experienced the Civil War as it had encroached upon St Louis, Kate seems more excited than frightened by the situation in Europe. In Schaffhausen, Germany, toward the end of July, she reports in her diary that their hotel is nearly empty of tourists; she spends her time reading Charles Dickens, and notes that the son of a Russian family 'calls me *die schöne Dame* not being able to master the intricacies of Chopin' (*KCM*, 79). The war news remains in the distance until they reach Paris, but on 4 September Kate writes in her diary, 'What an eventful day for France, may I not say the world? And that I should be here in the midst of it.... The Emperor was prisoner in the hands of the Prussians.... [After a meeting of the Corps Législatif] it seemed to pass like an electric flash from one end of Paris to the other – the cry "Vive la République!" I have seen a French Revolution!' (*KCM*, 88).

Because Kate Chopin's honeymoon travel diary is the most detailed of her autobiographical writings to have survived, it is possible to know more about her enthusiasms and her mode of casual expression at the age of 20 than at almost any other period of her life. European travel had been a dream for a long time, and it may have been her impatience to see that dream realized that caused Kate to be largely disappointed in the American cities that she and Oscar visited en route to their departure from New York. Although Cincinnati was 'a nice cheerful place', and she especially enjoyed its beer gardens, Philadelphia struck her as 'a gloomy puritanical looking city' where the 'people all look like Quakers'. She found Philadelphia's rows of red brick houses with white shutters quite boring, and playfully wondered, 'why will not *some one*, out of spite, out of anything, put up a black blind, or a blue blind, or a yellow blind – any thing but a white blind' (*KCM*, 68). Kate agreed with Oscar that New York was 'a great den of swindlers', and she found their two weeks there 'dull, dull!' (*KCM*, 69). Once in Europe, however, Kate was an enthusiastic traveler; uniformity in a city's appearance did not bother her in Germany, as she noted approvingly that in Bremen, Germany, 'the houses were all thatched and the cows all black' (*KCM*, 70). If beer gardens had been the high point of Cincinnati, Germany was noted for its wines, and the Chopins visited the Bremen Rathskeller, 'the most celebrated wine cellar in the world' (*KCM*, 70). In Bonn, she reveled in sensual indulgence: 'What quantities of that maddening Rhine wine I have drunk today. The music – the scenery – the bright waters – the wine – have made me excessively gay' (*KCM*, 74–5). Later in the same entry, Chopin alludes to her habit of smoking cigarettes – a habit which would raise some eyebrows in New Orleans and Cloutierville: 'Dear me! I feel like smoking a cigarette – think I will satisfy my desire and open that sweet little box which I bought in Bremen' (*KCM*, 75).

Now an adult married woman away from the watchful eye of relatives and neighbors, Chopin reveled in her freedom. Although she and Oscar visited numerous European cathedrals, Kate several times mentions with guilty pleasure having failed to attend Sunday mass. In Schaffhausen, Germany, on 31 July, she noted, 'Sunday! *Intended* to go to church – but what is it they say of the paving stones of the lower realm? Did not rise till ten and the church is three quarters of an hour from here' (*KCM*, 78). In Lucerne on 15 August, she similarly records, 'It is ... the feast of the Assumption, which fact I discovered when it was too late to attend Mass' (*KCM*, 82). As she would in New Orleans, Chopin enjoyed taking solitary walks, and seems to have enjoyed at least as much the knowledge that such freedom was considered improper. In Zurich on 12 August, Chopin records that while Oscar took an afternoon nap, 'I took a walk alone. How very far I *did* go.... I wonder what people thought of me – a young woman strolling about alone. I even took a glass of beer at a friendly little beer garden quite on the edge of the lake' (*KCM*, 81). Like all tourists, the Chopins bought souvenirs of their journey, and Kate notes the purchase of a watch and some books and sheet music in addition to her Bremen cigarette box. One shopping expedition in Stuttgart, however, served to remind her that her stay in Europe would soon give way to the realities of married life. In addition to a 'black lace shawl', Kate purchased 'some brussels and valenciennes lace – table and bed linnens [sic] &c in anticipation of that house keeping which awaits me on the "other side"' (*KCM*, 77).

When the Chopins returned to the United States to take up domestic life in a duplex on Magazine Street in New Orleans in the fall of 1870, Kate was already pregnant with her first child, Jean Baptiste, who was born the following May and named after Oscar's father. New Orleans was not unfamiliar to her; she had visited there in the spring of 1869, and declared that she liked the city 'immensely; it is so clean – so white and green' (*KCM*, 64). In truth, despite its flourishing semi-tropical flower gardens and graceful architecture, New Orleans was a dirty and unhealthy city, especially in the summer, when deadly fever epidemics were common. Between 1860 and 1880, the population grew from 168, 675 to 216, 010; the system of sanitation was rudimentary, and disease-carrying mosquitoes abounded in the warm months. By contrast to St Louis, however, the city lacked the grey smoke of manufacturing, and the mixture of cultures – French Creoles, African-Americans (who were nearly half the population), Irish, and many others contributed by New Orleans' status as a major port – gave it a cosmopolitan atmosphere more like a European than an American city. The Victorian strictures regarding women's behavior had less force in Southern Louisiana than they did in most parts of the country. While the Creole culture into which Kate Chopin had married was in some ways patriarchal in the extreme, especially regarding the sexual double standard, women were relatively free to participate in the sensual pleasures of food and drink, music, brightly colored clothing, and lively social gatherings. When she was not visibly pregnant or recovering from childbirth, Kate Chopin enjoyed her long, solitary walks around the city, a practice apparently sanctioned by Oscar, although frowned upon by some members of his family, who visited the city frequently from Natchitoches Parish.

By 1872, Oscar Chopin was established as a cotton factor – a middleman between those who grew cotton and those who bought it for foreign markets or domestic manufacture. Before the Civil War, when the institution of slavery made possible the relatively inexpensive cultivation of huge cotton plantations, the position of cotton factor was a lucrative one; during Reconstruction, the unstable Southern economy made the job more risky. Nonetheless, Oscar Chopin prospered in the early 1870s. In 1873, he moved his office to a more prestigious address, and the Chopins moved their growing family to successively better addresses twice during the decade, settling finally on Louisiana Avenue in the Garden District. Meanwhile, Oscar Chopin became involved in the racial tensions and confrontations that characterized the Reconstruction South. Having avoided the direct conflict of the Civil War itself because of his father's decision to wait out the war in France, Oscar became embroiled in its aftermath by joining the First Louisiana Regiment, an offshoot of the Crescent City White League, in 1874. In September of that year, Oscar's regiment joined with other White Leaguers in an armed skirmish that became known as 'the Battle of Canal Street'; the White League demanded the resignation of the mayor of New Orleans, who was in turn defended by the Metropolitan Police. More than two dozen men were killed in the urban battle, in which the White Leaguers were briefly victorious; but federal troops soon returned the Reconstruction leaders to power, and Oscar seems not to have seen further military action in the cause of white supremacy and states' rights. The incident, however, serves as a reminder of the racial and political volatility of the deep South in the 1870s, when Kate Chopin was observing the milieu in which most of her fiction was to be set.

No diary survives from the period of Kate Chopin's marriage, so many details of her life in New Orleans must be reconstructed from anecdotal evidence and gleaned from her later writing. For some reason, she returned to St Louis for the births of her second and third sons: Oscar Charles in September of 1873, and George Francis, in October of 1874. It was not unusual for young women of the period to want the comfort and assistance of their mothers or other female relatives when they gave birth, and because Oscar Chopin's job required some travel, she may have needed help caring for her other children at such a time. Her mother, Eliza O'Flaherty, had traveled to New Orleans to be present at the birth of Kate's first child, and stayed on while Oscar traveled to France to settle his father's estate; circumstances may have prevented her from doing so in 1873 and 1874. Certainly Kate Chopin expressed no dissatisfaction with the doctor who delivered her first son, and at least as she remembered the event in 1894, the experience of giving birth was one of immense satisfaction – more closely resembling the experience of Madame Ratignolle than that of Edna Pontellier in *The Awakening*. As she recalled it on Jean Baptiste's twenty-third birthday, she awoke from the chloroform to see her mother holding 'a little piece of humanity all dressed in white which they told me was my little son!'. Chopin recalled the feeling of maternal joy as being instantaneous and overwhelming: 'The sensation with which I touched my lips and my fingertips to his soft flesh only comes once to a mother. It must be the pure animal sensation; nothing spiritual could be so real – so poignant' (*KCPP*, 183). Kate maintained a close relationship with her mother throughout her life, and the bond may have deepened after her brother Tom was killed in a buggy accident shortly after Christmas in 1873 (her only other sibling, her half-brother George, had died ten years earlier of typhoid fever while serving in the Confederate Army).

Chopin's fourth and fifth sons – Frederick and Felix Andrew – were born in New Orleans, in January of 1876 and 1878, respectively. In naming Frederick, Chopin honored her St Louis doctor, who was as noted for his participation in the city's intellectual circles as for his obstetrical skills. A visitor to the Chopin home during the late 1870s recalled for Daniel Rankin a boisterous household in which Oscar enjoyed playing with his children and in which there was always music and laughter. Kate and the children spent the summer months on Grand Isle, an island in the Gulf of Mexico near New Orleans, where Oscar visited them on weekends. At the time, Grand Isle was the favored vacation destination for well-to-do Creole families; accommodations were far from elegant, but the island had an atmosphere of exclusivity and miles of sandy beaches where children could play in the warm Gulf waters. At least as importantly, it was considered a healthier environment than New Orleans during the months when the mosquitoes that transmitted malaria and yellow fever were most active. A yellow-fever epidemic killed 4,000 New Orleans residents in the summer of 1878 alone; the sea breezes that swept Grand Isle offered some protection against the insects carrying the diseases. At Grand Isle in the summers of 1875 and 1877, Kate was in the early stages of pregnancy, a condition she transferred to Madame Ratignolle in *The Awakening*.

Conventional critical wisdom has held that Kate's marriage to Oscar Chopin was a happy one, and that the distant, rather businesslike relationship between the Pontelliers in *The Awakening*, in which Léonce regards Edna as a 'possession', and she gradually withdraws from both marriage and motherhood, is not drawn from Chopin's own marital experience. Yet certain of Edna's habits and attitudes are shared with her creator. Kate was known for her solitary walking explorations of New Orleans, and there is no evidence that Oscar sought to deny her this freedom. She delighted in observing the colorful bustle of the city and listening to the variety of dialects, including Creole, Acadian, and Irish. Those people to whom Daniel Rankin spoke for his 1932 biography recalled that Kate Chopin had a talent for imitating the speech she heard on the streets: 'With her intimate friends, and to the hilarious delight of Oscar, she occasionally demonstrated her power of mimicry that perfectly simulated the manners, actions, and tones of voice of anyone who attracted her insatiable curiosity' (82). Rankin is certainly correct when he asserts that 'without literary intentions, she was ... gathering impressions for the materials of her stories in future years', and almost certainly wrong when he states that 'during the ten [actually nine] years of her married life in New Orleans, Kate Chopin never attempted to write or take notes' (92). She did keep a diary, although apparently one not as detailed as her honeymoon diary; more importantly, she wrote letters to friends and family in St Louis – letters sufficiently lively and detailed to prompt more than one recipient to encourage her to write fiction when she returned to St Louis in 1884.

Letters were important to nineteenth-century culture not only as a means of communication. For women in particular, letters could serve as a prelude to or part of a career in writing; at the very least, they served as an important means of self-expression. While Kate Chopin was growing up in St Louis, the women whose families were crossing the Mississippi River to settle in the West kept diaries to send to friends and family members, and these in turn became part of the historical record of the frontier. At the same time, Emily Dickinson wrote letters that contained some of her more than 1,700 poems; until a few years after her death, this dissemination of her work constituted her major form of publication. The importance of letters to Chopin can be seen in the frequency of mail as a trope in her fiction. The protagonist of 'Elizabeth Stock's One Story' is the postmistress in a small town. The plot of 'For Marse Chouchoute' turns on the heroic and tragic effort of the young black boy, Wash, to be sure that the Cloutierville mail bag gets to the train on time. 'The Going Away of Liza' begins with the exchange of mail at a train station. In *The Awakening*, Edna keeps up with Robert while he is in Mexico through his letters to Mlle Reisz; in chapter XXI, one of his letters is connected to art more broadly as Edna begs Mlle Reisz to both show her the letter and play the Chopin 'Impromptu' for her.

There is nothing surprising about the fact that Chopin seems not to have entertained serious thoughts about writing fiction during the 1870s. Her formal education, while instilling in her a lifelong love of books, had not fostered career aspirations; indeed, Kate Chopin in her twenties was living precisely the life that the Sacred Heart nuns would have envisioned for her: marriage and motherhood. And although servants took care of the more onerous aspects of cooking, cleaning, and child care, the fact remains that she gave birth to six children within nine years, which required a considerable physical and emotional investment. Then, too, little in Chopin's background would have led her to see herself as part of a tradition of women writers; most of her reading had been – and would continue to be – in the work of European male writers. Although New Orleans was rich in music and art forms – including the annual gaudy displays of Mardi Gras, which began to be celebrated in its current form in 1871, the first spring the

Chopins lived there, the Chopins' social circle tended to consist of Oscar's business associates, who were preoccupied with the price of cotton and the indignities of Reconstruction. Whereas Harriet Beecher Stowe's literary aspirations had been fostered by her participation in the Semi-Colon club in Cincinnati in the 1830s, when she was in her early twenties, New Orleans did not offer Chopin a similar opportunity. Chopin's contemporary, Grace Elizabeth King, did not begin publishing her stories and sketches about New Orleans until the 1880s, by which time Kate Chopin's life had changed dramatically.

By the late 1870s, Oscar Chopin's prosperity was imperiled by successive poor cotton crops, and mounting debts persuaded him to move his family to land in Natchitoches Parish that he had purchased earlier in the decade. With the move in the fall of 1879, Oscar was returning to the area in northwestern Louisiana where he had grown up, but Kate, although she was closer to St Louis, was for the first time living in a rural area, populated by Acadians – 'Cajuns' – whose French ancestors had immigrated from Canada. The town in which Oscar Chopin went into business as a shopkeeper, Cloutierville, could hardly have been more different from New Orleans. It had been founded in 1822, but had scarcely grown beyond a single street during the intervening half century. The New Orleans that Chopin wrote about in such stories as 'A Pair of Silk Stockings' (1897) had restaurants with 'spotless damask and shining crystal, and soft-stepping waiters serving people of fashion' (*CW*, 503), but the Cloutierville where she set such stories as 'For Marse Chouchoute' (1891) was 'simply two long rows of very old frame houses, facing each other closely across a dusty roadway', and the mail that the title character is proud of carrying 'was a meagre and unimportant one at best' (*CW*, 105). In New Orleans, Kate Chopin could walk or take a streetcar by herself, and even smoke cigarettes, without exciting undue attention, but in Cloutierville she was quickly noteworthy for her fine clothes and her habit of riding astride her horse rather than sidesaddle, as ladies were supposed to do. Both Oscar and Kate had relatives in Natchitoches Parish, a fact which only increased the scrutiny with which their behavior was regarded, and small-town gossip persisted through several generations of residents.

Chopin's last child and only daughter, Lélia, was born on the last day of 1879. Given the fact that she was not quite 30 when Lélia was born, Kate may have made a conscious decision to have no more children. Methods of contraception – some of them crude and none of them sanctioned for Catholic families – did exist, and additional children would have strained the now-precarious financial circumstances of the Chopins. The eight-member family lived in one of the largest houses in Cloutierville, and employed servants to do cooking and laundry, but life in Natchitoches Parish did not offer the upward financial trajectory that New Orleans had once promised. Plantation lands once worked by slaves were now divided into tenant farms, and although Oscar's store stocked the essential goods for the community, from food to farm equipment to clothing, most residents bought on credit and were slow to pay their bills – and Oscar Chopin seems to have been disinclined to press them for payment. But in the informal rural atmosphere of Cloutierville, social class lines were less firmly drawn than they were in New Orleans, and the residents mingled freely at social gatherings, dancing, playing cards, and enjoying the often spicy regional dishes such as gumbo and meat pies. Entire families attended such parties, which frequently lasted far into the night, and descriptions of these festivities made their way into a number of stories that Chopin set in Natchitoches Parish, including 'For Marse Chouchoute', 'At the 'Cadian Ball', and 'A Night in Acadie', in which 'the musicians had warmed up and were scraping away indoors and calling the figures. Feet were pounding through the dance; dust was flying. The women's voices were piped high and mingled discordantly, like the confused, shrill chatter of waking birds, while the men laughed boisterously' (*CW*, 491).

Although Kate Chopin's daughter, Lélia, later recalled her mother as having been a 'Lady Bountiful' in Cloutierville, 'dispensing advice and counsel, medicines, and, when necessary, food to the simple people around her' (Rankin, 102), the very phrase 'simple people' suggests that the Chopins distanced themselves to some extent from their Cloutierville neighbors, or at least that Lélia remembered it that way. Kate seems in fact to have remained a controversial figure, taking solitary horseback rides, smoking Cuban cigarettes, and preferring the cross-section of humanity to be found at Oscar's store to the more domestic chores of needlework and child care. An attractive woman, she 'dressed up in the evenings, and young men flocked about her. She was not domestic, she was powerful socially, and she was considered rather aggressive for a woman. She was much more popular with men than with women' (Toth, 154). Less visible to her Cloutierville neighbors was Chopin's intellectual life. She read avidly, and particularly important to her during this period were the works of Charles Darwin, Thomas Huxley, and Herbert Spencer, whose beliefs in biological evolution ran counter to the teachings of her religious background, and whose theories of social evolution were having a profound effect on the competitive, increasingly market-driven economy and culture of late-nineteenth-century America. Such reading would have interested Chopin not only because of her interest in people, which a friend later described as 'her constant delight' (Toth, 152), but also because she was no stranger to the world of business and finance. In New Orleans, she had become familiar with Oscar's business, recording in her diary a 'journey with Oscar through the district of warehouses where cotton is stored', where she witnessed 'the whole process of weighing, sampling, compressing, boring to detect fraud, and the treatment of damaged bales', and heard laments about 'too much rain for cotton' (Rankin, 94–5). In Cloutierville, she observed business on a less grand scale, working occasionally in Oscar's store. When she created the character of Thérèse Lafirme in her novel *At Fault* as 'a clever enough business woman' (*CW*, 744), the description could have fit Chopin herself. By the time Chopin created Edna Pontellier's husband Léonce in *The Awakening*, she was familiar with business from personal experience as well as observation.

The description of Thérèse Lafirme on the first page of *At Fault* is in some ways a description of Kate Chopin in 1882: 'a handsome, inconsolable, childless Creole widow of thirty'. Chopin was by no means childless, she was not truly a Creole, and she was 32, but with Oscar's death on December 10 – apparently from malaria – she was a young, handsome widow. Thérèse has inherited a 4,000-acre plantation; Kate Chopin inherited Oscar's store and some land, but also his accumulated debts, including unpaid taxes on his New Orleans property, which she gradually paid off over the course of more than a year, using the proceeds of the store and money from the sale of some of the Natchitoches Parish land. Worry about his creditors could have made Oscar susceptible to the fever that killed him; at any rate, he had been ill off and on for more than a year, and had even traveled to Hot Springs, Arkansas, in the summer of 1881 to seek help from rest and the famous waters. Although quinine had been known as an effective remedy for malaria for a long time, it was not administered until late in Oscar's illness, probably because it took a skilled diagnostician – not readily available in rural Natchitoches Parish – to distinguish between malaria and the other mosquito-borne fever common in damp, low-lying areas: yellow fever, which was often fatal. Oscar Chopin was buried in Cloutierville, and Kate stayed on there to manage both the business and domestic affairs of the family.

Whether Kate Chopin, like Thérèse Lafirme, was 'inconsolable' at her husband's death remains a matter of some conjecture. Her 1895 diary entry, suggesting that she would gladly give up the 'real growth' she had experienced during the previous decade if her mother and her husband were restored to life, indicates a continuing devotion to Oscar's memory, and her industry in paying off his debts – including the doctor bills incurred in his illness – suggests that she at least wished his name to retain its honor. Emily Toth, however, finds evidence that the relationship was strained during the Cloutierville years. She points out that Kate made an extended visit to St Louis shortly after Oscar returned to Louisiana from Hot Springs, and notes that 'since Louisiana residents did not commonly go north for the winter, such a trip ... could be taken as a sign of marital troubles' (158). Toth also reads Chopin's fiction for signs of how she might have felt about Oscar's death, concluding, accurately, that 'few of Kate Chopin's widowhood stories are portraits of grief' (163). The best-known of these stories is 'The Story of an Hour', in which Mrs Mallard looks forward to years in which 'there would be no powerful will bending hers in that blind persistence with which men and women believe they have a right to impose a private will upon a fellow creature', and pronounces herself 'free, free, free!' (*CW*, 353). Reading an author's work autobiographically, however, produces more speculation than certainty, and in the case of a woman writer, such readings come perilously close to reinforcing nineteenth-century critical views that women were capable of describing what they had experienced, but not of imagining what they had not. Small-town gossip passed from one generation to the next is scarcely more reliable, and the rumors that Kate Chopin had an affair – possibly beginning even before Oscar's death – with her Cloutierville neighbor Albert Sampité must remain just that, despite the fact that Toth is convinced of their truth, taking as evidence the recollections of a descendant of one of Chopin's contemporaries: 'The general talk was that [Sampité] was in love with the pretty widow, and there were those who believed that she, too, was in love with him. And that may be why she suddenly gave up the store and the plantation and went back to St Louis' (Toth, 172).

In fact, Eliza O'Flaherty had been urging her daughter to return to St Louis since Oscar's death. Whether or not she stayed for some time in Cloutierville because of a love affair, it is a matter of record that she proved to be an able businesswoman, overseeing the general store and chipping away at the various debts that Oscar had left: land taxes, money owed for merchandise for the store, and interest on loans. She also made sure that Oscar's relatives received the appropriate sums they were entitled to inherit from his estate, and went through the legally required process of petitioning to be named the official guardian of her children. Remarriage would have been a logical step for a young, attractive widow, especially when, debts finally paid, she was still a landowner, but Kate Chopin returned to St Louis in 1884, leaving her older boys to stay for a time with Oscar's brother, and resumed life with her mother. St Louis schools offered more for her children than did those of Natchitoches Parish, and life in a city provided Chopin with a level of intellectual and cultural stimulation that Cloutierville lacked. Then, too, during her 14 years as a resident in Louisiana, Chopin had spent a good deal of time in her native city, and had remained in touch with friends such as Kitty Gerasché and Dr Frederick Kolbenheyer, who had delivered the two of her sons who were born there. She returned neither as a young woman requiring the financial assistance and emotional support of her immediate family nor as a dutiful daughter called to care for an aging parent – Eliza O'Flaherty was only 56, and apparently in good health – but as a mature, competent woman selecting the environment in which she would live the next phase of her life.

At the time that Chopin moved to St Louis, her mother was living with her widowed sister, Amanda McAllister, and Amanda's two grown children, but shortly thereafter – presumably needing more room – Eliza, Kate, and Kate's children moved to a house across the street from Kate's Aunt Amanda. The children were enrolled in St Louis public schools, and settled into life with their grandmother, whose Creole-accented way of speaking English would have been familiar to them from the experience of Louisiana. Less than a year later, however, in late June of 1885, Eliza O'Flaherty died suddenly, and Kate Chopin's family circle was once again disrupted. The funeral was held at Holy Angels Church, where Kate had been married 15 years earlier. Her response to this loss was by all accounts unambiguous: she was grief-stricken, left without any immediate family except her children, the eldest of whom was 14 years old. While Chopin was not financially destitute, she inherited little from her mother, who had been the victim of unscrupulous management of her estate. The seriousness with which Kate Chopin began writing during the next few years seems the result of several convergent realities of the mid-1880s. Grief and loneliness fostered the need to explore in writing the ways individuals respond to change – not only loss, which Mrs Mallard assumes is the case in 'The Story of an Hour', but also positive alterations: the possession of a few extra dollars in 'A Pair of Silk Stockings', a joyous sexual encounter in 'The Storm'. The need for adult companionship made her welcome the visits of Frederick Kolbenheyer, who had kept her letters from Louisiana and detected in them a talent for writing fiction, and through whom she came to know other St Louis intellectuals. And extra income would be welcome.

Further, by the mid-1880s the popularity of regional literature meant that a variety of voices and accents had entered American literature. The publication of Mark Twain's *The Adventures of Huckleberry Finn* in 1885 not only revolutionized narrative by being related in the voice of an unschooled adolescent, but also gave prominence to a black character, the runaway slave Jim. In the same year, Joel Chandler Harris published *Mingo and Other Sketches in Black and White*, and George Washington Cable published his non-fiction study *The Creoles of Louisiana*, followed the next year by his novel *Dr. Sevier*, set in New Orleans at the time of the Civil War. Rose Terry Cooke's *Root-Bound* and Sarah Orne Jewett's *A Marsh Island* represented New England in 1885, and Jewett's *A White Heron and Other Stories* appeared the following year. In a few years, following her long apprenticeship as keen observer and recorder, Kate Chopin would take her place among such writers.

3
The Early Stories and *At Fault*

> About eight years ago there fell accidentally into my hands
> a volume of Maupassant's tales.... I read his stories and
> marveled at them.... Here was life, not fiction.... Here was
> a man who ... looked out upon life with his own eyes;
> and ... told us what he saw.
>
> (Kate Chopin, 'Confidences', 1898)

In crediting Guy de Maupassant for her own literary 'awakening',
Kate Chopin dates this revelation as occurring about 1890. In fact,
Chopin had been preparing for a literary life since she listened to
her great-grandmother's stories when she was five years old, and
read the novels of Sir Walter Scott when she was six. The years in
Louisiana had nourished a fiction-writer's imagination with the
settings and, more importantly, the people whose inner lives
became as important to her as were the colorful speech patterns she
liked to imitate. The appeal of Maupassant's stories may well have
lain in the French author's insistence on the solitude of the individual – a core 'self' that remained unknowable by other people.
Certainly the Maupassant stories that Chopin translated into
English – several of which were published in *St. Louis Life* and *The
St. Louis Republic* in the 1890s – deal with this theme. In the
Maupassant story 'Solitude', for example, a character says that
'since I have realized the solitude of my being I feel as if I were
sinking into some boundless subterranean depths', and the story's
narrator confirms his own inability to penetrate his companion's
essence: 'Was he drunk? Was he mad? Was he wise? I do not know'

(*KCC*, 195–7). Although Chopin's own fictional investigations of human solitude tend to be more lighthearted than Maupassant's accounts of madness and obsession, she did originally title *The Awakening* 'A Solitary Soul', and she exhibited a lifelong tendency to stand apart from the crowd. In her relationships with others, Kate Chopin was sometimes perceived as holding herself apart while achieving an understanding of her companions. She wrote as much in her commonplace book in 1869:

> A friend who knows me as well as anyone is capable of knowing me – a gentleman of course – told me that I had a way in conversation of discovering a persons [sic] characteristics – opinions – and private feelings – while they knew no more about me at the end than they knew at the beginning of the conversation. Is this laudable? Bah! I'll not reason it, for whatever my conclusion I'll be sure to follow my inclination.
>
> (*KCPP*, 83)

During the years immediately following her return to St Louis, Chopin set about remaking her life in ways that gave her greater independence. In 1886, a year after her mother's death, she bought a house in a newer part of the city, moving herself and her children away from her remaining relatives. Although she remained nominally a Catholic, she no longer attended mass regularly, and her associates were increasingly selected from among the St Louis intelligentsia, which included artists and journalists as well as Dr Frederick Kolbenheyer, whom Daniel Rankin describes as 'a decided agnostic; genial, witty, determined, a man of tremendous mental capacity, whose cultured insinuating conversations carried conviction to Kate Chopin' (106). In addition to encouraging Chopin to write fiction, Kolbenheyer served as an informal critic of her early work. Chopin recorded in the notebook in which she kept meticulous accounts of her literary career that she gave Kolbenheyer a 30,000–word draft of a story she then called 'Euphrasie', which she had completed in 1888, in April of 1890, and that he returned it in June and she began to revise it in January of 1891 (Rankin, 114). The story, considerably shortened and titled 'A No-Account Creole', was eventually published in *Century* magazine in 1891. Others – primarily journalists – also critiqued Chopin's early work. John

Dillon, editor of the St Louis *Post-Dispatch*, read a story titled 'A Poor Girl' in December of 1889 after it had been returned from the *Home Magazine*, which had found its subject matter not 'desirable'; following revision, Chopin submitted it to the *New York Ledger*, for which Fanny Fern had been a popular columnist in the 1850s and 1860s, and when the story was again rejected, she destroyed it (Rankin, 115). Journalist Charles Deyo was another of Chopin's willing local critics as she worked to establish herself.

The fact that newspaper editors and writers considered themselves appropriate critics for a fiction writer points to certain realities of the nineteenth-century literary market. Not only did many authors work as both journalists and fiction writers, but newspapers routinely printed short stories and poetry. Stephen Crane began his career as a fiction writer with *Maggie: a Girl of the Streets* (1893) and *The Red Badge of Courage* (1895), and then became a war correspondent who turned his experience on a sinking ship near Cuba in 1896 into his well-known story 'The Open Boat'. Of the handful of Emily Dickinson's poems that were published during her lifetime, the majority appeared in a newspaper, the *Springfield* (Massachusetts) *Republican*. Despite the increasing prominence of literary journals such as *The Atlantic* and *Century*, newspapers remained an important outlet for authors of fiction and poetry into the early decades of the twentieth century. Kate Chopin's close association with leading St Louis journalists during the 1880s was therefore important to the development of her career; several of her early short stories were first published in St Louis newspapers, which made her a local celebrity and widened her intellectual circle within the city. Just as the line between newspapers and literary journals as venues for serious writers was not as firmly drawn as it would later be, so the distinction between authors who wrote for children and those who wrote for adult readers was by no means firm. Both Louisa May Alcott and Mark Twain moved easily between the two audiences, and both Alcott's *Little Women* and Twain's *Huck Finn*, originally intended for adolescent readers, have become part of the adult literary canon. Some of Chopin's fiction similarly appealed to more than one audience: 12 of the stories collected in *Bayou Folk*, and three of those collected in *A Night in Acadie*, were originally published in such periodicals for young people as *Youth's Companion* (founded by Fanny Fern's father, Nathaniel Willis, in 1827) and *Harper's Young People's Magazine*.

As she established her own life in St Louis during the late 1880s, Chopin by no means severed her ties with Louisiana. In the summer of 1887, she and her children visited Natchitoches Parish. She still owned the house in Cloutierville where she and Oscar had lived, and the rent its occupants paid was one of her sources of income. She also remained close to Oscar's family, and on this visit was the guest of his brother Lamy. Oscar's sister Marie had been married shortly after Kate moved back to St Louis to an engaging ne'er-do-well named Phanor Breazeale, and during this visit Kate first met Phanor, whose irreverence appealed to her, and with whom she enjoyed smoking cigarettes and playing cards. In the spring of 1889, Kate returned to Cloutierville to take an action that signaled continued devotion to Oscar's memory: she had his body removed from the Cloutierville cemetery and sent by train to St Louis, where it was buried in the O'Flaherty family plot in Calvary Cemetery in April. She continued to own the Cloutierville house, however, until December of 1898, and kept in touch with Oscar's family in Natchitoches Parish with visits and letters.

By the time of her visit to Cloutierville in 1889, Kate Chopin had become a published writer. Although she had begun writing fiction by this point, her first published work was a poem – one of the few she ever published, and one of the 20 or so of her poems that have survived. 'If It Might Be' was published in January of 1889 in the Chicago magazine *America*. The publication was auspicious in the sense that *America* had a national readership, and it had published work by the venerable James Russell Lowell, who had edited THE *Atlantic* when Kate was growing up in St Louis, and by the popular Wisconsin poet Ella Wheeler Wilcox, who was known for her sentimental verse. In her literary debut, Kate Chopin had more in common with Wilcox than with Lowell. 'If It Might Be' is conventional in style, consisting of two four-line stanzas featuring rhymed couplets and such standard poeticisms as 'thou didst' and 'twixt'. The speaker in the poem offers both her love and her life to one who has only to declare his need for either; the tone is submissive and pensive, and the subjunctive 'if' conveys a resigned hopelessness. Chopin biographer Emily Toth suggests that she may have had Albert Sampité in mind as she wrote the poem, but any evidence of this is external to the poem itself.

Chopin's first published story, 'A Point at Issue!', which appeared in the St Louis *Post-Dispatch* in October of 1889, conveys a very different, and more characteristic, picture of relationships between men and women. If Chopin used the medium of poetry to express desires and yearnings, she used fiction to work out her ideas about the differences between social conventions and the individual's need for freedom and self-development. Although she had also been working on a story with a Louisiana setting, tentatively titled 'Grand Isle' (which she destroyed without, apparently, attempting to publish it), Chopin made her debut as a fiction writer not as a regionalist, but instead by reflecting the challenges to convention that circulated in the intellectual circle of which she was a part in St Louis. 'A Point at Issue!' is set in the non-regionalized town of Plymdale (whose name vaguely suggests 'Plymouth', and thus points to New England rather than to the South) and in Paris. It concerns the unconventional marriage between Charles Faraday, a professor of mathematics at Plymdale University, and Eleanor Gail, a young woman 'possessed of a clear intellect: sharp in its reasoning ... that *rara avis*, a logical woman' (*CW*, 49). The couple are intellectual companions, 'knocking at the closed doors of philosophy; venturing into the open fields of science' (*CW*, 50), for whom marriage seems a logical extension of an established friend-ship, characterized by 'readiness to meet the consequences of reciprocal liberty' (*CW*, 50). Thus, when Gail decides she wants to become fluent in French, the couple decide that she will move to Paris, where he will visit her during his summer vacations, for as long as is necessary to reach her goal, despite the views of a society that feels, 'It was uncalled for! It was improper! It was indecent!' (*CW*, 51). In spite of their unconventionally egalitarian views of marriage, Charles and Gail both prove to be susceptible to jealousy, she of a young female acquaintance whose charms Charles describes in too much detail in a letter, and he of a male Parisian who turns out to have been painting Gail's portrait as a gift for Charles. But the two quickly overcome these obstacles to their happiness and return to Plymdale together. Chopin's second published story, 'Wiser Than a God', similarly deals with a woman determined to follow her ambitions, which transcend conventional marriage; this story, like 'A Point at Issue!', emphasizes theme rather than setting, taking place in an unnamed city among people of German ancestry. Following her mother's death, Paula rejects a proposal of marriage to pursue a career as a concert pianist, telling her suitor that '[marriage] doesn't enter into the purposes of my life' (*CW*, 46). When he protests that she is speaking 'like a mad woman', she likens her vocation to that of a nun, asking whether he would 'go into a convent, and ask to be your wife a nun who has vowed herself to the service of God' (*CW*, 46–7).

By the time 'Wiser Than a God' was published in the Philadelphia *Musical Journal* in December of 1889, Chopin had assembled a circle of friends to whom the personal freedom explored in these stories would have been congenial. Like other American cities in the 1880s and 1890s, St Louis had its share of people who, like Chopin, read Darwin and Spencer and the latest fiction, who questioned traditional institutions, and who were engaged in social reform movements. Chopin's youngest son, Felix, later recalled that his mother 'belonged to a liberal, almost pink-red group of intellectuals, people who believed in intellectual freedom' (Toth, 182). Although Chopin herself was not an activist, among her friends were women who advocated women's suffrage and such clothing reforms as 'bloomers' – a trouserlike garment that gave women greater freedom of movement. Although St Louis still served as an important transition point for westward migration, it was also an intellectual center for the region, with two private universities and several periodicals in addition to newspapers, including *St. Louis Magazine*, *St. Louis Life*, *St. Louis Spectator*, and *Fashion and Fancy*. The editors of these periodicals – some of them women – were among Kate Chopin's friends, replacing her extended family and the Church as centers of her life.

As Chopin's first two published stories suggest, emotional and intellectual or artistic freedom were more important to her than was political freedom in the form of the right to vote, which she never openly advocated. When her stories featured women who were writers, one of her fictional purposes was to express her resistance to the sentimental or otherwise formulaic literature that had become associated with women. In 'Miss Witherwell's Mistake', the satirically treated title character writes fiction and articles for the Boredomville *Battery*. The fact that Miss Witherwell is a spinster does not stop her from writing articles such as 'A Word to Mothers', and she regards fiction and real life as entirely separate realms: 'two such divergent cupids, as love in real life, and love in fiction, held themselves at widely distant points of view' (*CW*, 60).

When Miss Witherwell's niece, Mildred, asks her aunt's advice about the story of two separated lovers that she does not know how to conclude, Miss Witherwell offers formulaic plot elements, such as having the young man rescue the girl's father from a railway accident or a shipwreck. Her niece protests that she wants a realistic story, which prompts Miss Witherwell to expostulate, 'the poison of the realistic school has certainly tainted and withered your fancy in the bud', and she suggests the only two endings that seem to her appropriate for fiction: 'Marry them, ... or let them die' (*CW*, 65). In 'Elizabeth Stock's One Story', the title character is rebuffed when she attempts to write realistic stories. When she writes one about 'old Si' Shepard that got lost in the woods and never came back', it is her uncle who protests that life and fiction are different: 'this here ain't no story; everybody knows about old Si' Shepard' (*CW*, 586). Elizabeth Stock is therefore persuaded that if she wants to be a writer, she must write about 'a murder, or money getting stolen, or ... mistaken identity' (*CW*, 587). Chopin further comments on the difference between realistic and formulaic fiction by having the narrator who introduces Elizabeth's 'one story' – a true account of her life – refer to it dismissively as the only item among her papers that 'bore any semblance to a connected or consecutive narration' (*CW*, 586).

'Elizabeth Stock's One Story' remained unpublished during Chopin's lifetime; it was included in the 1969 *Complete Works*, and then in *A Vocation and a Voice* (1991). The earlier-written 'Miss Witherwell's Mistake' was rejected by five national periodicals before being published in the St Louis *Fashion and Fancy* in February of 1891. Two months before, Chopin had published her first children's story, 'With the Violin'. Having also sought national publication for this story, after several rejections she placed it with the St Louis *Spectator* for December 1890. While Chopin appreciated the publication opportunities afforded by her growing local reputation and her network of St Louis friends, she continued to look to the major periodicals of the Northeast for recognition of her talent. When, in 1894, Chopin reviewed Hamlin Garland's *Crumbling Idols* for *St. Louis Life*, she took Garland to task for declaring that the dominance of the East as a literary center was soon to be at an end, replaced by such places as Chicago and California:

His attitude in regard to the East as a literary center is to be deplored; and his expressions in that regard seem exaggerated and uncalled for. The fact remains that Chicago is not yet a literary center, nor is St Louis (!), nor San Francisco, nor Denver, nor any of those towns in whose behalf he drops into prophecy. There can no good come of abusing Boston and New York. On the contrary, as "literary centers" they have rendered incalculable service to the reading world by bringing to light whatever there has been produced of force and originality in the West and South since the war.

(*CW*, 694)

By the time Chopin wrote in praise of Boston and New York as publishing centers capable of serving the needs of writers and readers in other parts of the country, her first collection of stories, *Bayou Folk*, had been published by the Boston firm of Houghton Mifflin; she could therefore feel assured that her own work had sufficient 'force and originality' to merit recognition on a national level. Such recognition required, however, that she make use of the Louisiana materials that she had accumulated during her 14 years of residence there. To become a 'national' writer, in other words, she first had to become a 'regional' writer.

Some of Chopin's earliest published efforts at using regional materials took the form of stories for children. Whether consciously or not, she thus took advantage of two of the most widely sanctioned modes for women writers of her era: using the powers of observation to create 'local color', and teaching young people moral lessons through fiction. Three of these stories are set in and around Cloutierville, in Natchitoches Parish, Louisiana. 'For Marse Chouchoute', which was published in *Youth's Companion* in August of 1891, is a story of self-sacrifice. When the 16-year-old Creole Armand Verchette, nicknamed 'Chouchoute', is given the job of delivering the Cloutierville mailbag to the railway station, his responsibility to 'Uncle Sam' awes his young Negro friend, Wash, to such an extent that when Chouchoute stops at a party on his way to the station and loses track of time, Wash takes it upon himself to deliver the mailbag, and suffers a serious injury in the process. The interracial theme of the story is interestingly complex. The black Wash is clearly the story's hero, risking his life to fulfill

Chouchoute's responsibility; at the same time, the relationship between the two recalls the days of slavery: 'Marse' is a term for 'Master', and when the station-master informs Chouchoute that Wash has been hurt, he refers to him as 'that poor little fool darky of yours' (*CW*, 109), suggesting ownership. 'A Very Fine Fiddle', which appeared in *Harper's Young People's Magazine* in November of 1891, features a poor white family living on the fringes of plantation culture. This story, too, is a cautionary tale, though one with less dire consequences. Fifine, one of six children of the destitute Cléophas, grows tired of her father playing his fiddle to take his children's minds off their hunger, and trades the rare old fiddle for a newer fiddle and some cash, but Cléophas is too disheartened by the loss of his 'very fine fiddle' to play the new one. 'Boulôt and Boulotte', also published in *Harper's Young People's Magazine*, the following month, similarly deals with a large family in rural Natchitoches Parish. Less didactic than the other two stories, 'Boulôt and Boulotte' is an amusing account of the 12-year-old twins of the title going to town to buy the first pairs of shoes they have ever owned, but carrying the shoes home rather than wearing them because, as Boulotte defiantly announces, 'You think we go buy shoes for ruin it in de dus'? *Comment!*' (*CW*, 152). The Creole syntax and French words in such stories demonstrate the accuracy of Chopin's ear for Louisiana dialects.

Both Louisiana and St Louis figure as settings in Chopin's first novel, *At Fault*, which she had privately published in 1890. Chopin's notebook records that she began writing the novel in July of 1889, a few months after she brought Oscar's body back from Cloutierville, and completed it the following April. By this point a committed writer, despite her initial difficulty in placing her work in the leading national periodicals, Chopin completed four short stories, a translation of a story by the French writer Adrien Vely, and the manuscript of *At Fault* between the early summer of 1889 and the spring of 1890. A recollection of her daughter, Lélia, presents the picture of a woman writing quickly, with little revision, in the midst of a busy household that included six children between the ages of 10 and 18:

She always wrote best in the morning, "when the house was quiet," as she said. She always wrote rapidly with a lead pencil on

[a] block [of] paper. When finished, she copied her manuscript in ink, seldom changing a word, never "working over" a story or changing it materially. She did not have a study or any place where she ever really shut herself off from the household. I know now that she often desired to do this when writing, but on the other hand, she never wished to shut us children out of her presence, and with the natural selfishness of children, we never tried to keep her undisturbed as she should have been.

(Rankin, 116)

Chopin biographer Emily Toth points out that Lélia's statement that the writer 'did not have a study' is not really accurate, and that Chopin 'kept her own writing room, furnished with bookcases, a comfortable Morris chair, and a very naked Venus on the bookshelf' (*KCPP*, 132). Both Lélia's description and some of Chopin's own comments about her writing habits seem calculated to create the sense that, like Jane Austen, she wrote without what Virginia Woolf would call 'a room of [her] own', combining her domestic and professional lives. In fact, Chopin's stories, many of them quite short, read like the quick outpourings she claimed they were, with sustained style and tone betraying little hint of domestic interruption. A novel was a different matter, and after completing *At Fault*, Chopin suffered just one rejection of the manuscript before paying the Nixon-Jones Printing Company of St Louis to produce 1,000 copies in September of 1890. She also served as her own publicist for the novel, noting in her account book that in late September and early October she sent review copies to the St Louis and New Orleans newspapers as well as to the national periodicals *The Nation*, *The Critic*, and *Literary World* (*KCPP*, 160).

At Fault, while not the major artistic achievement that *The Awakening* is, is interesting for its blending of literary genres and styles and for what it reveals of Chopin's participation in the intellectual dialogues of the late nineteenth century. As Chopin's only work that provides a sustained contrast between St Louis and rural Louisiana, the novel also suggests the depth of her interest in and affection for the culture and landscape of the region inhabited by Creoles and Acadians. In its plot structure and a number of its fictional elements, *At Fault* is informed by the popular romance novel of the nineteenth century. The would-be lovers, Thérèse

Lafirme and David Hosmer, must overcome significant obstacles before finally being united in marriage. Chief among these obstacles is David's divorce from his first wife, Fanny. As a Catholic (although, like Chopin, not a deeply committed one), the widowed Thérèse cannot countenance marriage to a divorced man, and it requires David's and Fanny's remarriage and the *deus ex machina* of Fanny's accidental death to allow the happy ending. In her insistence that David 'do the right thing' and return to his ex-wife, Thérèse exerts the moral force of the romance heroine, and even the language in which she delivers her ultimatum to David recalls the romance tradition:

> You married a woman of weak character. You furnished her with every means to increase that weakness, and shut her out absolutely from your life and you from hers. You left her then as practically without moral support as you have certainly done now, in deserting her. It was the act of a coward.
>
> (*CW*, 768–9)

Like a number of other romance heroines, such as Fleda in Susan Warner's *Queechy* and Christie Devon in Alcott's *Work* (1873), Thérèse is at the same time strong and competent, running her deceased husband's cotton plantation as capably as David runs the sawmill he has established on part of Thérèse's land, and earning the respect of those who work for her, most of whom are former slaves.

Also in keeping with the women's romance tradition is Chopin's use of settings. Much of *At Fault* takes place in domestic spaces that reflect the characters' moral standing, taste, and/or emotional state. The house that Thérèse has had built on her plantation following her husband's death, is deliberately comfortable and old-fashioned; in planning Place-du-Bois, Thérèse has 'avoided the temptations offered by modern architectural innovations, and clung to the simplicity of large rooms and broad verandas: a style whose merits had stood the test of easy-going and comfort-loving generations' (*CW*, 742). The house is thus a correlative to Thérèse's open, generous nature and solid virtues. When David's rather flighty sister Melicent comes to visit the plantation, she immediately redecorates the guest cottage, 'effacing the simplicity of her rooms with certain bizarre decorations that seemed the promptings of a disordered imagination. Yards of fantastic calico had been brought up from the store, which Grégoire with hammer and tacks was amiably forming into impossible designs at the prompting of the girl' (*CW*, 754–5). And one of the ways in which Chopin signals the anti-intellectualism of Fanny Hosmer's St Louis friend Belle Worthington is her refusal to allow her husband's books to be openly displayed in their apartment, 'averring that to have them lying around was a thing that she would not do, for they spoilt the looks of any room' (*CW*, 782). In contrast is the 'long, low, well-filled book-case' in the living room of Thérèse Lafirme at Place-du-Bois, whose shelves hold works by Balzac, Scott, Racine, Molière, and Shakespeare (*CW*, 845). The characters' response to the natural landscape is similarly revealing. Thérèse is deeply tied to the land, observing the fields and woods of the plantation from the back of her horse and from the veranda: 'she could see beyond the lawn ... a quivering curtain of rich green which the growing corn spread before the level landscape, and above whose swaying heads appeared occasionally the top of an advancing white sun-shade' (*CW*, 743). The city-bred Fanny, on the other hand, finds no beauty in the Louisiana countryside she sees from the train window, 'as they whirled through forests, gloomy with trailing moss, or sped over an unfamiliar country whose features were strange and held no promise of a welcome for her' (*CW*, 794).

While the central characters in *At Fault* are complex and realistic, Chopin also makes use of familiar nineteenth-century stereotypes that serve both sentimental and satiric purposes. Although Chopin often dealt sensitively with racial issues and relationships, several of the black characters in this novel are merely two-dimensional representations of white Reconstruction-era wish fulfillment. Uncle Hiram is the faithful, obsequious servant who, on the first page of the novel, warns Thérèse that thievery is taking place on the plantation and thus rouses her from her grief to take charge of the business her husband has left her. In the same category is the black Creole Marie Louise, whom Thérèse calls 'Grosse tante'. Marie Louise had been Thérèse's 'nurse and attendant from infancy'; now too old for service, she lives in a cabin across the river, which she will cross only to superintend the cooking at a fancy dinner party or to minister to Thérèse when she is ill, 'when she would install herself at her bedside as a fixture, not to be dislodged by any less inducement than Thérèse's full recovery' (*CW*, 807). Yet when Fanny Hosmer is killed when the river bank beneath Marie Louise's cabin is eroded by a storm, Chopin makes no mention of the fate of the elderly black woman. These honest and devoted black characters are reminiscent of Uncle Tom and Aunt Chloe in Stowe's *Uncle Tom's Cabin*, and Chopin makes reference to this novel when Grégoire tells Melicent about the grave of 'ole McFarlane', who, local legend has it, was the model for Simon Legree – or, as Grégoire puts it, 'the person that Mrs. W'at's her name wrote about in Uncle Tom's Cabin' (*CW*, 751). The young ne'er-do-well Jocint similarly merely serves the atmospheric romance by burning down David Hosmer's sawmill; the deed brings out a latent violence in Thérèse's nephew, Grégoire, who kills Jocint and is himself later shot to death in a fight. Neither death contributes materially to the central plot of the novel; instead, these characters provide a dark, violent contrast to the moral drama enacted between Thérèse and David.

It is the social satire that counterbalances the romance which ties *At Fault* to the final decades of the nineteenth century and reflects Chopin's awareness of and involvement in the intellectual controversies of her day. Religious skepticism is an important thread in the novel despite – or perhaps because of – the fact that Thérèse Lafirme's Catholic opposition to divorce is a central element of the plot. The most skeptical character of all never appears in the novel. David Hosmer's friend Homeyer – who seems to some extent based on Chopin's friend Frederick Kolbenheyer – is described as an 'individualist' who believes that a man has 'the right to follow the promptings of his character' (*CW*, 746). According to Homeyer, 'all religions are but mythological creations invented to satisfy a species of sentimentality – a morbid craving in man for the unknown and undemonstrable' (*CW*, 792). In his rejection of religion as mere 'mythology', Homeyer is at one end of a spectrum of beliefs in the novel. At the opposite extreme is Belle Worthington's daughter, Lucilla, a pious Catholic girl who attends – as had Kate Chopin – the Sacred Heart Academy in St Louis, and who intends to become a nun. Chopin's own reservations about Catholicism seem reflected in a comic conversation between Lucilla and Thérèse's black servant Aunt Belindy; when Lucilla remarks superciliously that 'the religious never get married, ... and don't live in the world like others', Aunt Belindy responds, 'Gwine live up in de moon?' (*CW*, 841). The other characters occupy positions between these two extremes. Belle Worthington is described as 'a good Catholic to the necessary extent of hearing a mass on Sundays, abstaining from meat on Fridays and Ember days, and making her "Easters"' (*CW*, 784). For her bookish husband, religion is an intellectual pursuit, not a matter of faith; he studies the history of religions, and is particularly interested in their similarities, 'the points of resemblance which indicate in them a common origin'. But Mr Worthington does not reject religion, as does Homeyer: 'the world is certainly to-day not prepared to stand the lopping off and wrenching away of old traditions' (*CW*, 792–3). Such discussions also reflect late-nineteenth-century controversies about the efficacy of social reform. While Mr Worthington seems to adopt a philosophy of gradual social evolution, David Hosmer is sympathetic to his friend Homeyer's more activist leanings, representing Homeyer as 'a little impatient to always wait for the inevitable natural adjustment' (*CW*, 793).

Just as Mr Worthington is present in *At Fault* only to represent such late-century intellectual discussions, his wife and other St Louis women offer Chopin the opportunity to comment satirically on urban pretentiousness, especially in contrast to Thérèse Lafirme's natural beauty and morality. Unlike Thérèse, these women do no meaningful work, but instead engage in a social life that includes drinking and card-playing. Chopin describes Belle Worthington and her friend Lou Dawson in scathing terms: 'These were two ladies of elegant leisure, the conditions of whose lives, and the amiability of whose husbands, had enabled them to develop into finished and professional time-killers' (*CW*, 781). Lou Dawson, whose husband is a traveling salesman, tests the limits of propriety by openly flirting with other men when her husband is away. None of the St Louis women is a model of motherhood. Lou Dawson has no children, and Belle Worthington has turned the care of 12-year-old Lucilla largely over to the Sacred Heart nuns. Chopin comments wryly that this nominally Catholic woman, by having only one child, 'had done less than her fair share ... as [a] propagator of the species' (*CW*, 782). David Hosmer's former wife, Fanny, had been less than devoted to the couple's one son, who died at the age of three, and David seems to feel that the child's death was in some ways a blessing. The time that Belle Worthington might have spent on parenting, she spends instead on adorning herself for social events, and Chopin takes care to point out the artificiality of her public appearance. As Belle pins to her hair blond curls which she has taken from her 'top drawer', her own blonde hair has 'a suspicious darkness about the roots, and a streakiness about the back, that to an observant eye would have more than hinted that art had assisted nature in coloring Mrs. Worthington's locks' (*CW*, 779).

In her comparison between the artificiality and decadence of an urban area such as St Louis and the natural environment of rural Louisiana, Chopin both borrows from the nineteenth-century romance tradition and pokes gentle fun at the life she was leading in St Louis. The identification of the city with corruption and the countryside with moral purity long pre-dated the nineteenth century, but such a distinction gained force with the growth of American cities, especially as immigration and industrialization led to crowding and magnified social-class differences. As early as the 1830s and 1840s, the Transcendentalists had touted the natural world as the source of moral lessons, and the association of female fictional characters with flowers, moonlight, and other natural phenomena signaled their essential purity. Ralph Waldo Emerson is one of the authors to whom Chopin frequently refers in her fiction (in *At Fault*, one of Mr Worthington's prized possessions is a volume of Emerson's essays); in her response to a review of *At Fault* in the *Natchitoches Enterprise*, Chopin quotes Emerson as saying, 'Morals is the science of substances, not of shows. It is the *what* and not the *how*' (*KCPP*, 202). Although Chopin does not 'code' Thérèse Lafirme as many nineteenth-century writers did their female heroines, she closely associates her with the natural as opposed to the artificial. When describing Thérèse's beneficial effect on Fanny Hosmer, for example, Chopin describes Thérèse as 'this woman so wholesome, so fair and strong; so un-American as to be not ashamed to show tenderness and sympathy with eye and lip' (*CW*, 801). The Louisiana setting is, to be sure, the scene of three violent deaths during the course of the novel – Jocint, Grégoire, and Fanny – but each of these deaths occurs in the service of the novel's moral drama.

In contrast to the Louisiana countryside, St Louis is depicted as busy, crowded, and impersonal. Although there is admiration for the city in Chopin's notation of the 'push and jostle of the multitudes that thronged the streets' and the 'intoxicating life', David Hosmer can only 'shiver' as he makes his way through the crowd in chapter IX, and Chopin emphasizes the 'ultra fashionable tendencies' of those on the sidewalks (*CW*, 775). The growth of St Louis since David has last been there is also presented in a negative light. A formerly quiet street now has a cable-car 'come to disturb its long repose, adding ... nothing to its attractiveness', and new apartment buildings merely reinforce the crowded nature of city life: 'marvelous must have been the architectural ingenuity which had contrived to unite so many dwellings into so small a space' (*CW*, 776). The characters' attitudes toward the novel's two locales are one index of their positions on the moral scale. Chopin indicates that David Hosmer belongs in Louisiana when, in an early conversation with Thérèse, he reveals his antipathy for St Louis: 'I resisted anything so distasteful as being dragged through rounds of amusement that had no attraction whatever for me' (*CW*, 767). In contrast, the women who are engaged in St Louis social activities are disdainful of life further south. When David visits St Louis intending to be reunited, however reluctantly, with his former wife, Fanny announces, 'I don't like the South. I went down to Memphis ... last spring ... ; and I don't see how a person can live down there' (*CW*, 778). Later, learning that Fanny is to move to Louisiana with David, Belle Worthington expresses her hope that the couple are to settle in New Orleans, 'the only decent place in Louisiana where a person could live' (*CW*, 788).

While Chopin ran certain personal risks in poking fun at her native city and modeling some of her characters on her St Louis friends and acquaintances, the truly controversial aspects of the novel lay not in its satiric elements, but in her treatment of such subjects as religious skepticism, divorce, and alcoholism. No one in the novel is conventionally pious; for most, religion is a matter of forms to be dutifully observed or the object of intellectual curiosity, and the convent-bound Lucilla is presented as a priggish fanatic. Even Thérèse, who is paradoxically the moral center of the novel and the one 'at fault' for some of its tragic outcomes, acts out of a vague sense of Catholic propriety rather than deeply held religious convictions. When Grégoire is killed, she asks the Catholic clergymen of the region to say masses for his soul, but does so as a response to custom rather than faith: 'Not that Thérèse held very strongly to this saying of masses for the dead; but it had been a custom holding for many generations in the family and which she was not disposed to abandon now' (*CW*, 853). Even her rejection of the divorced David and her insistence that he re-marry Fanny is based on what Chopin terms 'the prejudices of her Catholic education' rather than a deep conviction that divorce is a sin; Thérèse 'felt vaguely that in many cases [divorce] might be a blessing', and that it 'must not infrequently be a necessity' (*CW*, 764). And when she and David are reunited following Fanny's death, Thérèse regards herself as 'at fault in following what seemed the only right' (*CW*, 872). The fact that the reason for the divorce was Fanny's alcoholism is another audacious element of *At Fault*. In both the popular fiction and the temperance literature of the nineteenth century, the figure of the dissolute alcoholic was typically male – a man to be reformed by a virtuous woman, or whose drinking would be legally curtailed through the efforts of a largely female temperance movement. Nor is Fanny the only woman in the novel who is intemperate in her use of alcohol. As if to underscore the fact that women are not above the lure of strong drink, Chopin has Mr Worthington, perusing a volume of the lives of the saints while visiting Place-du-Bois, become fascinated by the story of St Monica, who, although ultimately cured of her addiction by 'Heaven', spent much of her life suffering from a 'dangerous intemperance' (*CW*, 846).

Interestingly, the reviewers who criticized *At Fault* tended to focus not on these obvious thematic issues, but on matters that to readers today seem merely incidental. To be sure, some reviewers adopted a moralistic stance, and the conservative *St. Louis Republic* addressed the topic of divorce obliquely by characterizing the novel as a story about 'women who love other women's husbands' (Toth, 191). The St Louis *Post-Dispatch*, in an otherwise positive review, objected to the fact that Melicent, David's sister, had been engaged five times, and *The Nation* – the only national periodical that reviewed *At Fault* – seeking the character who is 'at fault', refers to Fanny as 'the lady who drinks' (Toth, 192). And the *Natchitoches Enterprise* found 'improper' what it referred to as the 'love-making' between Thérèse and David when their lives should remain on a 'pure and high plane' (Toth, 193). But some reviewers took issue with Chopin's style; the *Republic* reviewer objected to her use of 'depot' to refer to a railway station and 'store' instead of 'shop'. Chopin chose to respond to two reviews of *At Fault*. In response to the *Republic*'s critique of her language, she wrote, 'I cannot recall an instance, in or out of fiction, in which an American "country store" has been alluded to as a "shop", unless by some unregenerate Englishman' (*KCPP*, 201). And when the *Enterprise* referred to Fanny as the 'heroine' of the novel, Chopin was compelled to set the record straight:

> Fanny is not the heroine. It is charitable to regard her whole existence as a misfortune. Thérèse Lafirme, the heroine of the book is the one who was at fault – remotely, and immediately. Remotely – in her blind acceptance of an undistinguishing, therefore unintelligent code of righteousness by which to deal out judgments. Immediately – in this, that unknowing of the individual needs of *this* man and *this* woman, she should yet constitute herself not only a mentor, but an instrument in reuniting them.
>
> (*KCPP*, 202).

Chopin's response to the *Enterprise* review reveals an interesting ambivalence to the woman she regarded as the central character of *At Fault*. She refers to Thérèse as the 'heroine' of the novel, and both her positive characterization of Thérèse and the novel's happy ending – in the tradition of the 'marriage plot' – argue for the author's admiration of her heroine. Yet Chopin also blames Thérèse for exercising a God-like power over the lives of others, and thus interfering with the individual autonomy that Chopin argues for in much of her fiction – most compellingly in *The Awakening*.

Foreshadowing the direction that Chopin's critical reputation would take during the 1890s, the aspect of *At Fault* that was most consistently praised by reviewers was Chopin's rendering of her Louisiana characters and settings. Even the reviewer for the *St. Louis Republic* acknowledged that the novel was 'a clever romance of Louisiana life', and noted that 'the local color is excellent' (Toth, 190–1). The more favorable review in the St Louis *Fashion and Fancy* placed Chopin in 'that bright galaxy of Southern and Western writers who hold today the foremost rank of America's authors', and the *New Orleans Daily Picayune* noted that the novel 'charmingly related' the life of 'a handsome Creole widow' (Toth, 192). The *Natchitoches Enterprise* balanced its negative critique of the novel's morality with praise for Chopin's depictions of the region.

The character and speech of the Creole Grégoire were 'true to nature', and Chopin's depictions of her black characters were singled out for special praise:

> The negro character[s] are exceedingly well reproduced and the authoress traces with a mistress hand the peculiarities of the African's dialect.... [T]he light and shade thrown in by Belinda's remarks are perfect specimens of negro mannerism. Marie Louise and Morico form exquisite pictures of old time darkies and remind the writer of the race and characteristics of his old nurse and yard-servant of the long ago.
>
> (Toth, 193–4)

Such statements as this reveal prevailing attitudes toward women writers and local-color literature, and also indicate why the identification of female authors with this literary genre led to the denigration of both by the early twentieth century. By using terms such as 'authoress' and 'mistress', the reviewer underscores Chopin's gender, and her depiction of the 'darkies' in *At Fault* appeals to the reviewer's sense of nostalgia for a bygone era. While Chopin's portrayals of African-Americans in this novel are admittedly stereotypical, in her use of dialect, her choice of such words as 'depot', and her treatment of the theme of divorce, she was striving for the kind of realism advocated by William Dean Howells, whose 1882 novel *A Modern Instance* she greatly admired.

One of the objects of Chopin's passing satire in *At Fault* is women's social clubs. Even the flighty Melicent is filled with 'horror' when she recalls the 'hundred cackling women' she observed playing cards in St Louis (*CW*, 855). Never much of a joiner, Chopin became a charter member of the elite St Louis Wednesday Club toward the end of 1890. The Wednesday Club was devoted more to intellectual exchange than to card-playing; one of its founders was Charlotte Stearns Eliot, whose son Thomas Stearns (later T. S.) Eliot was then a small child. The Wednesday Club was formed as 'a center of thought and action among the women of St. Louis' (Toth, 208), and among its members were women who had been active in the women's suffrage movement in Missouri. By now a dedicated and increasingly successful author, Chopin was more attracted to the club's intellectual than its reformist activities. Just as Chopin held her character Thérèse Lafirme 'at fault' for telling other people how to live their lives, she was suspicious of reformers. In her 1894 diary, Chopin wrote satirically about a Mrs Stone, who 'accepts life as a tragedy and has braced herself to meet it with a smile on her lips':

> The spirit of the reformer burns within her, and gives to her eyes the smouldering, steady glow of a Savonarolas. The condition of the working classes pierces her soul; the condition of women wrings her heart. "Work" is her watch word. She wants to make life purer, sweeter, better worth living.... She does not live for herself but for others and she is just as willing to reach the "world" through her personal work as through the written word. Intentions pile up before her like a mountain, and the sum of her energies is Zero!
>
> (*KCPP*, 185–6)

Chopin returned to this theme in her 1898 essay, 'Confidences'. 'Some wise man', she wrote, 'has promulgated an eleventh commandment – "thou shalt not preach"', which interpreted means "thou shalt not instruct thy neighbor". It is a commandment about as difficult to observe as the other ten.' Having been made miserable by such 'preachers', Chopin reports that she 'turned to and played "Solitaire" during my thinking hours' (*CW*, 702). As a version of playing Solitaire, Chopin resigned from the Wednesday Club after less than two years of membership.

About the same time that she resigned from the Wednesday Club, Chopin completed the story 'Miss McEnders', which continued the satire on her St Louis acquaintances she had begun in *At Fault*, and expressed in fictional form her resistance to reformers – this time on the grounds of hypocrisy. The title character is a wealthy young woman who plans to deliver her paper on 'The Dignity of Labor' to the Women's Reform Club and join a 'committee of ladies to investigate [the] moral condition of St. Louis factory girls' on the day of the story. But first she goes to meet Mademoiselle Salambre, who is sewing part of Miss McEnders' trousseau, because she 'liked to know the people who worked for her, as far as she could' (*CW*, 204). When she discovers that Mlle Salambre has a child but no husband, she erupts in moral indignation and demands that the seamstress cease work on her clothing. Mlle Salambre, whose occupation allows her to learn many of the city's secrets, challenges Miss McEnders to find out how her father has acquired his wealth, and she discovers what everyone except her seems to know: that her father is engaged in the illicit sale of whiskey. Gone are Miss McEnders' thoughts of 'the dignity of labor' and the 'moral condition of factory girls' as she 'sank into a chair and wept bitterly' (*CW*, 211). In an era of ardent reform movements, the satiric 'Miss McEnders' was not easy to place with a publisher. Chopin submitted the story to five periodicals, including *New England Magazine* and *Vogue*, before ceasing to send it out. Five years later, in March of 1897, the story appeared in the *St Louis Criterion*, under the pen-name 'La Tour'. The pseudonym would have protected Chopin from the anger of St Louis residents who recognized the model for the title character as Ellen McKee, a well-known philanthropist and daughter of William McKee, who had been convicted in the 1870s for stealing tax money from illegally brewed whiskey.

Kate Chopin risked alienating her St Louis readers by selecting such easily recognized targets for her satiric talent, but she ran different risks in some of the fiction she wrote in the early 1890s. 'Mrs. Mobry's Reason', written in 1891, deals with hereditary syphilis; her title character's 'reason' for being reluctant to marry, and then for determining that her daughter will never marry and have children, is her knowledge that she is a carrier of this disease, which, at the end of the story, has begun to manifest itself in her daughter, Naomi. The fact that the terms 'syphilis' and 'venereal disease' do not appear in the story is evidence of both Chopin's discretion and also widespread public familiarity with syphilitic symptoms. Nevertheless, 'Mrs. Mobry's Reason' was rejected by 14 publications (*KCPP*, 163–4) before finally being published in the New Orleans *Times Democrat* in April of 1893. Chopin was familiar with both Ibsen's 1881 play *Ghosts* and Sarah Grand's 1893 novel *The Heavenly Twins*, both of which dealt with syphilis, and both of which were read and discussed among Chopin's circle of friends. Sarah Grand's novel was intended in part as a warning to women about marrying men whose previous sexual experiences could expose them to venereal disease, and in her diary for 2 June 1894, Chopin makes reference to an acquaintance who believed the novel to be 'a book calculated to do incalculable good in the world: by helping young girls to a fuller comprehension of truth in the marriage relation!'. Chopin suggests that she agrees with this assessment when she adds, 'Truth is certainly concealed in a well for most of us' (*KCPP*, 185).

At the same time that Chopin's fiction of the early 1890s demonstrates her engagement with the controversial issues of the day, she was also writing the stories that were to comprise her 1894 collection, *Bayou Folk*. The fact that of the 23 stories in *Bayou Folk*, 19 were published separately in periodicals between 1891 and 1894 – 17 of these in publications with national circulations – testifies to the rapid pace of Chopin's growing reputation. By the same token, however, nine of the stories were first published in either *Youth's Companion* or *Harper's Young People's Magazine*, which provides evidence that it was fiction with 'safe' subject matter – including stories considered appropriate for children – that could make her work acceptable to a wide reading public. That public, at least as editors perceived it, also preferred stories set in Louisiana to those set in Missouri; the dialects and customs of Cajun and Creole characters seemed far more exotic than the more recognizable people of Missouri, and Chopin found it easier to place her Louisiana sketches.

Although the 1890 publication of *At Fault* had not brought Chopin the prestige she might have hoped for, she was undaunted in her commitment to writing and publishing, and 1891 constituted a sort of turning point in her career: she experimented with writing drama, had her first short story published in the prestigious *Century* magazine, and recognized that Louisiana was the most appropriate setting for her fiction. The one-act social comedy 'An Embarrassing Position', which is Chopin's only extant play, was not published until 1895, when it appeared in the St Louis *Mirror*. With its stereotypical characters and contrived plot, the play, like scores of others that enjoyed popularity in the 1890s, borrows from the conventions of the French farce and the English drawing-room comedy. Working in a genre that by its very nature does not permit a great deal of originality, Chopin nonetheless demonstrates considerable skill in creating social satire – an aspect of her career that has been largely overlooked. The plot turns upon the danger to a candidate for public office of even the appearance of sexual impropriety: when young Eva Artless shows up at the home of Willis Parkham late at night intending to spend the night as a guest,

Parkham hastily arranges to marry her rather than risking negative publicity. While Eva, Willis, and the opportunistic journalist are standard characters of farce, Chopin uses the figure of Cato, the 'respectable old negro servitor' in the Parkham household, to make fun of white southerners' penchant for dramatizing their Civil War experiences. When Willis Parkham summons Cato to go for a minister to perform the marriage ceremony and asks whether Cato can be trusted, the elderly Negro launches into the family story about burying the valuables as Yankee troops advance on the property: 'Ole Marse Hank, he come tu me, an' he 'low "Cato you's de on'iest one on de place w'at I kin tres' – ... Take dis heah gole, an' dis heah silver" – ' (*CW*, 171). Unlike Hiram, who in *At Fault* is a sentimental stereotype, Cato illustrates the comic potential of Southern myth-making.

The story 'A No-Account Creole', which the *Century* published in August of 1891, was a revision of one of the earliest stories that Chopin had written. After completing a 10,000–word version – then titled 'Euphrasie's Lovers' or 'A Maid and Her Lovers' – in 1888, Chopin submitted the story to six periodicals, including *Harper's* and *Cosmopolitan*, before seeking the editorial assistance of Frederick Kolbenheyer and then sending it to Richard Watson Gilder, the *Century* editor. At least two previous editors had complained that the story was too long, and Gilder also required revisions, but accompanied his critique with a 'flattering letter', which inspired Chopin to complete her revision within a week and return it to Gilder on 12 July. On 3 August, she could note that it had been 'accepted by Century – $100.00' (*KCPP*, 165). Chopin's letter to Gilder with her revision reveals an author eager to please an influential editor:

> The weakness which you found in "A No-Account Creole" is the one which I felt ... I thank you more than I can say, for your letter. My first and strongest feeling upon reading it was a desire to clasp your hand.... I shall confess that your letter has given me strong hope that you may find the story worthy of publication.
>
> (*KCM*, 106)

'A No-Account Creole' is set in both New Orleans and Natchitoches Parish, homes of the two men who vie for the affections of

Euphrasie, but New Orleans is mere backdrop, even during the scenes that take place during Mardi Gras. In contrast, the Natchitoches Parish setting comes alive in the dialects of its black and Creole inhabitants and in the physical descriptions of the land, with its live-oak trees and mockingbirds. Not only does this emphasis parallel the plot, as Wallace Offdean is drawn to the countryside as much as he is to Euphrasie – 'he had never known ... how charming a place an old, dismantled plantation can be' (*CW*, 91) – but it also reflects Chopin's fascination with rural Louisiana, where the stories that would comprise *Bayou Folk* are largely set. Following a visit to Natchitoches Parish late in 1891, Chopin returned to St Louis full of Louisiana stories to write during the winter months.

Shortly after Chopin and her son Oscar visited Marie and Phanor Breazeale in Natchitoches, the *Natchitoches Enterprise* reported on the visit, identifying Chopin as 'the authoress of that charming story *At Fault*', and noting that she 'has lately written another novel which will make its appearance in one of the leading American Magazines [sic.]' (Toth, 204). Assuming this new novel to be *Young Doctor Gosse and Théo*, the *Enterprise* was overly optimistic. Chopin's notebooks indicate that she sent this 50,000-word novel, which she wrote between May and November of 1890, to seven different publishing companies in Chicago, Boston, and New York in 1891, only to have it rejected by all seven. Later in the decade, the manuscript was rejected by three additional publishers, and Chopin ultimately destroyed it (*KCPP*, 162–3). Little is known about the novel except that the plot began in Paris and concluded in the United States. Chopin later recorded her frustration with the judgments of editors, whom she describes as 'really a singular class of men; they have such strange and incomprehensible ways with them'. She found particularly distressing assessments of her work which seemed contradictory:

> I once submitted a story to a prominent New York editor, who returned it promptly with the observation that "the public is getting very tired of that sort of thing." I felt very sorry for the public; but I wasn't willing to take the man's word for it, so I clapped the offensive document into an envelope and sent it away again – this time to a well-known Boston editor. "I am delighted with the story," read the letter of acceptance, which

came a few weeks later, "and so I am sure, will be our readers" (!) ... I wonder if the editor, the writer, and the public are ever at one.

(*CW*, 717–18)

Also disappointing during 1891 was Chopin's failure to win several literary competitions that she entered, including a *New York Herald* drama contest to which she submitted 'An Embarrassing Position'.

Such setbacks, however, hardly affected the pace of Chopin's writing in the early 1890s. Most of the stories in *Bayou Folk* were written in 1892 and 1893; indeed, in January of 1892, Chopin wrote three of the *Bayou Folk* stories in two days: 'The Bênitous' Slave', 'A Turkey Hunt', and 'Old Aunt Peggy'. Never a disciplined writer with set routines or goals for a day's work, Chopin wrote when inspired to do so, often accomplishing a great deal in a short time. In describing her writing process, Chopin anticipated and perhaps influenced her daughter Lélia's portrait of a woman balancing her professional life with her domestic responsibilities. Because this description was written for publication in the St Louis *Post-Dispatch* in November of 1899, and particularly because it was written several months after the publication of *The Awakening*, it seems likely that Chopin exaggerated the attraction of domestic activities such as sewing and cleaning:

I write in the morning, when not too strongly drawn to struggle with the intricacies of a pattern, and in the afternoon, if the temptation to try a new furniture polish on an old table leg is not too powerful to be denied; sometimes at night, though as I grow older I am more and more inclined to believe that night was made for sleep.... There are stories that seem to write themselves, and others which positively refuse to be written – which no amount of coaxing can bring to anything.... [W]hat is called the polishing up process has always proved disastrous to my work, and I avoid it, preferring the integrity of crudities to artificialities.

(*CW*, 721–2)

Chopin's aversion to the 'polishing up process' is more a commentary on her work habits than a reflection of her willingness to take constructive criticism from those whose opinions she respected. As the letter to *Century* editor Gilder indicates, she could respond with grace to suggestions that were intended to improve her work. In the same letter, in fact, she speaks to changes that she has made to her portrayal of Euphrasie: 'I hope I have succeeded in making the girl's character clearer. I have tried to convey the impression of sweetness and strength, keen sense of right, and physical charm beside'; and despite her defense of 'the integrity of crudities', she assures Gilder that she has 'further changed and eliminated passages that seemed to me crude' (*KCM*, 106). In the initial stages of composition, however, Chopin preferred to pour out her first conception of a story with few alterations.

By the spring of 1893, Kate Chopin decided that she had enough stories – many of them already published or accepted for publication – to comprise a book-length collection, and set about trying to find a publisher for it. She wrote to Marion A. Baker, editor of the New Orleans *Times-Democrat*, that she was about to leave for 'a two weeks absence in New York and Boston, and shall combine the business of seeking a publisher with the pleasure of – well, not seeking a publisher' (*KCM*, 107). In her quest for a publisher for her 'collection of Creole stories', later titled *Bayou Folk*, she had the support of Richard Watson Gilder, who had agreed to see that it was read by the editors at the Century Company. She was simultaneously attempting for the last time to find a publisher for her novel *Young Doctor Gosse*, and on 10 May 1893, she wrote to Gilder from her hotel in New York to assure him that she would not use his endorsement of her short fiction to help sell her novel:

> I have left the MS of a novel ... with the Messrs. Appleton. In using your kind note of introduction, however, I explained that it had no connection with the novel, of which you know nothing, but had been written in reference to a collection of short tales that you had subsequently consented to have read by the Century company.
>
> (*KCM*, 108)

Both Appleton and Century turned down Chopin's collection of stories, and in the summer she sent the manuscript to Houghton Mifflin, which accepted it for publication in 1894 as *Bayou Folk*. With the publication of this volume in late March, Kate Chopin was poised to be considered a major contributor to Southern local color literature.

In advertising *Bayou Folk* in the 17 March 1894, *Publishers Weekly*, Houghton Mifflin emphasized the strangeness for most readers of Chopin's subject matter. The stories, featuring 'life among the Creoles and Acadians of Louisiana', deal with characters who are 'semi-aliens', but who are nonetheless 'picturesque and altogether worthy of description and literary preservation'. Potential readers are advised that although dialect is used for authenticity, it is not used 'at such length as to be tedious', and the paragraph concludes by promising that 'these stories are quite unlike most American tales, and cannot fail to attract much attention' (Toth, 223). A glance at the table of contents of *Bayou Folk* would have signaled to readers in other parts of the country that they were entering distinctive linguistic territory; many of the story titles feature the names of people and places that would have seemed exotic to readers in the midwest and northeast, including 'Madame Célestin's Divorce', 'Boulôt and Boulotte', and 'La Belle Zoraïde'. As such titles also suggest, Chopin's central interest lay in characters rather than plot, and other titles convey a sense of place: 'In and Out of Old Natchitoches', 'A Visit to Avoyelles', 'A Gentleman of Bayou Teche', 'A Lady of Bayou St John'. Houghton Mifflin was optimistic about the success of *Bayou Folk*, producing an initial printing of 1,250 copies to be sold at $1.25 each.

Bayou Folk was the subject of a long review in the *New York Times* a little more than a week after it was published, and the anonymous reviewer provided ample evidence that Chopin's subject matter was indeed 'alien' to him or her. Whereas most of the stories in *Bayou Folk* are set in Natchitoches Parish, in the northwestern part of Louisiana, the reviewer wrote at some length about the Mississippi River, which forms the state's eastern border. Chopin's Creole and Cajun characters seem to the reviewer like anthropological specimens rather than citizens of the United States in the 1890s: they are 'barbarians softened by Catholicism', and have a 'pagan primitiveness' (Toth, 226). The reviewer for *The Critic* also stressed the exotic locale of Chopin's stories, writing with her own hyperbole about the Louisiana landscape, with its 'terrifying alligator', 'melodious mosquito', and 'dazzling heron' (Toth, 226). Although most of the reviews of *Bayou Folk* were positive, as with many contemporary responses to local-color writing they gave the writer scant credit for artistry, suggesting that she had merely recorded what she had observed without the power of invention. The *Times* reviewer, for example, complimented Chopin on possessing 'the art to let these stories tell themselves', and the writer for *The Critic* noted Chopin's 'shrewdness of observation and ... fine eye for picturesque situations'; in the same vein, *The Atlantic* commented that 'the entire ease with which she uses her material is born not less of an instinct for story-telling than of familiarity with the stuff out of which she weaves her stories' (Toth, 226). Also characteristic of such reviews was the frequent use of the words 'picturesque', 'quaint', and especially 'charming' – words which reviewers intended in a positive sense, but which just a few decades later would be used to denigrate the local-color genre.

A few reviewers compared Chopin's stories to those of Maupassant, but almost none dealt at any length with her artistic skills. An exception was *The Literary World*, which pointed out that many of the stories in *Bayou Folk* were 'little more than *croquis* – just a brief incident [or] idea sketched in with a few rapid strokes and left to the imagination of the reader to be *materialized*', but even this tribute to the suggestive economy of Chopin's style was overshadowed by the reviewer's sense of the strangeness of Chopin's subject matter: 'that subtle, alien quality which holds the Creole apart from the Anglo-Saxon – a quality we do not quite understand and can never reproduce, but which is full of fascination to us from the very fact that it is so unlike ourselves' (Toth, 227). In St Louis, where Louisiana scenes and characters were less 'alien', *Bayou Folk* and its author were fulsomely praised, and Chopin was declared a better author than the popular Southern local-colorists George Washington Cable and Mary Noailles Murfree. But local pride tended to obscure serious literary assessment, and Chopin was largely disappointed in the reviews of her book, despite the fact that her publisher was pleased. Houghton Mifflin might have been happy that the collection of stories was consistently considered 'charming', but Chopin had higher ambitions, as she wrote in her diary:

> In looking over more than a hundred press notices of "Bayou Folk" which have already been sent to me, I am surprised at the very small number which show anything like a worthy critical

faculty. [Serious reviews] might be counted upon the fingers of one hand. I had no idea the genuine book critic was so rare a bird. And yet I receive congratulations from my publishers upon the character of the press notices.

(Toth, 228)

Chopin did not respond to specific press notices of *Bayou Folk*, so there is little way of knowing how she felt about the remarks included in two of the longest articles occasioned by the publication of her collection of stories – remarks that to readers today seem calculated to deny her status as a professional writer. St Louis resident William Schuyler, in a profile of Chopin published in *The Writer* in August 1894, acknowledged that Chopin had shown a flair for writing while she was still a student, but pointed out that she was 'not distinguished as a scholar', and that following her marriage she became 'engrossed in the manifold duties which overpower a society woman and the conscientious mother of a large and growing family' (*KCM*, 116). Later in the article, Schuyler suggests that writing fiction was for Chopin more whim than vocation as he describes her method of composition: 'When the theme of a story occurs to her she writes it out immediately.' Schuyler, who had interviewed Chopin for his article, next stresses Chopin's appearance and demeanor, calling her 'attractive' and 'charming', and noting that 'her manner is exceedingly quiet' (*KCM*, 118). Closer to home, Chopin's friend Sue V. Moore took even greater pains to distance Chopin from the image of the professional woman writer in her article in *St. Louis Life*. While Moore calls Chopin 'one of the foremost writers of American fiction' (*KCM*, 111), she, like Schuyler, posits that such a ranking has come to her almost accidentally:

[Kate Chopin] is the exact opposite of the typical bluestocking. She has no literary affectations; has no "fads" or "serious purpose" in life; declares that she has never studied. She takes no notes and has never consciously observed people, places, or things with a view to their use as literary material.

(*KCM*, 114)

It is worth noting that in her commonplace book early in 1869, not long after she had graduated from Sacred Heart Academy, Chopin had indicated her interest in the concept of the 'bluestocking' by copying from an unnamed source the history of the term, including its current meaning of 'a title for pedantic or ridiculous literary ladies' (*KCPP*, 67).

Moore concludes her article by emphasizing Chopin's attractive appearance and her closeness to her children, with whom she makes 'a most attractive family group' (*KCM*, 115). Such comments served to contain the writer within a proper feminine role, which the character of the stories in *Bayou Folk* did nothing to violate. As she gained national recognition for her first collection of short stories, Kate Chopin was largely writing in a genre that reviewers and readers considered above all 'quaint' and 'charming', but her standards and aspirations were those of the serious artist.

4
'Local Color' Literature and *A Night in Acadie*

> How immensely uninteresting some "society" people are!
>
> (Kate Chopin, 'Impressions', 1894)

Besides her 1870 honeymoon journal, the only extant diary that Kate Chopin kept was written in 1894 and titled 'Impressions'. Her 4 May notation about the dullness of 'society people' is strikingly similar to her remarks in her commonplace book in the late 1860s about the fatigue and boredom of the debutante season. Then she had been a young woman who resented the time that parties and banal conversation took from her intellectual pursuits; in 1894, she was in a sense reaping the rewards of her intellectual and professional development by being asked to read her stories to people she often did not respect. The paragraph in which this exclamation occurs reveals Chopin reluctantly forgoing her own pleasures in order to promote *Bayou Folk*, which had been published about six weeks earlier:

> Have missed the euchre club again because Mrs. Whitmore insisted upon having me go to her house to meet Mrs. Ames and her daughter Mrs. Turner, who were anxious to know me and hear me read my stories. I fear it was the commercial instinct which decided me. I want the book to succeed. But how immensely uninteresting some "society" people are! That class which we know as Philistines. Their refined voices, and refined speech which says nothing – or worse, says something which offends me. Why am I so sensitive to manner.
>
> (*KCPP*, 179–80)

As in her commonplace book, Chopin presents herself not as anti-social, but rather as a woman who preferred to choose her own social events – in this case an opportunity to play cards – rather than being compelled to associate with people she considered 'Philistines'. The remark about giving in to her 'commercial instincts' speaks to Chopin as a professional writer, obligated to promote her own work by reading from it to people she presumed were more interested in her celebrity than her artistry.

'Impressions' also offers other evidence of Chopin's status as a professional author with two published books to her credit. She reports on a dinner party with William Schuyler, who had been asked to write a profile of her for *The Writer*, and his wife, and professes to be quite pleased with the account of her life that Schuyler had developed – perhaps because it preserved her feminine gentility and protected her from the epithet 'bluestocking': 'I don't know who could have done it better; could have better told in so short a space the story of my growth into a writer of stories' (*KCPP*, 183). Being a published author also brought with it requests that she critique the work of those who aspired to be writers, and Chopin responded with generosity, while expressing in the privacy of her diary her reservations about their talent. She remarks of a Mrs Sawyer that she is 'a harmless poet', and of a Mrs Blackman that she has 'the artistic temperament – woefully unballanced [sic] I am afraid' (*KCPP*, 185). Chopin devotes the most detailed entry to a neighbor, Mrs Hall, who has asked her to read some stories she has written. While Chopin readily agrees to do so – 'I never pick up such a MS but with the hope that I am about to fall upon a hidden talent' – she is critical of both Mrs Hall's naive faith in her own abilities and, ultimately, Mrs Hall's skill as a writer. 'She knows she can write as good stories as she reads in the magazines (such belief in her own ability is a bad omen).' One of Mrs Hall's stories concerns a young mulatto girl who rejects the attentions of a white man who loves her, and finally dies of consumption. Chopin has no objections to the theme, 'which [George Washington] Cable has used effectively', but she finds Mrs. Hall's handling of it conventional: 'no freshness, spontaneity or originality or perception'. The lessons that Chopin had learned about brevity are apparent when she writes that whereas Mrs Hall has taken a thousand words to tell how the girl had gotten her name, 'it should have been told in five lines' (*KCPP*,

180). Most surprising in Chopin's account of Mrs Hall are the remarks about her age, in which the 44-year-old Chopin suggests that it is too late for her neighbor to begin a career as a writer. Having remarked that Mrs Hall is 'nearly fifty', Chopin notes after reading her stories that 'if she were younger I would tell her to study critically some of the best of our short stories' (KCPP, 180–1). Coming from a woman who was 39 when she published her first story, such comments seem to suggest either that Chopin was forgetting her own publishing history or, more likely, that she had considered herself a writer serving an apprenticeship long before her work saw print.

A similar sense of self-importance characterizes Chopin's response to attending her first (and only) conference of writers, which she recorded in her diary and which was subsequently published in *The Critic*. The Western Association of Writers met annually in Warsaw, Indiana, and Chopin joined the group in late June of 1894. Besides Chopin, the attending writers whose work was well-known to contemporary readers were the 'Hoosier Poet', James Whitcomb Riley; Mary Hartwell Catherwood, who wrote historical romances set in the midwest; and Lew Wallace, best-known for his 1880 best-seller, *Ben-Hur*. Most of those attending the four-day conference, however, were aspiring poets, whom Chopin found largely untalented and 'provincial': 'Their native streams, trees, bushes and birds, the lovely country life about them, form the chief burden of their often too sentimental songs.' The conference participants seemed to Chopin mired in convention and unwilling to question received wisdom:

> The cry of the dying century has not reached this body of workers, or else it has not been comprehended. There is no doubt in their souls, no unrest; apparently an abiding faith in God as he manifests himself through the sectional church and an overmastering love of their soil and institutions.... Among these people are to be found an earnestness in the achievement and dissemination of book-learning, a clinging to past and conventional standards, an almost Creolean sensitiveness to criticism and a singular ignorance of, or disregard for, the value of the highest art forms.
>
> (CW, 691)

In her critique of these writers' fondness for 'book-learning' and their adherence to conventional forms, Chopin echoes Emerson's call for American writers to break with the past and to value experience over the information to be found in books. Further, by implicitly setting herself apart from these midwestern writers, Chopin claims for herself an originality that they lacked, and despite the popularity of her Louisiana stories, she downplays the significance of region by declaring that the 'big, big world' about which the writer should concern herself was 'human existence in its subtle, complex, true meaning, stripped of the veil with which ethical and conventional standards have draped it' (*CW*, 691).

Chopin also sounds a Transcendentalist note in the 1894 diary when she rhapsodizes about the natural world. Visiting rural Missouri in late May, she reveled in 'the pure sensuous beauty of it, penetrating and moving as love!'. From the porch of a hillside house, she 'could look across the tree tops to neighboring hills where cattle were grazing on the sloping meadows. Through the ravine deep down on the other side in a green basin, a patch of the Meramec [River] glistened and sparkled like silver' (*KCPP*, 184). On 7 June, Chopin noted that 'my love and reverence for pure unadulterated nature is growing daily. Never in my life before has the Country [sic] had such a poignant charm for me' (*KCPP*, 187). And on 2 June she extolled the value of life's simple pleasures: 'There are a few good things in life – not many, but a few. A soft, firm, magnetic sympathetic hand clasp is one. A walk through the quiet streets at midnight is another' (*KCPP*, 186). As rewarding as the intellectual life could be, Chopin expressed distrust for those who sought to live only through books, and preferred Emersonian direct experience. In her 7 June entry, she writes about St Louis *Post-Dispatch* editor Charles Deyo, who had discovered Plato and was living happily in the philosopher's world:

This is to me a rather curious condition of mind. It betokens a total lack of inward resource, and makes me doubt the value of the purely intellectual outlook. Here is a man who can only be reached through books. Nature does not speak to him, notwithstanding his firm belief that he is in sympathetic touch with the true – the artistic. He reaches his perceptions through others [sic] minds. It is something, of course that the channel which he

follows is a lofty one; but the question remains, has such perception the value of spontaneous insight, however circumscribed.

(*KCPP*, 187)

The spontaneity that Chopin favors over the 'channel' of another
person's thoughts had its corollary in her preferred method of
writing: the rapid capturing of character, scene, and incident as
they formed in her imagination.

Other people's books, however, had their uses. Chopin continued
to be an avid reader, and the 1894 diary affords insight into her
literary preferences in the mid-1990s. Guy de Maupassant
continued to be a favorite, and Chopin copied her translations of
three of his stories into her diary: 'A Divorce Case', 'Mad?' and 'For
Sale'. All three stories deal with obsessive love that leads to madness
or bizarre behavior, and none of them was published until they
were included in Thomas Bonner, Jr's *Kate Chopin Companion* in
1988. Of Chopin's American contemporaries, those singled out for
praise in the diary wrote, as did Chopin, fiction with distinct
regional settings. On her excursion to the Meramec River, a 'rough
looking fellow bending over a plow' reminds her of 'one of Hamlin
Garland's impersonations' (*KCPP*, 184), and the flavor of fresh
strawberries somehow makes her think of James Lane Allen's *A
Kentucky Cardinal*, which was being serialized in *Harper's* magazine.
Calling Allen's an 'exquisite story', she comments on its natural-
ness: 'What a refreshing idealistic bit it is, coming to us with the
budding leaves and the bird-notes that fill the air' (*KCPP*, 181).
Chopin reserved some of her highest praise for her female contemporaries. If her neighbor Mrs Hall had been young enough to
benefit from a model, Chopin would have recommended that she
read the stories of Sarah Orne Jewett, because 'I know of no one
better than Miss Jewett to study for technique and nicety of
construction' (*KCPP*, 181). But even better than Jewett in Chopin's
estimation was Mary E. Wilkins (Mary Wilkins Freeman, following
her marriage in 1902). Wilkins cannot serve as a model for the
aspiring writer, Chopin believes, 'for she is a great genius and
genius is not to be studied' (*KCPP*, 181). If Chopin was disappointed
in the quality and depth of the reviews of *Bayou Folk*, she was
equally disturbed by reviews of Wilkins' 1894 novel *Pembroke*,
which she called 'the most profound, the most powerful piece of

fiction of its kind that has ever come from the American press'. And yet, as with her own work, reviewers seemed to miss the point: 'I find such papers as the N. Y. Herald – the N. O. Times Democrat devoting half a column to senseless abuse of the disagreeable characters which figure in the book. No feeling for the spirit of the work, the subtle genius which created it' (*KCPP*, 187).

In addition to her translations of Maupassant's stories, Chopin copied the texts of six of her own stories into the 1894 diary, apparently doing so as soon as she was satisfied that they were finished. All six were published outside of St Louis – two in *Century* and one in *Vogue* – in 1895 and 1896, and three of the stories – 'Cavanelle', 'Regret', and 'Ozème's Holiday' – were included in Chopin's 1897 collection *A Night in Acadie*. The first of the stories, 'The Night Came Slowly', seems indistinguishable from one of Chopin's diary entries. Barely a page in length, it is a plotless reverie, with overtones of Maupassant, in which the first-person narrator begins by asserting disillusionment with both books and people – 'they make me suffer' – and a preference for nature. Lying under a maple tree at night, the narrator listens to the sound of katydids while 'abandoned to the soothing and penetrating charm of the night'. In the final paragraph, the mood is broken by a man with 'red cheeks and bold eyes and coarse manner and speech' bringing a 'Bible class' and arousing the speaker's anger with his claim to know Christ (*CW*, 366). This brief sketch, together with the next story, 'Juanita', was published in the Philadelphia periodical *Moods*. 'Juanita' begins as though it, too, could be a diary entry, with Chopin recounting an actual encounter with the title character, an overweight, ungainly young woman who, unaccountably, is rumored to have suitors. But the sketch begins to read like an invention as – with interesting foreshadowings of the fiction of Flannery O'Connor – Juanita settles her affections on a one-legged man by whom she becomes pregnant, and the couple is frequently seen heading for the woods, he 'upon a dejected looking pony which she herself was apparently leading by the bridle' (*CW*, 368). The four remaining stories in the diary are more characteristic of Chopin; all except one are clearly set in Louisiana, as opposed to the indeterminate settings of 'The Night Came Slowly' and 'Juanita', and they feature the sympathetic humor with which Chopin often regarded her characters. Not surprisingly, given Chopin's simultaneous work on translations, there are echoes of Maupassant; in 'Cavanelle', the narrator muses about the title character, 'is Cavanelle a fool? is he a lunatic? is he under a hypnotic spell?' (CW, 372).

The fact that some of Chopin's stories read initially like diary entries points to a characteristic of her regional stories that differentiates them from the local-color fiction of many of her contemporaries. As Susan V. Donaldson points out in *Competing Voices: the American Novel, 1865–1914*, one of the functions of the regional literature of the late nineteenth century was to reinforce white middle-class values by making people outside the mainstream appear exotic, magnifying the differences between the readers and the characters they read about. Donaldson likens the popularity of local-color fiction to the proliferation of ethnological exhibitions during the same period: 'Like exhibitions of "primitive" and "quaint" peoples, from Bushmen to South Sea Islanders, local-color narratives focused on subjects assumed to be marginal to the norm – New England spinsters and widows, ex-slaves, and newly arrived immigrants.'[1] Both exhibitions of exotic peoples and artifacts and local-color narratives served to define the boundaries of the 'normal' American through the latter's difference from that which was observed or read about. As Donaldson observes:

> What both ethnological collections and local color fiction shared was a dynamic demarcating the boundaries between the ordinary and the strange, the normative and the eccentric, and, above all, spectators and spectacles. These sets of symbiotic relationships implicitly situated both the viewer of the ethnological collection and the reader of local color fiction as members of the emerging white urban middle class. By definition the artifacts on display and the local stories being read represented everything that the audience was not, whether regional, traditional, quaint, foreign, or ethnic.

Reviewers of local color fiction reinforce Donaldson's point: by referring to characters and settings as 'charming', 'quaint', 'exotic', and even 'alien', reviewers positioned themselves as well as their readers as part of the normative group. The *New York Times* reviewer of Chopin's *Bayou Folk*, indeed, could seem to be describing an exhibition of 'Bushmen' or 'South Sea Islanders' by using the words 'barbarian' and 'primitive' to refer to Chopin's Louisiana characters.

Yet Chopin herself seldom employed a device used commonly by her contemporaries to underscore the difference between reader and 'spectacle': a narrative voice representative of the class and perspective of the reader, who introduces the 'different' characters and scenes and thus serves as a genteel barrier between the 'normal' and the 'odd'. Such a device can be traced back to the tall tales of the antebellum period – arguably the earliest form of American local-color writing – in which an educated Easterner venturing to the frontier on horseback or steamboat encounters the backwoodsman who boasts in dialect about his larger-than-life exploits. Such a narrator is implicitly somewhat condescending toward the characters who comprise the tall tale itself, maintaining an identification with the similarly situated reader. The narrators of late-century local-color stories are more often charmed by or sympathetic toward the regional characters to whom they introduce readers, but they are nonetheless outsiders who enter a different culture and serve as the reader's guide to it. At the beginning of Jewett's *The Country of the Pointed Firs*, for example, the observer of the Maine coastal town is described as 'a lover of Dunnet Landing', but she is a summer visitor from the city who notes the 'quaintness of the village with its elaborate conventionalities; all that mixture of remoteness and childish certainty of being the center of civilization of which her affectionate dreams had told'. Mary Wilkins Freeman's New England stories typically begin with a paragraph or more establishing the setting from an external perspective. Freeman's 'A Mistaken Charity' opens with a distant narrative gaze – 'There were in a green field a little, low, weather-stained cottage with a foot-path leading to it from the highway several rods distant' – and then introduces the characters: 'two old women – one with a tin pan and old knife searching for dandelion greens among the short young grass, and the other sitting on the door-step watching her, or, rather, having the appearance of watching her'. Harriet Beecher Stowe begins her story 'Uncle Lot' firmly established as the author: 'And so I am to write a story – but of what, and where?'. Having chosen New England as her setting, Stowe addresses the reader in familiar tones: 'Did you ever see the little village of Newbury, in New England?'.

Kate Chopin's stories, in contrast, are seldom mediated in this way by a perspective external to the setting and characters. When she employs a first-person narrator, as she does in 'Cavanelle', the narrator is neither an authorial voice nor a visitor, but rather a character in the story – in this case, a woman who shops frequently in Cavanelle's drygoods store. Although the narrator finds Cavanelle something of an enigma, their differences are not cultural or geographical, but instead stem simply from the difficulty that one individual has in understanding another's motivations. More commonly, Chopin employs no mediating narrative perspective at all, instead entering directly into the world her characters inhabit and take for granted, and leaving to the reader the task of becoming oriented there. Typical are the opening lines of 'At the 'Cadian Ball': 'Bobinôt, that big, brown, good-natured Bobinôt, had no intention of going to the ball, even though he knew Calixta would be there. For what came of those balls but heartache, and a sickening disinclination for work the whole week through, till Saturday night came again and his tortures began afresh?' (*CW*, 219). Similarly, the story 'Lilies' begins with action rather than exposition: 'That little vagabond Mamouche amused himself one afternoon by letting down the fence rails that protected Mr. Billy's young crop of cotton and corn' (*CW*, 194). Occasionally Chopin offers brief explanations for readers unfamiliar with her settings; near the beginning of 'The Return of Alcibiade', for example, she writes, 'Little more than twelve years ago, before the "Texas and Pacific" had joined the cities of New Orleans and Shreveport with its steel bands, it was a common thing to travel through miles of central Louisiana in a buggy' (*CW*, 249). But French words and Creole syntax pepper Chopin's Louisiana stories without translation, and the names of towns, rivers, and parishes are used as the residents of those places would use them – casually and without geographical coordinates to locate them on a map. Indeed, the story 'A Gentleman of Bayou Têche', which was first published in *Bayou Folk*, serves as a warning against the external and potentially condescending gaze of the outsider. Mr Sublet is an artist visiting Louisiana looking for 'bits of "local color" along the Têche'. When he sees the Cajun Evariste, he decides to paint this 'picturesque subject' and put the likeness, as Evariste tells his daughter, 'in one fine "*Mag'*zine"' (*CW*, 319). But the black servant Aunt Dicey, wise to the ways of exploitation, warns that the caption will read, '"Dis heah is one dem low-down "Cajuns o' Bayou Têche!"' 'I knows dem kine o' folks', Dicey comments (*CW*, 320), and, consequently, Evariste refuses to have his picture painted. The resolution of the story both establishes Evariste's humanity and allows him to resist being categorized as an exotic specimen; after Evariste saves Mr Sublet's son from drowning, the artist offers to let him choose his own caption for the picture, and Evariste insists on his dignity and individuality: 'Dis is one picture of Mista Evariste Anatole Bonamour, a gent'man of de Bayou Têche' (*CW*, 324).

Chopin thus positions herself as an inhabitant of the culture she depicts in her fiction, not a visitor or observer who wishes to point out the picturesque and exotic features of the region to underscore its difference from the rest of American society. Just as Louisiana is clearly preferable to St Louis in her novel *At Fault*, Chopin's delight in the language, customs, and landscape of the state is palpable in her short fiction. She seems to have been comfortable with the 'regional' label, particularly as her work attracted attention outside Missouri and Louisiana. Certainly, she expressed pleasure in being selected as one of the 'representative Southern Writers' to be featured in *Southern Magazine* in 1894. In early October, Chopin wrote to the author who was writing the sketches for the series, Waitman Barbe, enclosing newspaper articles about her life and work, and answering questions he had posed. In her letter, Chopin reiterates several central themes of the public story she had developed about herself during the previous few years. Describing her writing habits, she once more emphasizes the speed of her composition and effaces her own agency in the process:

> I have no fixed literary plans, except that I shall go on writing stories as they come to me. It is either very easy for me to write a story or utterly impossible; that is, the story must "write itself" without any perceptible effort on my part, or it remains unwritten. There is not a tale in "Bayou Folk", excepting the first ["A No-Account Creole"], which required a longer time than two, or at most three sittings of a few hours each. A story of more than 3000 words ["Azélie"] which will appear in Dec. Century was written in a few hours, and will be printed practically without an alteration or correction of the first draught.

> (*KCPP*, 205)

In addition to presenting herself as a writer to whom stories presented themselves whole, Chopin also places herself squarely in the domestic space: 'I work in the family living room often in the midst of much clatter' (*KCPP*, 205).

Even as Chopin continued to present herself to the public as a proper homemaker who dashed off stories at the dining room table, her reputation as a writer of some stature continued to grow, especially following the largely favorable critical reception of *Bayou Folk*. Her St Louis friends were more than once in a position to enhance her national reputation. Not only did *The Writer* call upon St Louis journalist William Schuyler to write a profile of Chopin; in the spring of 1895 her friend and former St Louis resident Rosa Sonneschein touted Chopin as the star author in the first issue of her magazine *The American Jewess*, published in Chicago. Sonneschein, a Hungarian immigrant, had been a leader in St Louis Jewish intellectual circles; following a messy and painful divorce from her rabbi-husband, she moved to Chicago and started *The American Jewess* as a progressive magazine of the arts and culture with a decidedly pro-women's rights stance. In her editorial for the first issue, Rosa Sonneschein extolled both the skill and the celebrity of Chopin, whose story 'Cavanelle' appeared in the issue:

> MRS. KATE CHOPIN whose gifted pen contributes to our initial number a delightful sketch of Creole life, is one of the most interesting and unique writers of the *fin de siecle*. Since the appearance of her book 'Bayou Folk', a collection of most charming tales, Kate Chopin has become an acknowledged literary power.
>
> (Toth, 247)

Although Sonneschein, like other editors and critics of the period, referred to Chopin's work as 'delightful' and 'charming', she nonetheless singled out the darkest and most daring story in *Bayou Folk*, 'Désireé's Baby', for special praise.

By the time Chopin published 'Cavanelle' in *The American Jewess*, her home had become a gathering place for a diverse group of St Louis intellectuals. Although Chopin's first biographer, Daniel Rankin, claimed that during the years between the publication of *Bayou Folk* and *A Night in Acadie* (1897) her life was 'in no way different from what it had been before literary success brought her from local to national prominence', and that she 'refused to be considered a literary person' (Rankin, 141), he was relying on her own public presentation of self. In fact, she was the frequent hostess of the closest thing St Louis had to a literary salon in the 1890s. One of the most notable attributes of the group that met for Sunday suppers and other gatherings at Chopin's unpretentious Morgan Street home was its ethnic diversity. Like many American cities in the late nineteenth century, St Louis had long been divided into separate enclaves based on ethnic and linguistic heritage, with the French and German residents maintaining their distance from one another – a situation exacerbated by the Civil War, when the French supported the Confederacy and those of German heritage were staunch Unionists – and the Irish at the bottom of the socio-economic heap. Chopin's friend and physician Frederick Kolbenheyer, who published his liberal political views in German-language newspapers in St Louis, had emigrated from Poland, where he had been a radical antimonarchist. George Johns was a native Missourian and a Princeton graduate, but in the 1890s he was a liberal editorial writer for the St Louis *Post-Dispatch* who was not afraid to take on the powerful conservative elements of the city. William Marion Reedy had grown up in St Louis' Irish ghetto; very much a self-made man, Reedy edited the *St. Louis Mirror*, which, by the time of his death in 1920, had a readership well beyond conservative St Louis. Reedy not only espoused liberal causes, but he also championed writers and challenged tastes: the *Mirror* was one of the first American periodicals to publish James Joyce, Amy Lowell, and Oscar Wilde.

Uniting these people and the others who frequented Chopin's home was an interest in books and ideas. Many in this circle were journalists with strongly held views on political and social issues; all were well-read in both American and European literature, and enjoyed discussing what they read. For some in the group, including Chopin herself, the gatherings represented an opportunity to indulge in behavior as well as ideas that would have been frowned upon by the more conservative elements of St Louis; women as well as men smoked cigarettes, argued, and, by all accounts, flirted. Even as she continued to present herself to the reading public as a mother writing stories in the midst of family chaos, Chopin enjoyed this social and intellectual life that was so different from the etiquette of calling cards and the assigned essays of the Wednesday Club. The views and behavior of some members of Chopin's circle would have been considered extreme by most standards. In the 5 July entry of her 1894 diary, Chopin noted that '[Charles] Deyo talked anarchy to me last night. There is good reason for his wrath against the "plutocrats" the robbers of the public.... He believes in equal opportunity being afforded to all men' (*KCPP*, 188). William Reedy became a figure of public scandal when, in 1893, he married the madam of a St Louis house of prostitution while on a drunken binge. After they were divorced in 1896, he eloped with a respectable young woman after the Catholic church refused to annul his earlier marriage, and he was excommunicated. Chopin, never a reformer or even a particularly political person, did not often share her friends' most radical views; in the diary entry about Charles Deyo, she expresses her view that his anarchic rhetoric seems based more in personal ambition than in concern for the public welfare, and wonders why he has not tried harder to effect change in his role as a journalist: 'He has had a pen in his hand for the past five years or more – what has he done with it?' (*KCPP*, 188). But Chopin was loyal to her friends, and Reedy, in particular, was a favorite, not least, perhaps, because he consistently championed women writers. When, toward the end of the decade, the New York periodical *Town Topics* put together a list of writers who should be selected for an American Academy of Letters if one were to be created, Reedy noted in the *Mirror* the complete omission of women, and asserted that 'we can turn over the best work that comes to mind and note that a great deal of it has been achieved by women'. Reedy's list of female nominees included, in addition to Kate Chopin, Mary E. Wilkins, Margaret Deland, Agnes Repplier, Gertrude Atherton, and Elizabeth Stuart Phelps (Toth, 267).

While her journalist friends made known their political views, Kate Chopin confined her public pronouncements primarily to matters of art and literature. Two review articles that she published in the fall of 1894 in her friend Sue V. Moore's *St. Louis Life* reveal a good deal about her taste and sensibility. An avid theater-goer, Chopin particularly admired the artistry of Edwin Booth, who was famous for his Shakespearian roles, and who may well have served as the model for the 'great tragedian' with whom the young Edna

Pontellier is infatuated in *The Awakening*. Chopin's reaction to the announced posthumous publication of some of Booth's letters, however, is quite negative; not only does she feel that such publication is an invasion of Booth's privacy, she also believes that the 'real Edwin Booth' – so proposed the title of the *Century* article announcing the publication – was to be found in his theatrical interpretations, not in his correspondence. 'No,' she writes, 'it is not here that we are to look for the real Edwin Booth, in a puerile collection of letters, expressions wrung from him by the conventional demands of his daily life.' Chopin defends the right of the artist to choose his own mode of public presentation: 'The real Edwin Booth gave himself to the public through his art. Those of us who most felt its magnetic power are the ones who knew him best, and as he would have wished to be known' (Rankin, 144). Her review of Emile Zola's novel *Lourdes* in the 17 November *St. Louis Life* bears directly on her own fiction-writing practices. She rejects as boring and overly didactic Zola's journalistic realism, making clear her preference for a compelling narrative over documentary detail:

> [T]he story is the merest thread of a story running loosely through the 400 pages, and more than two-thirds of the time swamped beneath a mass of prosaic data, offensive and nauseous description and rampant sentimentality. In no former work has Mons. Zola so glaringly revealed his constructive methods. Not for an instant, from first to last, do we lose sight of the author and his note-book and of the disagreeable fact that his design is to instruct us.
>
> (Rankin, 145)

Chopin's dislike of Zola's methods also found its way into her fiction. In her story 'Lilacs', also written in 1894, the French actress Adrienne Farival, annoyed by her servant, Sophie, threatens to throw a book at her: 'What is this? Mons. Zola! Now I warn you, Sophie, the weightiness, the heaviness of Mons. Zola are such that they cannot fail to prostrate you; thankful you may be if they leave you with energy to retain your feet' (*VV*, 140).

Chopin's resistance to both sentimentality and didacticism are demonstrated clearly in her story 'Azélie', which was published the following month in *Century*. Although on a fundamental level the story deals with social-class disparities in the post-Civil War south, Chopin frames the narrative as a gentle love story, allowing social issues to emerge subtly rather than using Zola's documentary detail. The title character, the daughter of an impoverished and lazy Cajun sharecropper, is first observed by the owner of the plantation, Mr Mathurin, 'from his elevation upon the upper gallery' (*CW*, 289), as she approaches the plantation store to secure, on credit, provisions for her family. The perspective then moves to that of 'Polyte, who, as the proprietor of the small store, occupies a social level between those of Mr Mathurin and Azélie, and who has the authority to determine what supplies Azélie may charge to her family's account, allowing her salt meat, coffee, and sugar, but denying her requests for tobacco, whiskey, and lard. But even as he thus exercises power over her family's desires and comfort, 'Polyte is falling in love with Azélie, and this feeling only increases when she breaks into the store one night to get what he had denied her: 'the very action which should have revolted him had seemed, on the contrary, to inflame him with love' (*CW*, 294–5). 'Polyte neither informs his employer about Azélie's burglary nor analyzes his own feelings, but he begins to charge her purchases to his own account and finally declares his feelings to her, hoping she will marry him. But Azélie resists him, neither offended by nor responsive to his kisses, and with the same passivity she accepts her family's move to Little River, an admission of their failure as sharecroppers. Rather than dwelling on the family's poverty, Chopin instead focuses the conclusion of the story on 'Polyte's decision to quit his job and follow Azélie to Little River. By giving the human love story primacy, Chopin manages to depict the complexities of the southern class structure without delivering a moralistic message. The issue of race, in fact, enters the story just once, in a casual although revealing way. When 'Polyte discovers Azélie in the store at night, she defends herself by claiming that her father is being discriminated against in favor of blacks: 'you all treat my popa like he was a dog. It's on'y las' week Mr. Mathurin sen' 'way to the city to fetch a fine buck-boa'd fo' Son Ambroise, an' he's on'y a nigga, après tout' (*CW*, 294). Neither 'Polyte nor Chopin comments on Azélie's assumption of white superiority; it was merely a fact of southern life.

The matter-of-fact realism of Chopin's stories of Creole and Acadian life – often, as in 'Azélie', touched with whimsy and wit – is quite different from the thorough reportage of Zola or the intense psychological drama of Maupassant's stories, but she continued to be drawn to the work of the latter author. Between 1894 and 1898, she translated eight of Maupassant's stories, and at one point she approached Houghton Mifflin, which had published *Bayou Folk*, about bringing out a collection of them, but the idea met with no enthusiasm. Chopin's career as a translator was thus limited to the publication of four stories, all in St. Louis periodicals: Adrien Vely's 'Monsieur Pierre' in the *Post-Dispatch* in 1892, and Maupassant's 'Solitude' and 'It?' in *St. Louis Life* (1895) and 'Suicide' in the *St. Louis Republic* (1898). Unlike those in Chopin's coterie, most American readers would have found Maupassant's fiction decadent or worse, and it was very likely Chopin's stature as a writer in St Louis that allowed publication of even these few stories. All three of the published Maupassant translations deal with extremes of human isolation. While the main speaker in 'Solitude' simply attempts to convince his companion of the essential unknowability of one human being by another, 'It?' and 'Suicide' depict characters driven to desperate action by their loneliness. The speaker in 'It?' explains that he is getting married, even though he considers 'legal mating a folly', in order 'to feel that [his] home is inhabited' so that he can avoid the hallucinations that beset his isolation (*KCC*, 189); 'Suicide' consists mainly of a suicide note in which a man explains the bleakness of his life, no 'great catastrophes', but instead 'the slow succession of life's little miseries' (*KCC*, 203). Bleak as these stories are, they were less controversial than those in which Maupassant presents traditional social institutions, such as marriage, in a perverse light. In 'A Divorce Case', a man becomes obsessed with the purity of flowers to the point that his wife's body disgusts him, and in 'Mad?' a woman transfers her affections from her husband to her horse, provoking the man to shoot both of them. The language as well as the themes of these stories would have made then unacceptable to many 1890s readers. Even *Vogue*, which published some of Chopin's more daring stories, would have hesitated at the following passage from 'Mad?': 'When she walked across my room, the sound of her every footfall awakened a turmoil in my whole being: and when she began to remove her garments, letting them fall about her to the floor, and emerging infamous and radiant, I felt in every member a fainting ignoble but infinitely delicious' (*KCC*, 186).

If Maupassant inspired Chopin to be more daring in her subject matter than were many of her contemporaries, the resulting fiction deals more with challenges to social convention than with states of obsession and despair. Some of these stories – including 'Désireé's Baby' and 'The Story of an Hour' – are among the best-known of Chopin's fictional works; the former deals with a young woman doomed by the suspicion that she is part Negro, and the latter presents a woman's relief at being widowed. These two stories, and more than a dozen others that Chopin published between 1893 and 1900, appeared in *Vogue*, a magazine more open than most to the experimental and unorthodox. Unlike *The Atlantic* and *Century*, the young *Vogue*, which began publication in December of 1892, did not attempt to reach a large segment of the American reading public, but rather was consciously intended for an economically and to some extent intellectually élite class. Founded as a weekly magazine of 'fashion, society, and "the ceremonial side of life",' and initially aimed at New Yorkers, *Vogue* had among its original backers Cornelius Vanderbilt, Mrs Stuyvesant Fish, and Mrs William D. Sloan.[2] In addition to forecasting trends in fashion, *Vogue* established a reputation for seeking out what was new in the arts, including literature. Chopin published six stories in *Vogue* during the magazine's first year: 'Désireé's Baby', 'A Visit to Avoyelles', 'Caline', 'Ripe Figs', 'A Lady of Bayou St. John', and 'Dr. Chevalier's Lie'. Two of these stories – 'A Visit to Avoyelles' and 'A Lady of Bayou St. John' – deal with unrequited love, in both cases the love of a man for a married woman, although in both stories proper decorum is ultimately maintained. The short sketch 'Dr. Chevalier's Lie' depicts a physician who hides the truth about a young prostitute, whose death by gunshot he attends, from her rural family, who a year earlier had been 'proud as archangels of their handsome girl, who was too clever to stay in an Arkansas cabin, and who was going away to seek her fortune in the big city'. Gossip ensues when Dr Chevalier arranges for the girl's funeral, but the matter is quickly forgotten: 'Society thought of cutting him. Society did not, for some reason or other, so the affair blew over' (*CW*, 147–8). Such stories went beyond the 'charming' and 'picturesque' to reveal extremes of human degradation and kindness.

Even as she paid homage to Maupassant in her translations and in some elements of her own fiction, Chopin also deepened her associations with the other regional writers with whom she was inevitably classified. One of these was Ruth McEnery Stuart, whom she met in St Louis in February of 1897. Stuart, a native of New Orleans, had moved to Arkansas upon her marriage, and returned to New Orleans to support herself by writing following her husband's death in 1893. There are striking parallels between the lives of Chopin and Stuart. Both had immigrant Irish fathers and mothers from distinguished southern families. Almost exact contemporaries (Ruth McEnery was born in 1849), both women became widows in the early 1880s and returned to their native cities to become writers; Stuart's first story was published in 1888. There are, however, significant differences. While Kate Chopin had several sources of income following Oscar's death, Stuart was dependent upon her writing to support herself and her son, a fact which may have a bearing on the themes and form of her work, which is more conventional and sentimental than is Chopin's. As Edwin Lewis Stevens wrote in the *Library of Southern Literature* in 1909: 'The anti-Christmas, anti-holiday, unchristianlike or unhappy side of life finds small expression from Mrs. Stuart's pen, for she is everywhere cheerful, looking on the bright side, and turning the flow of her drama away from tragedy and toward wholesome living, lightened by the play of comedy.' By the time she met Chopin, Stuart was living in New York and traveling around the country reading from her very popular stories set in Louisiana and Arkansas. Despite their differences, Chopin professed admiration for both Stuart and her work. After meeting her, Chopin wrote an admiring note to Stuart, crediting her with dispelling the chill of a snowy February day: 'the snow lay everywhere; but its silence and its chill no longer touched me. For the voice of the woman lingered in my ears like a melting song, and her presence, like the warm red glow of the sun still infolded [sic] me' (*KCPP*, 215–16). Later in the month, Chopin praised Stuart's fiction in the *Criterion*, noting first the 'fidelity' of her portrayal of the inhabitants of New Orleans and then sounding the same note that Stevens would by singling out the 'wholesome, human note sounding through and through' her stories (Rankin, 155–6).

But the *Criterion* article also reveals that Chopin was somewhat overwhelmed by her meeting with Stuart, and some of her comments about Stuart's fictional practice seem inexplicable unless seen in the context of a sense of personal awe. Chopin acknowledges that Stuart is a 'celebrity', one 'recognized throughout the length and breadth of these United States'. It is this very celebrity that initially made Chopin reluctant to meet Stuart: 'I had met a few celebrities, and they had never failed to depress me.' Stuart's sense of humor quickly dispelled Chopin's reservations: 'I might have known that a woman possessing so great an abundance of saving grace – which is humor – was not going to take herself seriously, or to imagine for a moment that I intended to take her seriously.' Given this personal 'saving grace', it is not surprising that Chopin praises Stuart for the 'rich and plentiful' humor in her fiction. More difficult to reconcile with a general avoidance of racial stereotypes in Chopin's own work is her endorsement of Stuart's portrayal of 'that child-like exuberance which is so pronounced a feature of negro character, and which has furnished so much that is deliciously humorous and pathetic to our recent literature'. Although there is little reason to doubt the sincerity of Chopin's admiration of Ruth McEnery Stuart and her talent as a writer, the *Criterion* article seems to be her attempt to present Stuart to the reading public as she presented herself to that public; toward the end of the article, Chopin insists on Stuart's femininity, calling her 'a delightful womanly woman', and she remarks that despite her intentions, when she met Stuart she 'did not speak of her stories', thus maintaining the social rather than the professional nature of their conversation (Rankin, 156–7).

Chopin's effusive remarks about Stuart are certainly not echoed in her *Criterion* articles about the work of two of her male contemporaries in March of 1897. Her commentary on Thomas Hardy's *Jude the Obscure* (1895) is framed as a larger discussion of book-banning, which Chopin, like the visitors to her salon, deplored. Hardy's novel has, she asserts, 'for some inscrutable reason ... been withdrawn ... from circulation at our libraries', and a visitor is shocked to see a copy of it in her home, 'with so many young people about'. But it is not for any offensive material that she criticizes Hardy's book, but rather for its dullness. 'The art is so poor that scenes intended to be impressive are at best but grotesque. The whole exposition is colorless. The hero arouses so little sympathy that at the close one does not care whether he lives or dies.' The novel *is*, Chopin concedes, 'immoral', but only because 'it is not true'. The sense of humor so important to Ruth McEnery Stuart's fiction is missing in Hardy's: 'From beginning to end there is not a gleam of humor in the book' (Rankin, 51–3). Chopin was far closer in spirit to Joel Chandler Harris, who had begun publishing his 'Uncle Remus' stories in 1879. Reviewing Harris' 1896 novel *Sister Jane: Her Friends and Acquaintances*, Chopin had the greatest praise for his creation of southern characters, 'every one of [whom] is a masterpiece of his creative genius'. Not surprisingly, Chopin admired most those traits of Harris' writing that were most similar to her own; individual chapters of *Sister Jane*, which read like local-color sketches, 'stand out like flaming torches'. But Chopin did not believe that Harris had the 'constructive faculty' to write a novel, and she found the plot of *Sister Jane* 'weak, unjointed [and] melo-dramatic'. She concludes her review by asking Harris to write more stories about 'those old-time people in their quiet, sleepy corner of Middle Georgia' (Rankin, 154–5).

As early as the fall of 1894, Chopin had envisioned a second collection of short stories. In her letter to Waitman Barbe in October, she noted, 'I have ready another collection of Creole tales which I hope to have published in book form after they have made their slow way through the magazines' (*KCPP*, 205). Her success to this point in her career had been with the short-story form, and she saw no reason to depart from it. When, however, she approached Houghton Mifflin, the publisher of *Bayou Folk*, about bringing out a second volume of her stories, the editors were not enthusiastic. When the firm's H. E. Scudder finally responded to her early in 1897, he complained that some of her stories seemed to have little plot. Further, he had made 'inquiries' about the success of *Bayou Folk*, and 'the result was not encouraging', despite the fact that the initial printing had sold out and 500 additional copies had been printed in 1895. Houghton Mifflin did wish to remain loyal to its published authors, Scudder told Chopin – '[we are] always loth to seem inhospitable to one whom [we] have once included in the lists' – but he suggested that a novel would be more successful than a collection of stories: 'You have now and then sent me a story long enough to run through two or three numbers in [*The Atlantic*]. Have you never felt moved to write a downright novel?' (Toth, 296). Scudder was apparently unaware of Chopin's novel *At Fault*, which she had had privately printed in St Louis, and he shared the common perception that both fiction writers and their readers preferred novels to shorter forms.

However Chopin may have responded to Scudder, she pressed ahead to find a publisher for her collection of stories. Despite her criticism of Hamlin Garland for predicting that cities such as Chicago would soon rival Boston and New York as centers of publishing, she next tried the Chicago publishing company Stone & Kimball, which published the avant-garde *Chap-Book*, a *fin-de-siècle* periodical that prided itself on the modernity of its authors, including Aubrey Beardsley, George Bernard Shaw, and Stéphané Mallarmé. Chopin's collection of 'Creole tales' may have seemed entirely too tame to Stone & Kimball, which had also rejected *Young Dr. Gosse and Théo*. Chopin had been for some time eager to publish with Stone & Kimball, especially in the *Chap-Book*, perhaps because such publication would give her the stamp of the 'modern' author – which some of her work surely deserved – as opposed to the more staid category of 'local-color' writer. In January of 1896, after she had sent Stone & Kimball her short-story manuscript, she wrote to suggest that two of the stories, 'Lilacs' and 'Three [Two] Portraits', might be appropriate for the *Chap-Book*, and closed her letter with an almost abject plea: 'I would greatly like to see one of them – some of them – something – anything over my name in the Chap-Book' (*KCPP*, 209). The two stories that Chopin identified as appropriate for the *Chap-Book* are definitely not local-color stories; both deal with the attractions of convent life in unconventional ways, and neither appeared in *A Night in Acadie*, but were deferred to the ill-fated *A Vocation and a Voice*. 'Lilacs' is the story of an actress for whom the convent-school of her youth is an annual refuge until, because of either the extravagant gifts she brings or the homoerotic relationship with a nun at which the story hints, she is forbidden to return. The 'Two Portraits' are of 'The Wanton' and 'The Nun', which together serve as a cautionary tale about the effects of the childhood environment on the development of a woman's self-esteem. The 'wanton' is raised with beatings and sexual promiscuity, and becomes a prostitute, and the 'nun', early taught the need to submit to God, has rejected the flesh in favor of the spirit, and is said to have visions. In presenting such extremes, Chopin implicitly argues for a middle ground, in which girls are taught to respect themselves without being abject. The

Chap-Book accepted neither story, and Stone & Kimball rejected the story collection, which Chopin eventually placed with their Chicago competitor Way & Williams, which published *A Night in Acadie* in 1897.

A Night in Acadie differs in several respects from *Bayou Folk*. Only four of the 21 stories – 'Polydore', 'A Matter of Prejudice', 'Mamouche', and 'The Lilies' – was initially published in a periodical for children, the first three in *Youth's Companion* and the last in *Wide Awake*. And although 'Mamouche' and 'Polydore' depict orphaned children who repent of behaving badly and are consequently rewarded with the love of wealthy benefactors, the stories are more complex than were Chopin's earlier brief cautionary tales, and much of the focus is on the stories' adult characters. In 'A Matter of Prejudice', an elderly Creole woman who, like Oscar Chopin's father, believes that 'anything not French had ... little right to existence' (*CW*, 282), has broken off relations with her only son for marrying an 'American' girl and living outside the French Quarter of New Orleans. When a little girl becomes ill at her grandson's birthday party, however, her maternal instincts are awakened and she goes to see her son, whereupon she discovers that the little girl is her own grandchild. 'Mamouche' is a sequel to 'The Lilies'. In 'The Lilies', the 'little vagabond Mamouche' appears only at the beginning of the story to perform the prank of letting down fence rails to allow the Widow Angle's calf to eat Mr Billy's cotton crop. When Mamouche reappears in the story that bears his name, he becomes the agent by which the reclusive Doctor John-Luis decides that he needs human companionship. Although the story involves the rehabilitation of the 'little vagabond,' Chopin is at least as interested in John-Luis, who had known Mamouche's grandfather and, it is suggested, was in love with his grandmother. Three of the stories in *A Night in Acadie* had appeared in *Vogue*, and three each in *Atlantic* and *Century*; none of the stories had been published in St. Louis periodicals, although three had appeared in the New Orleans *Times Democrat*.

The titles of the two collections suggest differences as well, 'bayou folk' conveying a sense of the picturesque and different, and 'night in Acadie' promising more sophisticated pleasures. Chopin biographer Emily Toth suggests that the name 'Acadie' was selected as a deliberate echo of the title of James Lane Allen's

Summer in Arcady, a novel first serialized under the title *Butterflies* in *Cosmopolitan* between December 1895 and March 1896 and published in somewhat revised form by Macmillan in 1896. Allen's novel pushed at the limits of propriety, describing the sexual attraction of a young man and woman during a hot summer in Kentucky. Although the consummation of their relationship does not take place until after they are married, in one scene the act is averted only by the intrusion of an angry bull. In language as well as in plot, Allen's novel was daring for its time, with such descriptions as 'laughing round-breasted girls', and the natural world is presented as conspiring with human desires: 'lashing everything – grass, fruit, insects, cattle, human creatures – more fiercely onward to the fulfillment of her ends'. Critical reaction to *Summer in Arcady* was predictable. *The Sewanee Review* wanted a story of a 'purer love' than that which Allen had presented, and even the more liberal *Vogue* called the book 'unclean'. Yet Allen remained a popular novelist, better able, as a man, to weather such criticism, and Chopin and her publisher may have wished to take advantage of that popularity. (Toth, 297–8)

The title story of Chopin's second collection – the only story not previously published – is not nearly as daring as Allen's *Summer in Arcady*. A mere plot summary, in fact, reveals elements of melodrama. Twenty-eight-year-old Telèsphore, with time on his hands and seeking a respite from trying to decide which of the neighboring young women to marry, takes the train from his plantation near Natchitoches to Marksville, a small town in central Louisiana. On the train he meets Zaida, who invites him to go to a dance that night. When, shortly after midnight, Zaida abruptly leaves the dance, Telèsphore discovers why she is dressed in white: she intends to meet her fiancé at the home of a justice of the peace and marry him over her family's objections. When the fiancé arrives drunk, Zaida's illusions about him are shattered, the two men fight, and the victorious Telèsphore drives Zaida away in her buggy, so infatuated that 'for the first time in his life, [he] did not care what time it was' (*CW*, 499). But despite the melodramatic elements of the chance meeting, the lovers' planned tryst, and the gallant Telèsphore besting the scoundrel, Chopin resists the closure of the melodramatic plot: the story ends with the couple riding slowly through the woods, making no plans for the future. One of

Chopin's main concerns in 'A Night in Acadie' is depicting the rebelliousness of her two central characters. Zaida's is the more conventional rebellion, declaring her parents 'perfec' mules' (*CW*, 494) for believing the rumors that her fiancé drinks, and prepared to marry him against their will. Telèsphore's rebellion is less orthodox, and verges on the comic. Named for an uncle to whom his family has been fond of comparing him, Telèsphore has determined to be his own person: 'His whole conduct of life had been planned on lines in direct contradistinction to those of his uncle Telèsphore', and the result has made him a successful young man. Because his uncle was illiterate, Telèsphore has learned to read and write; his uncle preferred hunting and fishing to work, and so young Telèsphore devotes himself to farming. 'In short, Telèsphore, by advisedly shaping his course in direct opposition to that of his uncle, managed to lead a rather orderly, industrious, and respectable existence' (*CW*, 485).

Many of the stories in *A Night in Acadie* deal with personal transformations, some of them as self-willed as that of Telèsphore, but most occurring because of external agency. The title characters in 'Polydore' and 'Mamouche', both young boys, learn to give up bad behavior, and the reclusive Mr Billy, in 'Lilies', gains a sense of the value of human contact after Marie Louise impulsively brings him an armful of lilies to make up for her calf's destruction of his cotton crop. While such stories, like the title story, have a touch of whimsy, Chopin seems to devote the most love and sympathy to her female characters who undergo transformative experiences, such as Madame Carambeau's decision to become reunited with her son in 'A Matter of Prejudice'. Two very different stories depict the complexities of the marital relationship and explore women's emotions regarding it; for different reasons, these stories were potentially the most controversial ones in the collection. The title character in 'Athénaise', which had been published in the *Atlantic* in August and September of 1896, married for only a short time to the much older successful planter Cazeau, leaves him to return to her parents' house, not because of any mistreatment or discord – indeed, Cazeau loves her tenderly – but because she finds marriage itself oppressive: 'I can't stan' to live with a man; to have him always there; his coats an' pantaloons hanging in my room; his ugly bare feet – washing them in my tub, befo' my very eyes, ugh!' (*CW*,

431). When her parents cannot convince Athénaise to return to her husband, her brother spirits her away to a boarding house in New Orleans, where she vaguely plans to become self-supporting, and where she is befriended by a journalist, Gouvernail, who becomes infatuated with her. Athénaise pays scant attention to Gouvernail or to much of anything else until she discovers that she is pregnant, whereupon she returns happily to Cazeau, and 'her lips for the first time respond to the passion of his own' (*CW*, 454). Gouvernail reappears in 'A Respectable Woman', which had appeared in *Vogue* in February of 1894, as a houseguest of Mrs Baroda and her husband. Imagining that her husband's friend will be 'tall, slim, cynical; with eyeglasses, and his hands in his pockets' (*CW*, 333), Mrs Baroda is prepared to dislike him, but as they talk one evening, she is drawn to him quite sensually:

> She wanted to reach out her hand in the darkness and touch him with the sensitive tips of her fingers upon the face or the lips. She wanted to draw close to him and whisper against his cheek – she did not care what – as she might have done if she had not been a respectable woman.
>
> (*CW*, 335)

Instead of giving in to her passionate impulse, Mrs Baroda goes to visit her aunt for the duration of Gouvernail's visit, but some months later she suggests to her husband that he come to visit again; the story concludes with her suggestive remark, 'This time I shall be very nice to him' (*CW*, 336).

In 'Athénaise', Chopin makes a brief, ironic comment on regional literature and its readers. When Gouvernail is looking through his books for something that Athénaise would enjoy reading, he suspects correctly that she has no 'literary tastes', and rejects philosophy, poetry, and novels before deciding to loan her a magazine. She later reports that 'it had entertained her passably', although 'a New England story had puzzled her ... and a Creole tale had offended her' (*CW*, 446). Chopin does not specify what 'puzzles' and 'offends' Athénaise, but she seems to suggest that portrayals of life in distant regions might indeed present 'alien' people and customs, while depictions of ways of life with which a reader was familiar – as Creole culture would have been to Athénaise – could offend through inaccuracy or condescension. After nearly ten years of writing and of testing the literary marketplace, Chopin had arrived at a balance between the 'picturesque' elements that editors demanded of regional writers, and ways of presenting the themes of human desire and self-fulfillment that interested her. While a few of the stories in *A Night in Acadie* are dependent upon the specific settings of central and southern Louisiana, most, without the place names and speech patterns, could take place anywhere. The very brief story 'Ripe Figs' is one of the former; Maman-Nainaine times family visits according to seasonal signals such as the ripening of the figs and the blooming of chrysanthemums. The story 'Regret', in contrast, could easily be transplanted to New England. The self-sufficient Aurélie had 'promptly declined' the proposal of marriage she received at the age of 20, and 'at the age of fifty she had not yet lived to regret it' (*CW*, 375). But when a neighbor must leave on a family emergency and asks Aurélie to care for her four small children, they quickly become an important part of her life, and after the children's mother comes to collect them, 'she cried like a man, with sobs that seemed to tear her very soul' (*CW*, 378).

As had been the case with *Bayou Folk*, however, reviewers of *A Night in Acadie* tended to evaluate Chopin's stories on the basis of their regional qualities rather than their thematic messages. The reviewer for the St Louis *Post-Dispatch* stressed Chopin's knowledge of 'the black race', 'the pure Congo African', and singled out for praise the story 'Tante Cat'rinette', which deals with a black woman's gratitude toward the white owner who had freed her (Toth, 303). Alexander DeMenil, reviewing the book in *The Hyperion*, which he had founded in 1894, was even more élitist, speaking of all of Chopin's Louisiana characters when he praised Chopin's depiction of 'a race and a life which are as innocent of the refinements and knowledge of higher civilization as it is possible for an exclusive, strongly opinionated, and self-isolated people clinging to the forms and traditions of a past civilization ... to be' (Toth, 305). The reviewer for the *Nation* pegged Chopin firmly as a regional writer, writing that 'her stories are to the bayous of Louisiana what Mary Wilkins's are to New England, ... in seizing the heart of her people and showing the traits that come from their surroundings' (Toth, 299). Chopin was also compared – favorably – to Joel Chandler Harris and George Washington Harris. In short, with the publication of her second volume of short stories, Chopin was critically ensconced as a major regional writer, a position which had both positive and negative effects on her career and her subsequent literary reputation.

While the reviews of A Night in Acadie were largely favorable, there were quibbles. The reviewer for The Critic noted that 'Athénaise' was 'marred by one or two slight and unnecessary coarsenesses'. While this reviewer was not specific about what elements of the story were 'coarse', there are some obvious candidates for such an accusation: Gouvernail's undisguised attraction to the married Athénaise, the clear references to her pregnancy (although the word is never used), and the passion of the embrace that closes the story. The St Louis Republic wanted some of Chopin's stories to have more conclusive endings. The ending of the title story would have been more 'satisfactory' if the justice of the peace had arrived to join Telèsphore and Zaida in marriage (Toth, 301) – the melodramatic 'marriage plot' ending that Chopin deliberately resists in the story. The reviewer for the St Louis Globe-Democrat, like others, concentrated primarily on Chopin's black characters and children, paying scant attention to the adult dramas in the stories. One of the risks of writing fiction that was immediately categorized in a sub-genre such as local color, as Chopin knew well by this point, was that reviewers brought to it a set of expectations against which to measure the work; as Chopin increasingly worked against the conventions of the genre, her friend Bill Reedy was one of the few who understood, as he wrote in the Mirror, that Chopin was dealing with 'human nature that is old as mankind and as puzzling and new to-day as when the first murderous instinct awoke to life in the heart of Cain or the first grand passion of love entered Eden' (Toth, 301).

By the time the reviews of A Night in Acadie appeared, Chopin had begun to work on The Awakening, and was thinking about a publisher for her third collection of stories, to be titled A Vocation and a Voice. Although she continued to wish for greater national visibility – she may briefly have considered a reading tour such as the one that had brought Ruth McEnery Stuart to St Louis – there was comfort in being a local literary celebrity. Almost all of the St Louis reviews of her second collection of stories, whatever their evaluation of the work, drew proud attention to the fact that

Chopin was a resident of the city. Her satiric sketches of parts of St Louis society in *At Fault* and her attack on hypocritical do-gooders in 'Miss McEnders' had angered some, and others had been at least slightly offended by what they perceived as 'coarseness' or 'indelicacy' in some of her stories, but no one could deny that Chopin was a widely known and respected writer. When, in mid-February of 1898, Chopin was invited to read two of the stories in *A Night in Acadie* to the St Louis Chart Club, the tribute to her by the club's president, reported in the *Post-Dispatch*, evidenced great pride at the same time that it offered a narrowly circumscribed view of her contribution to American literature:

> We are proud of the fact that a sister St. Louisan has made such valuable contributions to literature. The portrayal of characters, habits and manner in the Gulf States, with their phrases of French and Spanish creole, negro and Indian, is a marked feature of nineteenth century literature. Writers on these subjects have drawn on a deep mine of poetry and romance, and will give the next generation correct ideas of an institution and regime that has passed away. In the front ranks of the dialect writers stands Mrs. Kate Chopin.
>
> (Toth, 308)

In the view of the Chart Club president, Chopin's role as a writer was to chronicle a nearly bygone era, preserving its folkways for future generations; categorized as a 'dialect writer', her art is confined to the mimetic. But if such assessments continued to overlook the adult passions and the thematic emphasis on self-fulfillment in Chopin's fiction, she had already, by February of 1898, finished the manuscript of the novel that would challenge any reductive critique of her work.

Notes

1. Susan V. Donaldson, *Competing Voices: The American Novel, 1865–1914*. New York: Twayne, 1998. Subsequent references will be page numbers in the text.
2. Theodore Peterson, *Magazines in the Twentieth Century*. Urbana: University of Illinois Press, 1964, p. 64.

5
The Awakening and the Limits of Propriety

Throughout most of the time that she was an active publishing writer, Kate Chopin seems to have carefully crafted the self that she presented to the reading public, stressing that she wrote at home amidst domestic clutter and the tug of household responsibilities, and downplaying the effort she invested in her work. Such a presentation suited both the genteel standards of her social position and cultural expectations for a woman writer. No matter how much Chopin had pushed at 'proper' limits in her fiction – with the independent heroines of her early stories, her satire on St Louis society in *At Fault*, and her refusal to depict marriage as woman's supreme fulfillment – she remained a member of St Louis' social and intellectual élite. Her daughter, Lélia, was presented to society as a debutante late in 1899. Chopin's opinions were sought by journalists both locally and nationally, and her attendance at social events was reported in the society columns of the St Louis newspapers. When, in 1898, John Devoy published his *History of the City of St. Louis and Vicinity*, he accorded Chopin a prominent place in the volume, praising both her work and her personal characteristics. Her 1897 collection of stories, *A Night in Acadie*, had, according to Devoy, 'met with universal approval', and he noted the 'tenderness, humor, and true-to-life dialect' of her Louisiana stories. The 48-year-old Chopin also met Devoy's standards for respectable womanhood:

Mrs. Chopin is a well-preserved woman of commanding appearance and charming personality. Her conversation is always

111

polished and impressive. She is perfectly familiar with all the topics of the day, and on them she speaks fluently and intelligently. Mrs. Chopin resides with her family at 3317 Morgan Street, where she entertains her many friends.

(Toth, 307)

In a description not at all unusual for its period, Devoy gives equal weight to Chopin's intellectual capacity and her physical appearance, to her influential presence and her feminine qualities.

Two years earlier, however, Chopin drafted quite a different self-presentation, one which that blurred gender distinctions and challenged authority. Responding to an invitation by the editors of *The Atlantic*, in 1896, to write a profile of herself for the magazine's 'Men and Letters' series, she apparently decided to be playful with the series title by indulging in verbal cross-dressing. Invited to 'talk about myself' for *Atlantic* readers, Chopin decides to do so by adopting a male persona: 'I disguised myself as a gentleman smoking cigars with my feet on the table. Opposite me was another gentleman (who furnished the cigars) entrapping me into disclosures by well turned questions, after the manner of the middle men at the "minstrels".' She next notes that she has been persuaded to abandon her 'disguise' by 'a person of sounder judgment', who advised that the device was 'more clumsy than clever', but she rejects this person's assumption that she has adopted a persona because she is 'ashamed' of her real self: 'Like the colored gentleman in the Passemala I am sometimes "afraid o' myse'f" but never ashamed.' But if Chopin relinquishes her male disguise, she does not give up her defiant tone. After praising Guy de Maupassant for his escape from 'tradition and authority', for the way that his stories reveal that he has 'entered into himself and looked out upon life through his own being and with his own eyes', she declares her own independence as a fiction writer. To do so, she creates a figure drawn from her Catholic upbringing, the pious and didactic 'Madame Précieuse'. In the opinion of Madame Précieuse, Chopin's fiction lacks the proper spiritual quality. 'She often tells me that I have no soul (some people will tell you anything) and that my work consequently lacks that dignity and charm – which the spiritual impulse infuses into fiction.' But Chopin rejects such a critique and insists upon her own integrity:

'I can gain nothing by cultivating faculties that are not my own' (*CW*, 700–2).

By the time Chopin's 'In the Confidence of a Story-Writer' was eventually published in *The Atlantic* in January of 1899, most of its salient features – including the cigars, de Maupassant, and Madame Précieuse – had been edited out, so that the reading public was not treated to Chopin's wit and defiance. Only the essay's final statement rings with self-assertion: 'He who is content to reach his own group, without ambition to be heard beyond it, attains, in my opinion, somewhat to the dignity of a philosopher' (*CW*, 705). Chopin is not specific in this statement about what 'group' she considered her 'own' in the late 1890s, and in fact there were several actual or potential audiences for her writing. By far the largest was composed of those who enjoyed her Louisiana stories in periodicals and in book form; more locally, her circle of St Louis intellectual associates encouraged her, in the liberality of their own views, to move beyond fiction which critics could call 'picturesque' and 'charming'. When she expressed her opinions on literary or social issues in the pages of St Louis newspapers, readers could see hints of her resistance to conformity. When, for example, one of Chopin's Sacred Heart classmates, who now went by the name Sarah Maria Aloisa Spottiswood Mackin, published her memoir, *A Society Woman on Two Continents*, through a vanity press, Chopin's comments in the *St Louis Criterion* have just enough sarcasm to convey her opinion that her former friend might better have remained silent. The news that Sallie had written her memoirs, Chopin wrote, created in her 'an insane desire to do likewise', but 'I found that my memory was of that order which retains only the most useless rubbish'. Chopin remembered that when she and Sallie were schoolgirls, she was not allowed to stay overnight at Sallie's house because Sallie was not a Catholic, a circumstance that has undergone significant change: 'And to-day, here she is, not only a Catholic, but actually receiving a golden rose from the Pope! While I – Well, I doubt if the Holy Father has ever heard of me, or if he would give me a golden rose if he had' (Toth, 268).

Like other prominent citizens, Chopin was sometimes called upon by the local press to express her views on issues about which she was assumed to have some expertise, and on these occasions, too, she displayed skepticism about conventional pieties. In January of 1898, the St Louis *Post-Dispatch* sought the opinions of several women on the question 'Is Love Divine?'. Chopin was included in this group because, announced the *Post-Dispatch* writer, 'as a novelist [she] should know what love is'. But in contrast to the other respondents, who professed that love occupied a plane above human will and material circumstances, Chopin emphasized the inexplicability of love: 'It is as difficult to distinguish between the divine love and the natural, animal love, as it is to explain just why we love at all.' She also used the occasion to reveal that she had been working on a new novel, in which she was exploring just such questions: 'In a discussion of this character between two women in my new novel [*The Awakening*] I have made my heroine say: "Why do I love this man? Is it because his hair is brown, growing high on his temples; because his eyes droop a bit at the corners, or because his nose is just so much out of drawing?"'. Chopin concluded her response by stressing the 'animal' as opposed to the 'divine' nature of love, calling it 'an uncontrollable emotion that allows of no analyzation and no vivisection' (Toth, 310). Later in the month, the editors of the *Post-Dispatch*, alarmed by the fact that several young society women had recently committed suicide, sought an explanation for this phenomenon by soliciting responses to the question 'Has High Society Struck the Pace That Kills?'. While the first three women whose opinions appeared in the paper shared the view that wealthy young women who killed themselves did so because of some flaw of 'heredity' or because they tended to be 'morbid' or 'hysterical', Chopin refused to see suicide as a product of gender weakness. 'Business men commit suicide every day, yet we do not say that suicide is epidemic in the business world. Why should we say the feeling is rife among society women, because half a dozen unfortunates, widely separated, take their own lives?' Weary, as Virginia Woolf would be a generation later, of society's tendency constantly to analyze women's nature and motivations, Chopin concluded, 'Why all this talk about women?' (Toth, 310–12).

While social prominence did not, as the *Post-Dispatch* editors seem to have assumed, confer expertise on such issues as love and suicide, Kate Chopin had been devoting considerable thought to these matters as she wrote *The Awakening* between June of 1897 and January of 1898. In the years since the novel was published in 1899, there has been a great deal of speculation about the origins of the story of Edna Pontellier, who becomes infatuated with the Creole Robert Lebrun and dissatisfied with the requirements of her upper-middle-class marriage to Léonce Pontellier, awakens to the potential of her sensual nature, has a casual affair after she moves out of her husband's house, and finally swims into the Gulf of Mexico beyond her capacity to return. Chopin's first biographer, Daniel Rankin, reaches back to her early childhood and the story-telling of her great-grandmother, which gave her 'a keen interest in woman's nature, and its mysterious vagaries' (Rankin, 173). Rankin also locates the time of the novel's composition in a *fin-de-siècle* mood that featured a 'mania for the exotic that fed upon evocations of a barbaric past – Salome's dance, Cleopatra's luxury, the splendor and cruelty of Salammbo's Carthage' (Rankin, 175). Per Seyersted reports that Chopin's brother-in-law Phanor Breazeale believed that Chopin had based the novel on the actual life story of a woman with whom New Orleans Creoles were familiar, but Seyersted prefers the influence of literary models, such as Maupassant's 'Réveil' and Flaubert's *Madame Bovary*. Later commentators have sought autobiographical clues, and although Chopin and her heroine share a penchant for solitary walks and a resistance to social convention, there is little evidence that Chopin was unhappy in her marriage to Oscar, which seems to have granted her more emotional and physical freedom than Léonce is willing to give to Edna. The possibility of a woman losing her vitality and independence in marriage, however, was one with which Chopin had long been familiar. In the commonplace book that she kept while a student at the Sacred Heart Academy in the 1860s, one of the excerpts from her reading that she recorded was from a commentary on European life by Anna Brownell Jameson (1794–1860), who was best-known for her 1832 book about Shakespeare's heroines, *Characteristics of Women*. Writing of an 'accomplished' and 'elegant' German woman of her acquaintance, Jameson notes that she 'excused herself from going with me to a picture gallery, because on that day she was obliged to recon up the household linen'. Jameson adds that she 'met with cases in which the women had, without necessity, sunk into mere household drudges – women whose souls were in their kitchen and their house hold stuff – whose talk was of dishes and of condiments' (*KCPP*, 55). In her honeymoon diary in the summer of 1870, Chopin wrote of a meeting in Philadelphia with 'Miss Claffin', who 'discussed business extensively with Oscar, and entreated me not to fall into the useless degrading life of most married ladies – but to elevate my mind and turn my attention to politics, commerce; questions of state, &c. &c. I assured her I would do so – which assurance satisfied her quite' (*KCPP*, 102).

Whatever were the various inspirations for *The Awakening*, it was well known among Chopin's friends and relatives in late 1897 and early 1898 that she was completing a new novel. Her friend and St Louis *Mirror* editor William Reedy seemed to be reflecting conversations with Chopin – if not a reading of the manuscript – when, in January of 1898, he wrote an article for the *Mirror* titled 'Wives and Husbands'. Reedy's central message was that women needed a measure of independence, even within marriage, and he felt that women needed to claim it for themselves: 'Women who submit to complete obliteration in matrimony will find, in time, that they will not need to obliterate themselves, for they will be ignored'. The statement that most clearly echoes Edna's stance in *The Awakening* concerns the balance between duty and selfhood: 'Women's truest duties are those of wife and mother, but those duties do not demand that she shall sacrifice her individuality' (Toth, 309). Later in the year, the news of a forthcoming new novel by Kate Chopin had reached Louisiana. Chopin had visited Natchitoches Parish in June of 1897, just as she was beginning the novel, and she returned there in December of 1898, when one of her purposes was to sell the Cloutierville house in which she and Oscar had lived, and which she had rented out since her move to St Louis. The *New Orleans Times-Democrat* took note of her visit in glowing terms:

> Last Friday's train brought to Natchitoches one who, although she is not a native, has spent some years of her life in the parish, and has many relatives and friends who welcome her with open arms. This refers to that beautiful and talented woman, Mrs. Kate Chopin of St. Louis, who has made a brilliant success in the literary world. Her last novel has not yet been published, but judging from her former works there is indeed a treat in store for all lovers of fiction.
>
> (Toth, 322)

In July of 1899, however, the *Times-Democrat* had a very different view of Chopin's new novel; the paper's reviewer felt that Edna's 'senses' had overpowered her 'reason, judgment, and all the higher faculties and perceptions', which led to her 'totally unjustifiable conduct' (Toth, 347–8).

The potentially objectionable subject matter of *The Awakening* did not cause Chopin problems in finding a publisher for the novel. Almost as soon as she had finished the book, she submitted it to Way & Williams, which had published *A Night in Acadie*. She visited Chicago in the spring of 1898, at least in part to consult with a literary agency about ways to advance her career, including going, as had Ruth McEnery Stewart, on the lecture circuit to read from her work. Although such a reading tour never materialized, Chopin was warmly received in Chicago, where there was a great deal of literary activity, and a cordial relationship with Way & Williams encouraged her to send her third collection of stories to that publisher as well. By early summer, Way & Williams had accepted both the novel and her collection of stories *A Vocation and a Voice*, for which she had been seeking a publisher for several years. Soon thereafter, however, Way & Williams went out of business, and the publisher's contracts were transferred to Herbert S. Stone & Company, also in Chicago. Herbert S. Stone published *The Awakening* (which until that point had been titled *A Solitary Soul*) in the spring of 1899, but for reasons that have never been clear, Stone dropped *A Vocation and a Voice* from its lists. The negative publicity that *The Awakening* attracted within a few months of its publication could have made a publisher wary of offering to the public another volume by its author, especially a collection that included some of Chopin's most daring stories to date; alternatively, the highly competitive book publishing business could have prompted a reduction in the number of titles that Herbert S. Stone felt it could properly promote.

During the time that Chopin had worked on *The Awakening*, she had written little else, and shortly after she completed it, America's war with Cuba provided a considerable distraction from work. In early February 1898, the Cubans destroyed the United States battleship the *Maine*, eventuating in a declaration of war in April. Not only did many people in St Louis have ties with Cuba, but Chopin had two sons who were the appropriate age for military service. Felix, a high-school senior, was rejected by the Army because of his small size and frail appearance, but 22-year-old Fred enlisted and went off to Georgia for training. The brief war was over before his company saw action, but during the spring and summer of 1898 the Chopin household was occupied with talk of war with Spain. Just after victory was declared, however, following the famous march up San Juan Hill, Chopin wrote one of the few stories that she never attempted to publish, 'The Storm'. A sequel to 'At the 'Cadian Ball', written six years earlier, 'The Storm' is a frank story of sexual passion consummated during a thunderstorm by a man and a woman who are married to other people. The brief encounter has no negative consequences for anyone involved. Shortly after her encounter with Alcée, Calixta welcomes home her husband and young son; Alcée, meanwhile, writes a letter to his absent wife encouraging her to prolong her visit, which suggests that he hopes for a continuing relationship with Calixta. The story ends on a placid note: 'So the storm passed and every one was happy' (*CW*, 596).

'The Storm' contains some of the most openly sexual language found anywhere in Chopin's work. As the rain and thunder pound Calixta's house, 'the generous abundance of [Calixta's] passion, without guile or trickery, was like a white flame which penetrated and found response in depths of [Alcée's] own sensuous nature that had never yet been reached'. What follows is even more explicit: 'When he touched her breasts they gave themselves up in a quivering ecstacy, inviting his lips. Her mouth was a fountain of delight. And when he possessed her, they seemed to swoon together at the very borderland of life's mystery' (*CW*, 595). The language describing the sexual encounter between Edna Pontellier and Alcée Arobin in *The Awakening* is far more restrained – to the extent, in fact, that readers unfamiliar with nineteenth-century narrative codes often fail to realize what is happening. Chopin does write that Alcée touches Edna's shoulder, and 'could feel the response of her flesh to his touch', but the scene concludes with general language that draws a curtain between the reader and the textual moment: '[Alcée] did not say good night until she had become supple to his gentle, seductive entreaties' (*CW*, 976). Despite such caution, Chopin was aware that in Edna she had created a woman who 'sinned' – not only in terms of sexual infidelity, but also in withdrawing from her responsibilities as a wife and mother. In February of 1898, shortly after she had completed *The Awakening*, she wrote a poem, 'The Haunted Chamber', which seems to allude to the novel and which suggests that she had merely written an age-old story – one that would be better understood by women than by men:

> Of course 'twas an excellent story to tell
> Of a fair, frail, passionate woman who fell.
> It may have been false, it may have been true.
> That was nothing to me – it was less to you.
> But with bottle between us, and clouds of smoke
> From your last cigar, 'twas more of a joke
> Than a matter of sin or a matter of shame
> That a woman had fallen, and nothing to blame,
> So far as you or I could discover,
> But her beauty, her blood and an ardent lover.
> But when you were gone and the lights were low
> And the breeze came in with the moon's pale glow,
> The far, faint voice of a woman, I heard,
> 'Twas but a wail, and it spoke no word.
> It rose from the depths of some infinite gloom
> And its tremulous anguish filled the room.
> Yet the woman was dead and could not deny,
> But women forever will whine and cry.
> So now I must listen the whole night through
> To the torment with which I had nothing to do –
> But women forever will whine and cry
> And men forever must listen – and sigh –
>
> (*CW*, 733–4)

'The Haunted Chamber' was never published, and although Chopin later published a mock-serious defense of her novel, by the summer of 1899 it was clear that, whatever the reaction of individual readers, the critical response to *The Awakening* was largely a negative one.

The earliest reviews, however, were encouraging, and the first one to appear, in the March *Book News*, echoed the sentiment of 'The Haunted Chamber' that Chopin had written a universal woman's story. The review's author, Lucy Monroe (the sister of Harriet Monroe, who would establish the influential *Poetry* magazine in Chicago in 1912), found *The Awakening* 'remarkable', and felt that 'studying the nature of one woman reveals something which brings her in touch with all women – something larger than herself'. Although Monroe believed that Chopin's novel had 'audacity', she also felt that it was justified; as a woman, Edna was 'faulty', but she had a 'complex character' with a 'magnetism which is essential to the charm of the novel'. On the whole, in Monroe's opinion, the novel showed 'a very subtle and brilliant kind of art' (Toth, 328–9). The first notice of the publication of *The Awakening* to appear in St Louis also made a point of the story's universality, finding Edna's situation 'rare in fiction, but common enough in life'. The writer had no problem with the nature of Edna's 'awakening', merely noting that she goes from being 'quiescent' to realizing that 'she has never lived'. Chopin was praised as 'an artist who can suggest more than one side of her subject with a single line' (Toth, 329). Surprisingly enough, this March notice appeared in the *St. Louis Republic*, the city's most conservative newspaper, whose reviewer had criticized *At Fault* on the grounds of both morality and Chopin's use of language. Just as the negative reviews of *At Fault* chose to overlook such seemingly obvious targets as Chopin's satire on religion, instead focusing on such 'indelicacies' as Melicent Hosmer's multiple engagements, so those who criticized *The Awakening* seemed primarily concerned with Edna's adultery, largely ignoring the fact that Edna finds both Protestantism and Catholicism stultifying. Given the fact that most reviewers attacked *The Awakening* on moral grounds, it is remarkable that the critics were silent about Chopin's frank portrayal of Madame Ratignolle's pregnancy at a time when obviously pregnant women did not appear in public. *The Awakening* is in fact structured on the period of gestation, opening at the point when Adele Ratignolle announces to the vacationers at Grand Isle that she will bear another child, and closing shortly after she has gone into labor.

Apparently, the remarks about *The Awakening* which appeared in the *St. Louis Republic* in March were based on the publisher's publicity for Chopin's novel, because when the *Republic* printed an actual review at the end of April, the reviewer's scathing comments set the tone for much of what was to follow. Titled 'Kate Chopin's New Book is the Story of a Lady Most Foolish', the review consisted mainly of plot summary studded with quotations from the novel selected to emphasize Edna's departure from the feminine ideal. Whereas the *Republic* notice of a month before had described Edna before her awakening as 'quiescent', the April review characterized her as 'self-contained' and 'unthinking', and stated that the 'tragedy' of her awakening was that whereas she had 'learned to love', she 'did not love her husband'. The review ended by suggesting that Edna's cardinal quality was selfishness: 'So the woman who did not want anything but her own way drowned herself' (Toth, 336–7). The review that appeared in *The Nation* on 3 August similarly stressed what the reviewer perceived as Edna's self-ishness: '"The Awakening" is the sad story of a Southern lady who wanted to do what she wanted to. From wanting to, she did, with disastrous consequences; but as she swims out to sea in the end, it is to be hoped that her example may lie forever undredged.' The reviewer had admired Chopin's 'agreeable short stories', and so had begun reading *The Awakening* with 'high expectations', but finished the novel with 'real disappointment'. The reviewer was moved to offer Chopin's heroine advice about her conduct; she should have 'flirted less and looked after her children more, or even assisted at more *accouchements*'. Regarding Chopin herself, the *Nation* reviewer reports having '[dropped] a tear over one more clever author gone wrong' (*CEKC*, 52). The 4 June review in the *Providence Sunday Journal* is worth quoting in its entirety because of its similarly moralistic tone, its assumptions about the effect of literature on the formation of character, and the reviewer's resistance to fiction which depicted life's realities:

Miss Kate Chopin is another clever woman, but she has put her cleverness to a very bad use in writing "The Awakening". The purport of the story can hardly be described in language fit for publication. We are fain to believe that Miss Chopin did not herself realise [sic] what she was doing when she wrote it. With a bald realism that fairly out Zolas Zola, she describes the result upon a married woman, who lives amiably with her husband without caring for him, of a slowly growing admiration for another man. He is too honourable [sic] to speak and goes away; but her life is spoiled already, and she falls with a merely animal instinct into the arms of the first man she meets. The worst of such stories is that they will come into the hands of youth, leading them to dwell on things that only matured persons can understand, and promoting unholy imaginations and unclean desires. It is nauseating to remember that those who object to the bluntness of our older writers will excuse and justify the gilded dirt of these later days.

(*CEKC*, 53)

The reviewer's mistaken identification of the author as 'Miss' Kate Chopin underscores the sense that a woman writer should not sully her natural feminine purity by writing 'gilded dirt'.

Even before the *Providence Sunday Journal* review appeared, Chopin felt the need to somehow defend herself against the mounting attacks on Edna Pontellier's behavior. In late May of 1899, she wrote what even at the time would have been read as a mocking rebuttal to her critics. Instead of arguing for artistic freedom or defending literary realism, she adopted the pretense that her central character had merely escaped authorial control:

Having a group of people at my disposal, I thought it might be entertaining (to myself) to throw them together and see what would happen. I never dreamed of Mrs. Pontellier making such a mess of things and working out her own damnation as she did. If I had had the slightest intimation of such a thing I would have excluded her from the company. But when I found out what she was up to, the play was half over and it was then too late.

(*KCPP*, 296)

Chopin's remarks were published in *Book News* in July, by which time *The Awakening* had received considerable national attention, most of it negative. Chopin had established herself in the minds of reviewers and critics as an author of harmless, often amusing stories of Creole and Acadian life; when she veered from this 'safe' subject matter to address woman's selfhood and independence – issues she was by no means the only author to explore in the 1890s – she was regarded by many as having abdicated her sanctioned role and committed an act nearly as reprehensible as those of Edna Pontellier.

If the book reviewers for major urban newspapers and literary periodicals had the power to determine Chopin's literary reputation and influence the direction her career would take, she could take some solace in the fact that a number of individual readers of *The Awakening* regarded the novel as a major achievement. The St Louis poet R. E. Lee Gibson had admired Chopin's work throughout the decade, at one point referring to her short-story collections *Bayou Folk* and *A Night in Acadie* as 'almost my favorite volumes of the few, very select and fondly-cherished books that I possess' (Toth, 328). When Chopin sent him a copy of *The Awakening* shortly after the novel's publication, Gibson's praise knew no bounds. Reading it, he wrote to Chopin in late April, he had become 'so completely engrossed, so absorbed that I could not put the book by until I had finished it'. In Gibson's view, Chopin belonged in the first rank of American authors: 'one capable of writing stories like yours is wonderfully gifted above the balance of us, and is worthy of all possible praise and success' (Toth, 337). St Louis attorney Louis B. Ely was equally enthusiastic, although his note to Chopin reveals that he was aware that the novel could be controversial. *The Awakening* was, Ely believed, 'a *moral* tale rather than an immoral one ... a sermon against un-naturalness.... I think there is little in it to offend any body' (Toth, 338). At least one of Chopin's friends declared his admiration for *The Awakening* in public. Charles Deyo reviewed the novel in the *Post-Dispatch*, showing insight into Chopin's intentions to which professional literary critics would not be attentive for 50 years, and countering the attacks that had been and would continue to be launched against the novel. Deyo understood Chopin's portrayal of Léonce Pontellier as a man who believes he 'possesses' his wife, and also Edna's desire to be free of such ownership. Unlike those readers who could not see beyond Edna's deviations from conventional morality, Deyo assessed the novel as a work of art, praising Chopin's 'rare skill in construction' and her 'delicious English, quick with life, never a word too much'. To those who believed the novel would corrupt young readers, Deyo maintained, '*The Awakening* is not for the young person; not because the young person would be harmed by reading it, but because the young person wouldn't understand it.' Deyo acknowledged that Chopin's theme was a dark one, but he kept his focus on her artistic achievement: '[The novel] is sad and mad and bad, but it is all consummate art. The theme is difficult, but it is handled with a cunning craft' (Toth, 342–3).

It is likely that Charles Deyo had the benefit of discussions with Chopin about *The Awakening*; as part of her intellectual circle, he had frequently talked with her about her work, and he had critiqued some of her earliest stories. But positive responses to the novel arrived from outside St Louis, as well, sometimes identifying qualities that eluded contemporary reviewers. 'Lizzie L.', a friend of Chopin's in Louisville, Kentucky, pointed to humor as one of the strengths of the novel: 'the humor of the book is delicious – like Balzac – but still essentially your own. In many places I can hear you speaking, describing incidents in your own cute, inimitable way' (Toth, 345). In the fall of 1899, after several months of being buffeted by negative reviews, Chopin was delighted to receive two long letters in support of *The Awakening* from London. The first, signed by Lady Janet Scammon Young, expressed 'great ... interest' in Chopin's novel, which had 'deeply stirred some ... noble souls' to whom she had loaned her copy. As much as Lady Janet admired the book that Chopin had written, she had plans for Chopin's next novel, 'which you among living novelists *could* write'. Lady Janet wanted a story in which a woman like Edna has a husband capable of being sensitive to her awakening; whereas in *The Awakening* Dr Mandelet, whom Léonce Pontellier consults about his wife's strange behavior, offers vague, offhanded advice, Lady Janet proposed that the doctor could convince Léonce that he should assist with rather than resisting her blossoming sensuality. 'Show us', Lady Janet advised Chopin, 'how such a husband can save such a wife and turn the influence of sex to its intended beneficient end' (Rankin, 178–9). Although Chopin's surprise correspondent oversimplified the message of *The Awakening* in seeing Edna's 'awakening' as primarily a sexual one – as did many other readers – she nonetheless refrained from moralizing, and hoped that the novelist she admired would write a story about a more egalitarian marriage. Enclosed in Lady Janet's letter was a letter from one of the 'noble souls' who had borrowed her copy of the novel, a London physician named Dunrobin Thomson. According to Dr Thomson, *The Awakening* was 'easily the book of the year'. Although Thomson also construed Edna's awakening as primarily sexual, he spoke against those critics who found her foolish, sinful, or unnatural. 'You [Thomson's letter is written to Lady Janet] fancy *Edna's* case exceptional? Trust an old doctor – most common. It is only that *Edna* was nobler, and took that last clean swim. The others live'. The cause of the problem, for all the Ednas of the world, Thomson believed, was lack of understanding and openness about female sexuality:

The essence of the matter lies in the accursed stupidity of men. They marry a girl, she becomes a mother. They imagine she has sounded the heights and depths of womanhood. Poor fools! She is not even awakened. She, on her part is a victim of the abominable prudishness which masquerades as modesty or virtue.... The law, spoken or implied, which governs the upbringing of girls is that passion is disgraceful.

After propounding the lecture that Dr Mandelet might have given to Léonce, Thomson concludes with fulsome praise for Chopin's novel: 'This book has stirred me to the soul. *Edna* is like a personal friend. She is not impure. The art, the local colour, the distinctness of characterisation of even the minor personages are something wonderful' (Rankin, 180–2).

Emily Toth suggests that the letters from Lady Janet and Dr Thomson may have been fabricated by some of Chopin's friends; her search of London registries of physicians and members of the aristocracy failed to turn up either name. But there is also no evidence that Chopin knew the letters were invented – if they were – so that even if they could not publically counteract negative reviews, they could buoy Chopin's sense of herself as a writer. Then, too, in St Louis she was still a celebrity, even if some did not approve of her latest novel, and when, in November 1899, she was asked to write an essay about herself for the Sunday magazine section of the *Post-Dispatch*, her tone was jaunty, if at times a bit defensive. She writes as an experienced author who has published 'many short stories and a novel or two', one whom 'the public' has chosen to call 'an author'. As she had several times before, Chopin describes her method of writing as quite casual. She writes 'in a Morris chair beside the window', and is tempted to say that she writes 'any old time'. As to *why* she writes, it is 'the spontaneous expressions of impressions gathered goodness knows where.... I am completely at the mercy of unconscious selection'. A note of asperity enters the essay, however, when she writes of her books not being taken 'seriously'. She has grown tired of being asked where the books can be found, and responds with some exasperation, 'Why, you will find it, no doubt, at the bookseller's or the libraries'; if the questioner says that the libraries 'don't keep it', Chopin writes acidly, 'She hadn't thought of the bookseller's. It's real hard to think of everything! Sometimes I feel as if I should like to get a good remunerative job to do the thinking for some people.' Chopin concludes her essay with sarcasm about the unwelcome questions journalists ask 'a defenseless woman'. One of these is how many children she has: 'I have a good many, but they'd be simply wild if I dragged them into this.' She considers 'impertinent' the question of whether she smokes cigarettes: 'Suppose I do smoke cigarettes? Am I going to tell it out in meeting? Suppose I don't smoke cigarettes. Am I going to admit such a reflection on my artistic integrity, and thereby bring upon myself the contempt of the guild?' The essay ends on a bantering note: 'In answering questions in which an editor believes his readers to be interested, the victim cannot take herself too seriously' (Rankin, 182–4). If Chopin was at this point feeling herself to be a 'victim' regarding *The Awakening*, it seems telling that nowhere in the essay does she directly allude to the novel.

The reference in Chopin's *Post-Dispatch* essay to the possibility that libraries might not have some of her work on their shelves resonates interestingly with one of the most persistent rumors about *The Awakening*: that the book was banned by one or more St Louis libraries. Chopin's first biographer, Daniel Rankin, states that 'the book was taken from circulation by order of the librarian of the St Louis Mercantile Library' (Rankin, 173). Thirty-two years later, in his 1969 biography, Per Seyersted expanded the scope of the banning by writing that 'the public outcry against the book quickly led the city's libraries to ban it' (Seyersted, 175). Seyersted's source is a comment by Chopin's youngest son, Felix, then 75, in a 1953 issue of the *Post-Dispatch*; Felix stated that the novel was 'withdrawn from the Mercantile and St. Louis Public Libraries, later being restored to the Central Public Library in a 1906 reprint edition' (Seyersted, 224, n.26). Seyersted also relied on the long memory of Clarence E. Miller, in 1899 an apprentice at the Mercantile Library, who in 1961 reported that Chopin had requested *The Awakening* at that library, only to be told that it had been withdrawn from circulation (Seyersted, 175); in Miller's view, there had been 'bigoted people on the book-committee' (Seyersted, 224, n.27). However, when Chopin's 1990 biographer, Emily Toth, checked the records of St Louis libraries, she found no evidence that *The Awakening* had ever been removed from the shelves by anyone other than borrowers eager to read it, and she also points out that there is no record in the St Louis press of a protest against the banning of the novel – which would certainly have been launched by Chopin's liberal friends, who were firmly opposed to such suppression. Ironically, the persistence of the banning rumor was one factor in the revival of interest in *The Awakening* in the middle of the twentieth century, as scholars attempted to rescue controversial books from the prudery of previous generations. As Toth notes, 'and so, long after her death, gossip has, at last, been good to Kate Chopin' (Toth, 425).

A concomitant myth has been that the adverse response to *The Awakening* so disheartened Chopin that she ceased writing. This misrepresentation seems traceable to Chopin's daughter, Lélia, who was frequently an unreliable commentator on her mother's life and work, and who wrote in 1907 that 'My Mother ... never discussed the reception of *The Awakening* with me.... But I know how deeply she was hurt by many facts, principally that she never wrote again' (Toth, 422–3). As early as 1932, the records that Chopin kept of her writing and submissions to publishers convinced Daniel Rankin that she did not abandon her career in 1899. 'May I suggest', Rankin wrote, 'that the list of her writings after July 1899 be consulted?' (Rankin, 185). But Lélia's comment found its way into both the 1907 *Library of Southern Literature* and Fred Lewis Pattee's 1915 *American Literature Since 1870*, and hence took on an authority that proved difficult to dislodge. Further, the notion that Chopin's feminine sensibilities were mortally wounded by attacks on the morality of her novel no doubt appealed to those who tended to stereotype women writers during the first decades of the twentieth century.

While it is true that 1899 was far from Chopin's most productive year as a writer, it is also the case that throughout that year – until February of 1900, in fact – she expected Herbert S. Stone & Company to bring out her third collection of stories, *A Vocation and a Voice*. Her manuscript account books reveal that her creation and submission of new and previously written stories was largely limited to the early months of 1899, before *The Awakening* was published and began to be reviewed. In January, she sent the story 'Vagabonds' to the *Times Herald*, which rejected it, as had seven other periodicals to which she had sent it since 1895. A very short, nearly plotless story, 'Vagabonds' depicts a brief meeting between the female narrator and the itinerant Valcour, who is said to be distantly related to her. Although the narrator, who wears a 'shabby skirt' and 'clumsy old boots', is not far above Valcour on the social scale, she has a sense of propriety that causes her to chide the down-at-the-heels 'cousin' for kissing another man's wife and for spending what little money he has on whiskey. As they part, however, the narrator displays some envy of Valcour's freedom: 'I could not help thinking that it must be good to prowl sometimes; to get close to the black night and lose oneself in its silence and mystery' (*CW*, 470–2). Also in January, Chopin wrote 'One Day in Winter', subsequently titled 'A December Day in Dixie'. This story, too, was submitted to and rejected by the *Times Herald*, but was accepted by *Youth's Companion* in March. The same month the *Companion* also accepted the story 'A Little Country Girl', which Chopin had written in February, and sent her a check for $50.00 (*KCPP*, 146). Both stories feature unusual weather; in 'A December Day in Dixie', the residents of Natchitoches suspend their usual activities to frolic in a rare snowfall, and in 'A Little Country Girl' a severe thunderstorm disrupts the circus that the title character has yearned to see. Throughout 1899 and well into 1900, Chopin attempted to find a publisher for the story 'The Unwritten Law', also written in February, sending it to *Century*, *Atlantic*, *Cosmopolitan*, *Saturday Evening Post*, and *Scribner's*; all rejected it, and the manuscript has apparently been lost (*KCPP*, 145–6). During the winter of 1898–9, Chopin again turned her attention to writing poetry. Of the several poems she completed and submitted for publication, however, only 'I Opened All the Portals Wide' (alternatively titled 'O Fair, Sweet Spring') was accepted; it appeared in the July 1899 issue of *Century*. Like Chopin's other poems – except the brief ones she sometimes sent to friends, which were often teasing and witty – the *Century* poem is conventional and sentimental, featuring poeticisms such as 'fain' and peppered with exclamation marks.

In her fiction, in contrast, Chopin continued to explore themes of love and passion. The story 'The Godmother', which she completed in February 1899, deals with a woman in her fifties whose love for her godson, Gabriel, is so strong that when he comes to tell her that he has killed a man, she persuades him not to turn himself in and, without Gabriel's knowledge, retrieves and cleans his knife, makes the murder look like a robbery, and claims that on the evening in question Gabriel was ill and resting in her apartment. Tante Elodie, the godmother of the title, is a complex character who reclaims the story from the melodramatic aspects of the plot. A long-time resident of the old town of Natchitoches, she is in many ways a Southern conservative. She resents the intrusion of the teachers' college, known as the 'Normal School', regarding it as 'an unpardonable innovation, with its teachers from Minnesota, from Iowa, from God-knows-where, bringing strange ways and manners to the old town'. She considers the emancipation of the slaves to have been 'a great mistake' (*CW*, 598), and she is a deeply religious Catholic. 'Prayers were no trifling matter with her', and before going to sleep on the night that Gabriel comes to tell her of his crime, 'she had said her *Notre Père*, her *Salve Marie* and *Je Crois en Dieu* and was deep in the litany of the Blessed Virgin' (*CW*, 600). Yet Tante Elodie is also a woman with a romantic past – her 'brief passion' for Justin Lucaze, Gabriel's father, 35 years earlier. Chopin even hints subtly that perhaps Tante Elodie is Gabriel's mother; her parents had stopped her from marrying Justin, and she seems all too eager to deny any connection between her involvement with Justin and the 'deep and powerful affection' she feels for Gabriel (*CW*, 599). Certainly her efforts – which are successful – to protect Gabriel from an accusation of murder are those of a mother protecting a child, and when the news arrives that Gabriel has been killed in a fall from a horse, her thoughts turn to 'her own place down there beside Justin's, all dismantled, with bats beating about the eaves and Negroes living under the falling roof' (*CW*, 614). Chopin's account books do not record any attempts to publish 'The Godmother' before it was accepted by *Reedy's Mirror* in December 1901.

Although Chopin did little writing during the remainder of 1899, it was in other ways a busy year for her as she endured the stress of negative responses to *The Awakening*. Her active social life continued without hiatus, including the Thursday evening gatherings of writers and intellectuals at her home. A glimpse of one of these occasions is afforded by a letter written by the poet Madison Cawein, who was visiting from Louisville, Kentucky, on 17 August. Cawein had greatly admired *The Awakening* when he had read it in the spring, and he developed a corresponding admiration for

Chopin herself, whom he described as 'a lovely woman of fifty-two [she was actually forty-nine] but still fine-looking and capable of exciting the enthusiastic admiration of men much younger than herself'. Cawein, a believer in spiritualism, had enjoyed the story-telling at Chopin's salon:

> We passed a delightful evening of ghost stories and poetry. I thought of how you would have enjoyed it – the ghost stories especially. A Mr. Schuyler [writer and musician William Schuyler] told some interesting ones, but I flatter myself that mine – in subject, at least, if not as well-worded as his – were the most thrilling. Mrs. Chopin is great skeptic, but she seemed most interested; perhaps if given a chance I might be able to convert her to believing in them.
>
> (Toth, 356–7)

Chopin had other admirers outside of St Louis. During the summer, Richard B. Shephard, then a member of the Utah House of Representatives, evidently wrote to ask for a list of her published books, because on August 24 she sent him a list, offering to provide him with a copy of the privately printed *At Fault*. In early November, soon after she returned from several weeks in the Wisconsin lake country, she again wrote to Shephard to ask whether he had obtained her books, apologizing that 'a severe spell of illness' – which Emily Toth speculates might have been depression – had interrupted her correspondence (*KCPP*, 211–12). A never-published piece that Chopin wrote in the fall of 1899 perhaps hints at the toll that critical rejection had taken on her emotional state. Titled 'A Reflection', the essay presents Chopin as a person left out of a 'moving procession'. While some people, she writes, 'are born with a vital and responsive energy' that provides them with 'motive power' for the 'mad pace', she is not one of these 'fortunate beings', but is instead left 'by the wayside'. Chopin 'could weep at being left by the wayside' to watch the 'fantastic colors' of the human procession. Yet at the same time, she feels somehow superior to these energetic people, who 'do not need to apprehend the significance of things' as she presumably does; although she is left behind with 'the grass and the clouds and a few dumb animals', she feels 'at home in the society of these symbols of life's immutability' (Toth, 362–3). If indeed Chopin is referring in this piece to her literary career, she at least had the consolation of being more perceptive than the common herd, more attuned to life's truths.

By November Chopin was preparing for the debutante season of her daughter, Lélia, which began in December, but she was first and foremost an author and local literary celebrity. The élite Wednesday Club, to which Chopin had belonged in the early 1890s, and whose 250 members were active in social reform as well as in promoting the arts, invited her to participate in a special program at the end of the month. The program included a performance of several of Chopin's poems which William Schuyler had set to music, and Chopin's reading of her story 'Ti Démon,' which she had completed earlier in the month. Covering the Wednesday Club event, the *Post-Dispatch* referred to 'Ti Démon' as a 'touching little story of Creole life' (Toth, 371); actually, the story describes how one incident and ensuing small-town gossip combine to ruin the reputation of a gentle and loving man. The title character's nickname was given him by his mother because of his lusty crying as an infant, but he developed into a man more deserving of his given name, Plaisance. After one uncharacteristic outburst of violence, however, when he finds his fiancée walking with another man, the townspeople shun him as though he really was a demon long after his one violent act is forgotten. Chopin submitted 'Ti Démon' to four different periodicals, all of which rejected it, between December 1899 and May 1900 (*KCPP*, 146), and the story eventually became part of *A Vocation and a Voice*. Also in late November, Chopin was prominently featured in a *Post-Dispatch* article titled 'A St. Louis Woman Who Has Won Fame in Literature'. As testimony to the author's prominence, the article included two drawings – one of the house on Eighth Street where she was born, and the other a rendering of Chopin in her 'workroom', drawn by her son Oscar. The text of the article referred only obliquely to the controversy surrounding *The Awakening*, noting that whereas Chopin's novel 'has not had the vogue of Winston Churchill's "Richard Carvel", ... it has aroused more discussion and probably deeper interest'. In what could have been an allusion to the fact that *The Awakening* had not become a best-seller, the unnamed *Post-Dispatch* writer emphasized Chopin's dedication to her art: 'As a writer of fiction Mrs. Chopin appeals to the finer taste, sacrificing all else, even pecuniary profit, to her artistic conscience.' Most surprising, in light of most previous assessments of Chopin's contributions to American literature, is the writer's refusal to categorize Chopin as a regional author:

> Mrs. Chopin has been called a southern writer, but she appeals to the universal sense in a way not excelled by any other American author. She is not sectional, or provincial, nor even national, which is to say that she is an artist, who is not bound by the idiosyncrasies of place, race, or creed.
>
> (Toth, 363–4)

Such a statement, had it appeared in *The Nation* or *The New York Times*, could have had significant influence on Chopin's literary reputation, but in a St Louis newspaper it could be taken merely as pride in a local author.

A brief look at other books by American authors published during 1899 affords some sense of literary taste at the end of the century. Historical novels were popular, as they had been throughout the nineteenth century, beginning with Lydia Maria Child's *Hobomok* (1824), set in the colonial period. Winston Churchill, mentioned in the *Post-Dispatch* article and a participant with Chopin in the Wednesday Club's 'An Hour with St. Louis Authors' in November, was a generation younger, born in St Louis in 1871. His 1899 novel *Richard Carvel*, set in the period of the American Revolution, was the first of a number of historical romances in a career that lasted well into the twentieth century. What was still called 'local-color' writing – a category into which *The Awakening*, despite its New Orleans setting, decidedly did not fit – continued to enjoy popularity. The year 1899 saw the publication of Hamlin Garland's *Boy Life on the Prairie*, Sarah Orne Jewett's *The Queen's Twin and Other Stories*, Charles W. Chesnutt's *The Conjure Woman* and *The Wife of His Youth*, and Booth Tarkington's *The Gentleman from Indiana*. Humorous writing that played upon vernacular language had been in wide circulation for much of the century, and took on a note of common-sense morality at the end of it with such works as Finley Peter Dunne's *Mr. Dooley in Peace and in War* (1898) and George Ade's *Fables in Slang* (1899). William Dean Howells, Henry James, and Edith Wharton all published novels in 1899, but the only other novel that took stylistic and thematic risks comparable to those of *The Awakening* was *McTeague*, by Frank Norris, who was then at the beginning of his brief career. While Chopin's novel was said by some reviewers to have been influenced by the work of French naturalist Emile Zola – a comparison she resented – Norris embraced Zola's example in delineating characters who, like Chopin's Edna, are driven by inner compulsions to sometimes tragic ends.

In December, with the debutante season in full swing, Chopin recorded royalty payments from *The Awakening* of $102.00 (*KCPP*, 142). As had been the case 30 years earlier, during her own debut season, she was pulled between the social and the intellectual parts of her life. As much as she enjoyed socializing on her own terms, she did not participate as wholeheartedly as did most mothers in Lélia's round of parties; she chose not to attend, for example, a lavish reception honoring the English actress Ellen Terry, London's leading Shakespearian actress at the turn of the century. With the approach of the new century, Chopin was able to distinguish more clearly than ever before between two 'moving processions' and her part in each. She would be an invited (and paid) guest to read from her work at the Wednesday Club, but not a member. The St Louis newspapers would laud her as an important – if controversial – American author, but not always list her in their society columns. With all of her children grown up, Chopin, shortly before she turned 50, was free to be her own person, to make her own choices.

6
1900–1904

Kate Chopin's story 'A Little Country Girl' was one of the stories that *Youth's Companion* included in the list 'The Best of Reading for Girls' as the magazine announced its publication plans for the year 1900. Perhaps buoyed by this recognition of her prominence – at least within a certain literary market – in early 1900 Chopin resumed her writing by completing two more stories for young people. The first of these, 'Alexandre's Wonderful Experience', written in January, closely resembles the stories of Horatio Alger, which for three decades had chronicled the elevation of poor young urban boys to positions of comfort and respectability through a combination of hard work, virtue, and luck. Like the typical Alger hero, Alexandre is first presented eking out a minimal living, in this case polishing furniture at an antique store in New Orleans. When a lovely but obviously not wealthy woman comes to the store to inquire about selling the owner a chest of drawers, Alexandre is angered by the store owner's dismissal of her even though he knows that a doctor living on St Charles Avenue is looking for just such a piece of furniture. Unable to get the woman out of his mind, Alexandre foregoes his usual supper of coffee and a roll to visit both the woman and the doctor without his employer's knowledge. Like the title character in 'Elizabeth Stock's One Story', Alexandre's good deed leads to his becoming ill, and by the time he is released from the hospital he has lost his job at the antique store and is forced to resort to selling clothes poles on the street. But, also like the Alger hero, the boy's natural virtue has not gone unnoticed. A nurse at the hospital remarks that 'any one could see he had had good bringing up!' (*KCPP*, 265). More importantly, the meeting between the woman and the doctor has brought about more than a business transaction: the doctor has treated the woman's invalid daughter and then married the widow. Alexandre's 'wonderful experience' is being taken to the couple's plantation, where he can leave 'the grime and the noise of the city behind him' (*KCPP*, 268). While Chopin's story demonstrates the rewards of honesty and good manners, it is less didactic and more whimsical than the typical Alger story. As she had in some of her earlier children's stories, such as 'A Very Fine Fiddle', Chopin employs the child's perspective, which gives the reader glimpses of Alexandre's 'lively imagination' (*KCPP*, 262). Trying to imagine a rosier future for the widow than the continued sale of her furniture, Alexandre daydreams that she finds 'a long lost will' in a secret drawer of her writing desk, and envisions her 'descending the marble steps of her Chateau in France, in a trailing purple velvet gown' (*KCPP*, 265).

'The Gentleman from New Orleans', which Chopin completed in February, is less clearly a story for young people, although it does demonstrate the beneficial effects of the industry and hospitality of Sophronie, young housekeeper for the Bénoîte family; in fact, Chopin first submitted the story to *Century* magazine. When Sophronie is left behind to do the household chores while the Bénoîte family goes to an all-day barbecue, she is told to watch for a 'gentleman from New Orleans' who is making a business trip through the parish. During Sophronie's busy day of cleaning, a strange man appears and Sophronie extends to him the best the household can offer. Not until the Bénoîtes return does she discover that this is not the 'gentleman from New Orleans', but instead Mrs Bénoîte's father, who had opposed her marriage but who has come to take her to see her sick mother. Mr Parkins' pleasure at the welcome he has received smooths his reconciliation with Buddie Bénoîte, and the whole family prepares to go to visit Mrs Parkins. If Sophronie's dedication to duty is one moral message in the story, a second concerns the bond between parent and child. The hotheaded Buddie Bénoîte had vowed to take his shotgun to any member of his wife's family who set foot on his property, but when he sees his wife embrace her father, 'the realization that the tie which united those two clinging to each other out there was the same that bound his own to the cherished baby in his arms, was an overwhelming realization' (*CW*, 636).

Youth's Companion was quick to accept both stories. Chopin submitted 'Alexandre's Wonderful Experience' on 24 January 1900, and received word of acceptance and a check for $50.00 on 18 February; after *Century* rejected 'The Gentleman from New Orleans' on 21 February, she sent it the same day to *Youth's Companion*, and on 12 March was paid $40.00 for the story (*KCPP*, 146). Thus, between March 1899 and March 1900, *Youth's Companion* had accepted four of Chopin's stories and had paid her a total of $150.00 for them. Inexplicably, however, the *Companion* never published these stories. Had the controversy about *The Awakening* made the magazine's editors wary of publishing her work? Such an explanation is at odds with the fact that the magazine accepted two of the stories after the critical furor had erupted, and whereas acceptance of – and payment for – a story did not constitute the binding contract that it might today, it certainly implied approval of both story and author. Unfortunately, no correspondence has survived – if it ever existed – to explain the *Companion's* decision not to use the stories after all, but the fact that they did not appear in print during Chopin's life has fueled the assumption that Chopin produced little fiction after *The Awakening*. More direct rejections of her work marred the beginning of 1900. In January, THE *Atlantic* became the second magazine to reject her story 'Ti Démon', objecting that the story was too 'somber', that the 'sad note' was 'too much accented' (Seyersted, 182). It may be no accident that Chopin's note accompanying her submission of 'A December Day in Dixie' to *Youth's Companion* in February has a tone of diffidence, almost inviting rejection: 'I can't imagine that you will care for this little sketch, or impression of one snowy day last winter when I arrived in Natchitoches, but I send it anyway, hoping that you might' (*KCPP*, 213).

The most severe blow came in February, when Herbert S. Stone & Company notified Chopin that it would not, after all, publish her collection *A Vocation and a Voice*. If the publisher offered any reason for this decision, Chopin did not record it in her manuscript account book; her characteristically cryptic entry about the volume reads in full as follows:

A Vocation & A Voice

Collection

To Atlantic	Nov. 24 '96
R[eturned]	Jan. 2 '97
To Bodley Head	Jan. 5 '97
R[eturned]	
To F. Tennyson Neely	Mar. 14 '97
R[eturned]	Apr. '97
To Way & Williams	– '98
Accepted –	
Transferred to H. S. Stone	Nov. '98
R[eturned]	Feb. 1900

(*KCPP*, 138)

Over the years, Chopin's biographers have speculated about the reasons why the publisher decided not to bring out *A Vocation and a Voice*. Daniel Rankin assumed a connection to *The Awakening* controversy: 'Perhaps the bitter reception given *The Awakening*, though the novel sold well, intimidated the publishers' (Rankin, 195). Per Seyersted, in 1969, seemed certain that it was merely a business decision having nothing to do with Chopin's reputation: 'Not knowing that Stone had decided to reduce the number of titles to be published by his company, nor that he had been unafraid of censorship when he brought out, for example, [Hamlin] Garland's *Rose of Dutcher's Coolly* [1895], Kate Chopin might have thought the rejection meant that she had become a literary outcast' (Seyersted, 182). Emily Toth concurs with Seyersted, stating with authority (although without documentation) that 'the firm was cutting back on its list, and not necessarily making a judgment on Kate Chopin's writing' (Toth, 373). However Chopin understood the rejection in early 1900, there is no evidence that she attempted to find another publisher for the collection, although she did, with some success, submit some of the individual stories to periodicals.

By February of 1900, slightly more than half of the stories that eventually appeared in *A Vocation and a Voice* in 1991 had been published in periodicals, fewer than had been the case with *Bayou Folk* and *A Night in Acadie*. In addition, the pattern of submission, rejection, and acceptance of the stories that Chopin intended for this volume reveals that from the early 1890s on she had been writing stories that were quite different from the regional sketches on which her reputation had been established. The earliest of the stories, 'An Idle Fellow', which she wrote in June of 1893, was rejected by such disparate publications as *The Atlantic*, the New Orleans *Times-Democrat*, and *Chap-Book* between May and October of 1894, and the fact that she approached these different periodicals suggests that even before the middle of the decade she was searching for the proper market for work which did not fit the 'local color' mode. 'Lilacs', written in May 1894, was published in the *Times-Democrat* in December 1896, but it had been rejected by *Century*, *Atlantic*, *Scribner's*, *Chap-Book*, *Harper's*, *Vogue*, *Cosmopolitan*, and *Yellow Book* in 1984 and 1895. 'A Mental Suggestion', written in December of 1896, did not appear in print until the 1969 *Complete Works*, but Chopin circulated the story for three years, sending it in turn to *Scribner's*, *Vogue*, *McClure's*, *Cosmopolitan*, *Lippincott*, *Black Cat*, and *The Saturday Evening Post* between January 1997 and February 1900. Although the *Chap-Book*, known for publishing innovative fiction, never accepted one of Chopin's stories, the editors at *Vogue* continued to be receptive to her work. Ten of the stories eventually to comprise *A Vocation and a Voice* were published in *Vogue* between December 1894 and July 1900: 'An Egyptian Cigarette', 'The White Eagle', 'The Story of an Hour', 'Two Summers and Two Souls', 'The Unexpected', 'Her Letters', 'The Kiss', 'Suzette', 'The Recovery', and 'The Blind Man'. *Vogue* rejected only two of the *Vocation* stories that Chopin sent to the magazine, although 'The Story of an Hour' was initially turned down and accepted only when she resubmitted it six months later.

Most of the other *Vocation* stories that were published during Chopin's life appeared in two quite different St Louis periodicals. The title story and 'The Godmother' appeared in the *Mirror*, edited by the populist Irishman William Reedy, and 'The Falling in Love of Fedora' and 'An Easter Day Conversion' in the *Criterion*, the successor to *St. Louis Life*. Reedy had considerable contempt for the *Criterion*, which he described as being characterized by 'exalted aestheticism' (Toth, 285), but both periodicals, for different reasons, were open to Chopin's more innovative fiction. Chopin sent only one of the *Vocation* stories – the 'Ti Démon' that is also known as 'A Horse Story' – to *Youth's Companion*, which returned it, as did *Century*, *Atlantic*, *Cosmopolitan*, and *Saturday Evening Post*.

Chopin's 'horse story' is one of only four stories in *A Vocation and a Voice* to be set in Louisiana, and none of the four has the lightness of tone and the emphasis on region that had come to be associated with the local-color story. Both of the 'Ti Démon' stories, the sketch titled 'Suzette', and the longer story 'The Godmother' are set in the Acadian region of Natchitoches Parish, a fact revealed primarily by place names and the speech of the characters, but all of them deal with misunderstandings, death, and loss. The human Ti Démon is forever regarded as dangerous following his single act of violence, and Gabriel's similarly uncharacteristic killing of a man who is threatening him sets in motion Tante Elodie's elaborate deception in 'The Godmother'. The title character in 'Suzette' is as much relieved as saddened to learn that her suitor has drowned while drunk; his constant attention had begun to annoy her, and 'it was not her fault that he had grown desperate – that he was dead' (*VV*, 111). Shortly after receiving the news, she dresses carefully to impress a young man who is leaving on a cattle drive, but he pays no attention to her, and as she weeps in disappointment, 'the carnations drooped from their fastening and lay like a bloodstain upon her white neck' (*VV*, 113). The 'Ti Démon' in which the title character is a horse has touches of whimsy reminiscent of some of Chopin's earlier stories. Much of the story is told from the perspective of the aging horse, who understands human speech and is capable of untying the rope with which his owner, Herminia, has tied him to a tree. He is also proudly aware of his origins as an Indian pony, when he had been named 'Spitfire', and dislikes being compared to a mule as he grows older. But the story ends sadly.

After overhearing the suggestion that he is too old to be useful and should be shot, Ti Démon escapes to return to the Indian nation, but dies on the way. (It is not clear why Chopin gave two of her stories the same title, and she was aware that magazine editors might be confused. When she submitted the second 'Ti Démon' to *Century*, which had earlier rejected her 'horse story', she felt the need to differentiate between them: 'The title – "Ti Demon" is one which I have offered before to the Century, but the story is entirely new' [*KCPP*, 212]).

The title story, 'A Vocation and a Voice', includes one sequence set in Louisiana, but most of the story, like the majority of the stories in the collection, has no specific regional location. More important than geographic setting is the story's treatment of several thematic elements which characterize the collection as a whole. One of these is religion – specifically Catholicism – which Chopin treats more seriously than she had in *At Fault*, despite her own distance from religious observance by the late 1890s. The 'vocation' of the title belongs to the unnamed central character, who leaves the Irish ghetto of a large city, where the one stable element of his life has been his service as an altar boy, to travel with an itinerant couple who eke out a living telling fortunes and selling herbal medicines. When they arrive in Louisiana, he is befriended by a parish priest, and later, when he comes close to killing the man he is traveling with, he seeks refuge in a monastery, where hard physical labor is combined with religious devotion: 'The dreams of the youth found their object among the saintly and celestial beings presented to his imagination constantly, and to his pious contemplation' (*VV*, 33). Yet Chopin's depiction of religious commitment has a Transcendental component in this as well as other stories. The boy 'had no mind for books', but he 'knew by name every bird and bush and tree, and all the rocks that are buried in the earth and all the soil that covered them' (*VV*, 33). A similar preoccupation with the natural world as the source of faith is the message of 'An Idle Fellow', which takes the form of a monologue spoken by a genderless narrator who is 'tired' after a lifetime of reading books. His or her companion, the 'idle fellow' Paul, instead reads nature. 'He is listening to a thrush's song that comes from the blur of yonder apple-tree.... He turns away from me and the words with which I would instruct him, to drink deep the scent of the clover-field and the thick perfume from the rose-hedge.' The speaker concludes that Paul is 'very wise, he knows the language of God which I have not learned' (*VV*, 52–3). In two other stories, flowers lead the central characters to religious institutions. In 'Lilacs', which is set in France, the annual aroma of lilac blossoms draws the Parisian actress Adrienne Farival to the convent where she had spent her youth for a period of rest and renewal. And in 'An Easter Day Conversion' – alternately titled 'A Morning Walk' – the 40-year-old Archibald, a man who 'leaned decidedly toward practical science' (*VV*, 127), is captivated by a young woman carrying an armload of white lilies to church. He accompanies her, and the minister's message, 'I am the Resurrection and the Life', all at once has meaning for him: 'This was his text' (*VV*, 130).

The 'voice' in the title story is that of Suzima, the female fortune-teller with whom the boy travels. Originally named Susan, but renamed by her male companion to fit with her role as 'The Egyptian Fortune Teller', she once aspired to be an opera singer. 'I sang in the chorus of an opera when I wasn't more than sixteen', she tells the boy early in their acquaintance. 'Some people said if I'd had the means to cultivate my voice I'd be – well, I wouldn't be here to-day, I can tell you' (*VV*, 8–9). The boy responds to her voice, feeling that 'he had never heard anything more beautiful than the full, free notes that came from her throat' (*VV* 11), and it is her voice that draws him from the monastery at the end of the story. 'He was conscious of nothing in the world but the voice that was calling him and the cry of his own being that responded' (*VV*, 36). Susan's frustrated desire to be an opera singer has echoes in other stories. In 'Elizabeth Stock's One Story', the title character, postmistress in a small Missouri town, aspires to be a writer, but has neither the encouragement nor the education to achieve her goal. Adrienne, in 'Lilacs', is a successful stage actress, but finds the life unfulfilling and spends her time bickering with her servant and her manager. When she is told that she cannot return to the convent that has been her annual refuge, she weeps 'with the abandonment of a little child' (*VV*, 145). The unnamed woman in 'The White Eagle' is denied even the aspiration for a mean-ingful life. Gradually stripped of family, friends, and a steady income, she has for company only the cast-iron eagle from her childhood home. 'No mate came to seek her out. Her hair began to grizzle. Her skin got dry and waxlike upon her face and hands' (*VV*, 74).

Relationships between men and women do not fare well in this collection of stories. While at the end of 'A Vocation and a Voice' Susan and the boy who has become 'Brother Ludovic' seem to be on the verge of being reunited, far more frequently couples grow apart rather than together. Just as Chopin had declared in her remarks in the *Post-Dispatch* in January of 1898 that love was not 'divine', she demonstrates in her later stories that it is affected by whims, misunderstandings, and secrets. In 'Two Summers and Two Souls', a man declares his love for a woman after five weeks' acquaintance, but she is unwilling to commit herself and he leaves heartbroken. When, a year later, she writes him that she has decided she does love him, he has just succeeded in putting her out of his mind. Although he does go to see her, he does so with a sense of doom: 'As he would have gone unflinchingly to meet the business obligation that he knew would leave him bankrupt' (*VV*, 83). In 'The Unexpected', a man becomes ill while away on business and is told that his recovery depends on a stay in a southern climate; when he visits his fiancée before leaving and suggests that they marry immediately so that she may inherit his estate if he dies, she is repelled by his emaciated appearance and flees the house. Physical appearance is also a factor in 'The Recovery'. A 35-year-old woman who has been blind for 15 years regains her sight, and is shocked to see signs of aging when she first looks in the mirror. The man who loves her has waited patiently through the years of her blindness, but when he suggests that they now commit to each other in marriage, she realizes that what she had taken for love was instead youth: 'The blessed light had given her back the world, life, love; but it had robbed her of her illusions; it had stolen away her youth' (*VV*, 122). In 'Her Letters', a woman with a terminal illness at first decides to burn her love letters from another man, but then leaves them in a bundle with a note asking her husband to destroy them unopened at her death. The husband finally complies with her wishes and throws the letters into a river, but he is so tortured by the knowledge that she has kept a secret from him that he drowns himself in the same river. More lighthearted is the story 'A Mental Suggestion', but here, too, Chopin presents love as mysterious and unpredictable. Don Graham, a college professor, is also a hypnotist who has frequently used his powers on his friend Faverham. When Graham conveys to Faverham the 'mental suggestion' that he will find Graham's fiancée attractive rather than boring, the joke back-fires: Faverham and Pauline fall in love and eventually marry. Afraid that his 'mental suggestion' will wear off and the marriage will be destroyed, Graham attempts to plant a counter-suggestion, only to discover that the couple's relationship is beyond his power to control.

In dealing with hypnosis in 'A Mental Suggestion' and fortune-telling in 'A Vocation and a Voice', Chopin was responding to the late-nineteenth-century fascination with pseudo-scientific attempts to forecast or influence human behavior, but she was also risking the charge that her fiction was decadent. In these two stories, Chopin stops short of claiming the validity of these phenomena; 'Suzima' knows that her cards cannot foretell the future, and Graham recognizes that hypnosis cannot control human emotion. But in 'An Egyptian Cigarette', Chopin employs no such safeguards when she describes a drug-induced state. The first-person narrator accepts the gift of a small unmarked box from a friend who has obtained it from 'a species of fakir' in Cairo; the box contains six hand-rolled cigarettes, one of which the narrator smokes in the friend's 'smoking-den', whose 'appointments were exclusively oriental' (*VV*, 67–8). As soon as she begins to smoke, 'a subtle, disturbing current passed through my whole body and went to my head like the fumes of a disturbing wine' (*VV*, 68). In the ensuing visionary state, the narrator imagines herself alone in a desert, abandoned by her lover, who has ridden away on a camel; she is 'blistered' by the sun and hot sand, and yearns for the cooling waters of a nearby river. Although the narrator's tone of impassioned despair is in contrast to Edna's calm demeanor as she plans what will be her final swim in the Gulf of Mexico, the two scenes have strikingly similar imagery, which is not surprising given the fact that Chopin wrote 'An Egyptian Cigarette' in April of 1897, two months before she began serious work on *The Awakening*. In the short story, the narrator notes that the 'oracles' and the 'stars' had predicted that 'after the rapture of life I would open my arms inviting death, and the waters would envelop me' (*VV*, 69); at the end of *The Awakening*, Chopin writes that 'the touch of the sea is sensuous, enfolding the body in its soft, close embrace' (*CW*, 1000). Just before Edna begins her swim, she sees 'a bird with a broken wing ... beating the air above, reeling, fluttering, circling disabled down, down to the water' (*CW*, 999); similarly, the narrator in 'The Egyptian Cigarette' hears 'the wings of a bird flapping above my head, flying low, in circles' (*VV*, 70). At the end of the story, the narrator's report to her friend that she has had a 'dream' does nothing to detract from the reality of her vision (*VV*, 71). Chopin evidently knew better than to submit 'An Egyptian Cigarette' to *Century* or *Atlantic*; her manuscript account book shows that she first sent it to the *Chap-Book*, the *Criterion*, and a periodical identified only as 'Rep' before *Vogue* accepted the story in April 1900 (*KCPP*, 143–4).

Several of the stories in *A Vocation and a Voice* are frank in their depictions of sexuality. In the title story, the boy comes upon Suzima bathing naked in a river, and 'her image, against the background of tender green, ate into his brain and into his flesh with the fixedness and intensity of white-hot iron' (*VV*, 26). Shortly thereafter, when he and Suzima are together in the wagon, she initiates a sexual encounter, turning to hold him 'fast with her arms and with her lips' (*VV*, 29). In 'Two Portraits', the 'wanton', who has been sexually abused as a child, learns that her body is her only commodity and knows instinctively 'the ways of stirring a man's desire and holding it.... [T]he secret was in her blood and looked out of her passionate, wanton eyes and showed in every motion of her seductive body' (*VV*, 47). The husband in 'Her Letters' has perceived his wife as 'cold and passionless' (*VV*, 98), but she recalls the passion she had shared with her lover: 'This man had changed the water in her veins to wine, whose taste had brought delirium to both of them' (*VV*, 96). Two of the stories have homoerotic elements which recall the scene early in *The Awakening* when Madame Ratignolle takes Edna's hand 'firmly and warmly' and 'stroked it a little, fondly', and Edna, initially startled, 'soon lent herself readily to the Creole's gentle caress' (*CW*, 897). In 'The Falling in Love of Fedora', the title character, having begun to fall in love with a younger man, goes to the station to pick up his sister; the strong physical resemblance between the two stirs Fedora to announce, 'I shall be quite fond of you', and on the drive home, 'Fedora bent down and pressed a long, penetrating kiss upon her mouth' (*VV*, 117). And throughout the story 'Lilacs', Chopin provides suggestions that one of the reasons for Adrienne's regular visits to the convent – and perhaps the reason why she is barred from returning – is her attraction to Sister Agathe. Although the women's feelings remain unspoken, when Adrienne leaves the convent for the last time Sister Agathe 'knelt beside the bed on which Adrienne had slept. Her face was pressed deep in the pillow in her efforts to smother the sobs that convulsed her frame' (*VV*, 145).

In addition to their thematic differences from Chopin's local-color stories, many of the stories in her third collection are different in form and style. While many of the earlier stories had been quite short, some of them well under a thousand words in length, they nonetheless established distinct characters and locations, using names, dialect, and quick descriptive phrases to anchor them in recognizable reality. In 'A Very Fine Fiddle', for example, collected in *Bayou Folk*, the Louisiana setting is evoked by old Cléophas' exclamation '*Dieu Merci!*', the reference to 'great carryings-on up at the big plantation', and little Fifine counting her money beneath 'a big chinaberry-tree'. The texture of social-class disparity is conveyed by the contrast between the 'ladies and gentlemen from the city' and the 'shabby little girl' on the plantation veranda (*CW*, 149–50). The short sketches in *A Vocation and a Voice*, on the other hand, tend to be removed from such social contexts. Ideas take precedence over character and place, and because the stories could be set anywhere, they take on a universality that accords with their philosophical messages. In 'The Story of an Hour', Mrs Mallard could be any woman who receives the news of her husband's accidental death and feels first grief and then an exhilarating freedom. No regional setting exists to suggest that her reaction is the result of cultural conditioning or custom; Chopin instead presents marriage as an institution with the potential to crush individuality, a socially sanctioned 'blind persistence with which men and women believe they have a right to impose a private will upon a fellow-creature' (*VV*, 78). 'An Idle Fellow' lacks even the slender plot of 'The Story of an Hour', consisting of a meditation on whether knowledge is best acquired from books or through direct observation. The unnamed narrator and his friend Paul sit on a 'door-step' with a view of apple trees and roses, and then take a walk down a hill to a place where 'women and men and children are living' whom Paul understands because 'in their eyes he reads the story of their souls' (*VV*, 52–3).

Some of the stories resemble parables in which Chopin comments on the inevitable consequences of human choices. As she had in

The Awakening, Chopin presents relationships between men and women as unstable alliances resulting more from momentary whim or passion than from true commitment. In 'The Kiss', a young woman is attracted to the 'rather insignificant and unattractive Brantain' solely because of his wealth; she 'liked and required the entourage which wealth would give her'. When Harvy, to whom she had previously been committed, kisses her in Brantain's presence, she claims that instead of being lovers, she and Harvy are 'like cousins – like brother and sister, I may say'. Reassured, Brantain proposes to her, and at the wedding reception she thinks she will have both love and money when Harvy approaches to kiss her: 'She felt like a chess player who, by the clever handling of his pieces, sees the game taking the course intended.' But Harvy declares that he has learned that kissing women is 'dangerous', and the woman realizes that 'a person can't have everything in this world; and it was a little unreasonable of her to expect it' (*VV,* 106–8). The unnamed woman in 'The Recovery' is unable to accept the fact that she no longer looks like she did at 20, before she became blind, and so rejects the man who has waited for her with 'untiring devotion' (*VV,* 120). If these stories suggest that women are culturally conditioned to value wealth and physical appearance, in 'Two Portraits' Chopin leaves no doubt that she stands on the 'nurture' side of the heredity versus environment debate. These two accounts of a girl named Alberta are mirror images of one another; each begins with the same paragraph, in which Chopin emphasizes the power of early experience to mold a woman's sense of herself in the world:

> Alberta having looked not very long into life, had not looked very far. She put out her hands to touch things that pleased her and her lips to kiss them. Her eyes were deep brown wells that were drinking, drinking impressions and treasuring them in her soul. They were mysterious eyes and love looked out of them.
>
> (*VV,* 45)

In 'The Wanton', Alberta's thirsty soul is met with 'beatings which alternated with the most generous indulgence' from 'her mama who was really not her mama' (*VV,* 45). During a childhood in which there is little stability – 'The people about her seemed to be always coming and going' (*VV,* 46) – Alberta learns to rely only upon her own body, which by the age of 17 she is trading for money. By the end of the story Alberta has become a dangerous woman, 'for since [she] has added much wine to her wantonness she is apt to be vixenish; and she carries a knife' (*VV*, 47–8). As 'The Wanton' is a parable of the flesh, 'The Nun' is a parable of the soul. Here the young orphaned Alberta falls into the care of a nun, who teaches her that 'the soul must be made perfect and the flesh subdued' (*VV*, 48), and so Alberta enters a convent, where she submits entirely to the will of God: 'She does not walk upright; she could not, overpowered by the Divine Presence and the realization of her own nothingness' (*VV*, 50). Neither Alberta is capable of seeking the self-determination that Edna Pontellier begins to find in *The Awakening*; the 'wanton' ends as an alcoholic prostitute, and the 'nun' regards herself as merely 'a worm upon the earth' with her sights fixed on 'heavenly bliss' (*VV*, 50).

The fact that the characters in 'Two Portraits' are given little individual identity is paralleled by the namelessness of a good many of the characters in *A Vocation and a Voice*. Indeed, by naming both the wanton and the nun 'Alberta', yet engaging them in radically different life stories, Chopin calls into question the individuality that can be conferred by names, just as she names both a man and a horse 'Ti Démon' in the two stories with that title – and in both cases, this is not the character's real name: the man is actually named Plaisance, and the horse was originally called Spitfire, the only name the horse 'acknowledged officially' (*VV*, 151). As Peggy Skaggs points out, the central character in Chopin's title story is called 'the boy' as token of his lack of any real identity until he adopts the monastic name Brother Ludovic. 'But one day,' Skaggs writes, 'he learns that this self-image, too, is inadequate', when he hears Suzima sing and leaves the monastery to join her. '[T]he boy's conflicting needs, like Edna's, are universal, transcending sexual limitations.'[1] The universality conferred by namelessness works in such otherwise different stories as 'An Egyptian Cigarette', 'Her Letters' and 'The White Eagle' to focus attention on the story's message rather than the details of character and setting that characterize the local-color stories. The drug-induced reverie the narrator experiences in the whimsical 'An Egyptian Cigarette' makes no profound comment on the human condition, but the anonymous narrator represents the human attraction to that which is forbidden and exotic and the concomitant desire to maintain respectability; even though she wonders what 'other visions' the remaining five cigarettes might hold for her, she destroys them, and claims merely to have had a 'dream' (*VV*, 71). The woman in 'Her Letters' becomes any woman with a secret past, and 'The White Eagle' is a parable of human loneliness, as the cast-iron bird is the only constant companion of the unnamed seamstress.

Most of these stories also feature stylistic differences from Chopin's regional stories. In even the most serious of her Louisiana stories in *Bayou Folk* and *A Night in Acadie*, the regional descriptions and the use of dialectical speech lend lightness to the tone, and the emphasis on plot and incident creates quick movement. The story 'For Marse Chouchoute', for example, ends sadly, with young Wash seriously injured in his attempt to deliver the Cloutierville mail to the train, yet Chopin lightens the conclusion by closing with Wash recounting his wild ride to Chouchoute and reiterating his inverted sense of racial hierarchy that requires him to take care of his white friend: 'I boun' to git well, 'ca'se who – gwine – watch Marse – Chouchoute?' (*CW*, 110). In contrast to the immediacy of a style driven by plot and characterization, the *Vocation and a Voice* stories tend to feature lyrical, sometimes impassioned passages that connect characters not to each other in a community setting, but instead to questions of their position in a universal scheme. In the title story, the boy enjoys the solitude of night as he travels with Suzima and Gutro:

> To step his foot out into the darkness, he did not know where, was like tempting the Unknown. Walking thus he felt as if he were alone and holding communion with something mysterious, greater than himself, that reached out from the far distance to touch him—.
>
> (*VV*, 14)

The husband in 'Her Letters', troubled by the mystery of his wife's secret, similarly seeks answers outside the human community: 'He no longer sought to know from men and women what they dared not or could not tell him. Only the river knew.... It babbled, and he listened to it, and it told him nothing, but it promised all' (*VV*, 103). The speaker in 'The Night Came Slowly' also turns to nature when people cannot provide understanding: 'Can one of them talk to me like the night – the Summer night? Like the stars or the caressing wind?' (*VV*, 84). Such passages, in which night and darkness serve as correlatives for human isolation, recall the ending of *The Awakening*, when Edna leaves behind both New Orleans and Grand Isle and seeks the embrace of the sea. Even Elizabeth Stock, less given to philosophical musing than most of the other characters in this collection, ponders fate as she nears the end of her life and of her 'one story': 'what I got to do is leave everything in the hands of Providence, and trust to luck' (*VV*, 44).

In their emphasis on human isolation, depictions of the search for meaning, and substitution of extended conversations or monologues for traditional plot, these stories show the influence of Guy de Maupassant far more than do the stories in Chopin's earlier collections. While Chopin's characters seldom display the obsessive or even pathological behavior that some of Maupassant's characters do, she employs several devices to underscore their separation from supportive human communities. The boy in 'A Vocation and a Voice' is an orphan, as are the two Albertas in 'Two Portraits'. The boy has lived in 'The Patch' as an 'alien member' of the Donnelly household, and when he gets lost at the beginning of the story, he has the 'conviction that it would make no difference to any one' whether he finds his way back (*VV*, 3). Blindness serves as another isolating factor. The woman in 'The Recovery' has lived for 15 years 'in darkness with closed lids' (*VV*, 118), and when her sight is restored she finds that 'the sight of things confuses' her, and she chooses to 'go back into the dark' (*VV*, 122). In 'The Blind Man', the unnamed title character wanders the streets of a city trying to sell pencils; during his 'aimless wandering' he is nearly robbed of his pencils by some children and narrowly avoids being run over by a streetcar (*VV*, 124–5). The reverie induced by the 'Egyptian cigarette' is of being abandoned in the desert, Dorothea in 'The Unexpected' runs from the sight of her ill lover until 'she could perceive no human habitation' (*VV*, 92), and Elizabeth Stock ends her days alone in St Louis City Hospital, in 'a silence that remained unbroken until the end' (*VV*, 37). Even the Louisiana stories in this collection sound the note of loss and isolation. The title character in 'Suzette' learns of the death of one suitor and is ignored by another, and Tante Elodie in 'The Godmother', after learning of

Gabriel's death, sits 'alone in the corner, under the deep shadow of the oaks while the stars came out to keep her company' (*VV*, 188).

It is impossible to know what effect the publication of *A Vocation and a Voice* in 1900 would have had on Chopin's literary reputation and her career. Reviewers would surely have noted that few of the stories could be termed 'charming' and 'picturesque' like the stories in *Bayou Folk* and *A Night in Acadie*, and some would have complained that some of the stories were devoid of plot and action. The more genteel reviewers would have found such stories as 'An Egyptian Cigarette' and the references to sexuality in 'The Wanton', 'A Vocation and a Voice', 'Her Letters' and 'The Falling in Love of Fedora' disturbing and possibly 'immoral', especially coming from the pen of a woman. It was in 1900 that Theodore Dreiser's novel *Sister Carrie* was printed but then withdrawn from circulation because the publisher feared that the story, in which a woman lives with two different men to whom she is not married, would violate readers' moral standards. Among the popular books of the year were Frank L. Baum's *The Wonderful Wizard of Oz*, Finley Peter Dunne's *Mr. Dooley's Philosophy*, and novels by Hamlin Garland, Ellen Glasgow, Robert Herrick, and Booth Tarkington; only Mark Twain's *The Man That Corrupted Hadleyburg* would have been regarded as similarly a departure from its author's former, less dark, mode. On the other hand, the publication of Chopin's third collection – however it was received by critics – would have affirmed that the author of *The Awakening* possessed a fictional range and versatility that readers would not have suspected a decade earlier.

In April of 1900, Chopin wrote one of her longest stories, 'Charlie', which returns to the Louisiana setting and which features one of the most complex female characters in her short fiction. The story is a curious hybrid, incorporating elements of nineteenth-century senti-mental fiction and the 'New Woman' ideology, and using a planta-tion setting to develop a strong but conflicted young woman. Like many nineteenth-century heroines, Charlie is motherless; but she is hardly without family. One of seven daughters of plantation owner Laborde, Charlie, at 17 the next-to-oldest of the girls, is a curious mix-ture of masculine and feminine qualities. Named Charlotte, Charlie is the only one of the sisters who has a nickname, and the only one who resists the discipline of Miss Melvern, the governess imported from Pennsylvania to oversee the girls' education. Charlie wears her hair cut short and dresses in 'a costume of her own devising, something between bloomers and a divided skirt which she called her "trouser-lets"' (*CW*, 639). While her sisters study their lessons, Charlie rides her horse around the plantation, chiding the servants and visiting a Cajun family that lives on the edge of the Laborde property. Like a swaggering young man, she boasts to the Cajun children that she intends to shoot bears and tigers in the woods, and in fact carries a pistol. While Charlie's father has thought of sending his rebellious daughter away to boarding school to learn feminine behavior, he secretly admires her spirit; she 'could ride and shoot and fish; she was untiring and fearless. In many ways she filled the place of that ideal son he had always hoped for and that had never come' (*CW*, 644). When he sees her dressed for dinner one night, he finds the sight 'dismal': 'there was something poignant in the sight of his beloved daughter in this unfamiliar garb' (*CW*, 653). Yet Charlie also writes poetry, and when she finally is sent to a female seminary in New Orleans, she takes readily to the training in such feminine skills as dancing, and prides herself on the whitening of her sun-browned hands. Although Charlie's older sister, Julia, sees a 'revolution in Charlie's character' in New Orleans that seems 'violent and pronounced' (*CW*, 656), Chopin has established Charlie's balance of traditionally masculine and feminine characteristics early in the story:

> She was greatly celebrated for two notable achievements in her life. One was the writing of a lengthy ode upon the occasion of her Grandmother's seventieth birthday; but she was perhaps more distinguished for having once saved the levee during a time of perilous overflow when her father was away. It was a story in which an unloaded revolver played a part, demoralized negroes and earth-filled gunny sacks. It got into the papers and made a heroine of her for a week or two.
>
> (*CW*, 641)

When Mr Laborde is injured in an accident, it therefore seems natural that Charlie returns home to help run the plantation while he recovers. This is not the chastened nineteenth-century heroine returning home to take up properly domestic responsibilities, but a young woman fully aware of her capabilities, as she declares to her father when he asks for Gus Bradley, the young man from a neighboring plantation who has been helping him with his mail: 'I know as much as he, more perhaps when it comes to writing letters. I know as much about the plantation as you do, Dad; ... and from now on I'm going to be ... your right hand' (*CW*, 667–8). When, at the end of the story, Gus, who has been attracted to Charlie since her tomboy days, begins tentatively to declare his feelings, she responds in kind without out a trace of coquetry, and the reader is left to imagine an eventual union of equals.

'Charlie' was rejected by both *Youth's Companion* and *Century*, whereupon Chopin ceased to submit the story. The *Century* editors might have objected to Charlie's androgynous dress and behavior, and the story was very likely too long for *Youth's Companion*. Whatever the reasons for the rejections, Chopin's rate of composition and acceptance had slowed considerably by the middle of 1900. Only five more stories were published during Chopin's life: 'The White Eagle' in *Vogue* in July 1900, 'The Godmother' and 'A Vocation and a Voice' in *Reedy's Mirror* in December 1901 and March 1902, respectively, and 'The Wood-Choppers' and 'Polly' in *Youth's Companion* in May and July 1902 (Rankin, 305). 'The Wood-Choppers' has in common with 'Charlie' a man's admiration for a woman's spunk and determination. When the schoolteacher Léontine gets home one day to her 'poor little bit of a Southern house', she discovers that no one has cut firewood for her and her elderly mother, so she attempts to do so herself, and is observed by a new neighbor, Mr Willet, who sends her inside and cuts the wood himself. Rather than being grateful, Léontine, whom Chopin describes as 'spunky', suffers from injured pride, and when Mr Willet continues to assist the family with gifts of fruit and meat, she warns her mother that Mr Willet will marry a woman 'who may look down on us, who will be disagreeable, whom we will dislike'. But Mr Willet has in fact been courting Léontine herself, and when they marry and move to his plantation, he takes with him Léontine's wood-cutting ax, 'proclaiming that as long as he lived it should hold a place of honor in his establishment' (*CW*, 674–9). The story 'Polly', written in January 1902 and first called 'Polly's Opportunity', also ends with the marriage of the female character, but it is set in Missouri instead of Louisiana, and is more intent on conveying a moral message to young readers. When Polly receives an unexpected check for $100.00 from her uncle with instructions to spend it on herself, she instead buys gifts for her family, and is rewarded with the news that her fiancé, George, has gotten a better position and that, consequently, 'Polly was going to get a position which every well-meaning girl, at some time of her life, looks forward to as the beginning of better things' (*CW*, 680). With their Cinderella-like endings, the two *Youth's Companion* stories are conventional tales which lack the spark and distinctiveness of Chopin's earlier stories.

In 'Charlie', Chopin provides just one line of a poem her heroine has written, but with its abstractions and capitalizations it resembles Chopin's own poetry: 'Relentless Fate, and thou, relentless Friend!' (*CW*, 641). Soon after completing 'Charlie', Chopin herself turned again to poetry, composing 'Alone', which seems to speak to her state of mind in the summer of 1900. Whether she was thinking of Oscar or another lost love, at the age of 50 Chopin was nostalgic for 'our living Love in the Long Ago', when there was 'a Love not born to die'. Although there is darkness between her and her 'distant Star', she seems in the concluding stanza to foresee a reunion after death: 'Lovely the Life that shall live in The Life/When the Distance no longer my Kisses bar' (*KCPP*, 293–4). In August, Chopin's thoughts were again on the past; as she recorded having done 30 years earlier in her honeymoon diary, she remembered the birthday of her childhood friend, now a nun, Kitty Garesché, this time with a poem, 'To the Friend of My Youth: To Kitty':

> It is not all of life
> To cling together while the years glide past.
> It is not all of love
> To walk with clasped hands from first to last.
> That mystic garland which the spring did twine
> Of scented lilac and the new blown rose,
> Faster than chains will hold my soul to thine
> Thro' joy, and grief, thro' life – unto its close.

(Toth, 378)

Chopin's poetry is today of interest primarily for insights it may afford into her emotional preoccupations, not for its literary merit. As Barbara C. Ewell has noted, 'even in the context of most contemporary magazine poetry, Chopin's verse is not particularly distinguished. Her subjects tend to the conventional; her imagery and technical control are not remarkable; her diction is often artificial'.[2] Nonetheless, she enjoyed a reputation as a poet among her St Louis friends, among whom musical settings of poems had a particular vogue at the turn of the century. The three poems what William Schuyler had set to music for performance at the November 1899 meeting of the Wednesday Club were 'I've Opened All the Portals Wide', 'You and I', and 'Love Everlasting', and according to Daniel Rankin, 'because of Kate Chopin's local importance as an author these songs had considerable popularity as program pieces in St. Louis for many years' (Rankin, 113).

The local press continued to seek Chopin's opinions on literary matters. In early December of 1900, the *St. Louis Republic* promised that the question 'What books shall I buy just now?' would be answered by Chopin, who would address the increased prominence of Western literature. Despite Chopin's decade-long reputation as a Southern regionalist, the *Republic* now assigned her to this category, describing her as 'a St. Louis woman who has won a distinct place as a member of this same Western literary guild' (Toth, 379). In 1894, Chopin had written scathing denouncements of both the Western Association of Writers and Hamlin Garland's prediction that the West would become a major literary center, but by 9 December 1900, when the *Republic* published her 'Development of the Literary West: A Review', she had changed her mind. She opens the article by noting the impact of Bret Harte's story 'The Luck of Roaring Camp', first published in 1868:

> It was the first resounding note. It reached across the continent and startled the Academists on the Atlantic Coast, that is to say, in Boston. They opened their eyes and ears at the sound and awoke to the fact that there might some day be a literary West. Something different from the East, of course, and alien, but to be taken seriously, to be observed and considered.
>
> (*KCPP*, 223)

For Chopin, the origins of an authentic Western literary tradition could be traced to the work of the Jesuit missionary Pierre Jean De Smet, who worked among the Indians of the Northwest in the middle decades of the nineteenth century and who published several collections of sketches of native life in the 1840s and 1850s. De Smet, Chopin writes, wrote with 'simplicity and directness', and 'when one has read [his work] there is left upon the mind a well-traced picture of the early West, by no means devoid of atmosphere and color' (*KCPP*, 223).

Her own contemporaries, Chopin asserts, wrote about a different West than had either Harte or De Smet, a region where 'mining camps are not so very far from the police station, and the bucking broncho [sic] is colliding with the automobile'. The 'intensely interesting story' of this developing region was being told by 'hundreds of men and women' with 'keen … artistic perception', and although this fiction sometimes suffered from a 'lack of reserve' or 'tawdriness', these deficiencies were balanced by its 'vigor'. Of the dozen or so writers of these 'hundreds' that Chopin singled out for special mention, only a few – including Mark Twain and Hamlin Garland – are familiar to readers a hundred years later; while she has praise for the others, she also identifies some of the reasons why their work was devalued by twentieth-century critics. Of Mary Hallock Foote, author of such novels as *The Chosen Valley* (1892) and *Coeur d'Alene* (1894), Chopin notes the 'pleasure' she has taken in reading her work, which has 'a fine literary quality', but she also comments that the novels are 'damaged somewhat by a too conventional romanticism' (*KCPP*, 224). Owen Wister, whose collections of stories included *Red Men and White* (1896) and *Lim McClean* (1898), was 'greatly liked', Chopin wrote, but she detected something false in his writing: 'he gives the impression of a stagy fellow with an eye on his audience in the East' (*KCPP*, 224). Of the St Louis-born novelist Winston Churchill, Chopin remarked that he had had 'marvelous success with his historical romance', referring to Churchill's 1899 *Richard Carvel*, set in the Revolutionary War period. Chopin further noted that Churchill was said to be working on a novel 'depicting life in St. Louis during the days of Lincoln and Grant' (*KCPP*, 225), and in fact his Civil War novel *The Crisis* was published the next year, but twentieth-century readers were to place greater value on such grimly realistic Civil War accounts as Stephen Crane's *The Red Badge of Courage* (1895) than on Churchill's historical novels. Chopin's most unreserved praise went to writers who depicted Midwestern small-town and rural life with the realism and detail that she had employed in her Louisiana stories. Octave Thanet was the pseudonym of Alice French, who was born in the same year as Chopin in Massachusetts, but who lived in and wrote about Iowa and Arkansas. 'Sincerity', Chopin felt, marked Thanet's short stories, the most recent collection of which was *The Captured Dream* (1899):

> Her heart is essentially with the plain, everyday people. We meet her characters everywhere – crowding the department stores on bargain days, hurrying with bundles through the streets; thronging the lodge meetings and church sociables. She must walk about our Middle Western towns with her mental notebook open, chuckling to herself.
>
> (*KCPP*, 224)

But the writer who 'most subtly reflects the western spirit', in Chopin's view, was Hamlin Garland. Although Garland had been 'guilty of inexcusable crudities in handling men and women', Chopin greatly admired his depictions of the upper Midwestern landscape, with its 'bleak rainfall; the still and killing cold and great winding sheets of snow; the flaming splendor of the sun' (*KCPP*, 225).

As the new century began, Chopin's household included four of her children and a black servant. Her sons George and Fred had moved to boarding houses and were pursuing careers – George as a doctor and Fred as, in succession, a salesman, an insurance agent, and a clerk. In June of 1902, her oldest son, Jean, was married and moved to his own home in St Louis. As the size of her household diminished, so too did the energy with which Chopin had approached her intellectual and social lives and her writing career. In the fall of 1903, she sold her Morgan Street house and rented a newer house on McPherson Avenue, near Jean and his wife, who were expecting their first child. Fortunately, the new house was well-supplied with bedrooms; her son Fred decided to move back home, and when neither his wife nor his child survived childbirth, so did Jean, with a nervous breakdown that required his mother's care and support. Chopin herself, at 53, was no longer in robust health, and she had virtually quit writing. The year before, she had made a will, leaving her property and possessions to her children, and after 1902 she recorded no further royalties from her writing.

But as 1904 approached, there was much excitement in St Louis as the long-anticipated World's Fair prepared to open in Forest Park. Envisioned since the mid-1890s, the Fair had been scheduled to coincide with and celebrate the centennial of the Louisiana Purchase in 1803, but there had been numerous delays. When Chopin wrote to her sister-in-law Marie Breazeale on 4 February 1902, Marie's husband, Phanor, had just been elected to Congress, and Chopin hoped that travel to Washington might bring them through St Louis. The World's Fair would be an additional reason for such a visit, but Chopin expressed exasperation at the fact that it would not open when planned: 'You must have that Womens [sic] Federation send you up to our Worlds [sic] Fair. *It isn't going to be next year*, notwithstanding the assurances of the officers, not unless they can get some spooks and fairy godmothers to do the work for them' (*KCPP*, 214). When the Fair, officially known as the Louisiana Purchase Exposition, finally opened on 30 April 1904, Kate Chopin was one of its most enthusiastic visitors, traveling the few blocks from her home to Forest Park nearly every day to hear the music of Scott Joplin and inspect the new inventions that such fairs invariably featured, such as radios and electric clocks. On 20 August, after a long day at the Fair, Chopin suffered an apparent brain hemorrhage, and died on 22 August.

In spite of the decline in her literary productivity, Chopin was still a highly regarded local celebrity, and the news of her death made the front pages of some St Louis newspapers. While the articles praised both Chopin's social graces and her intellect, most of them spoke of her as the author of short stories about Louisiana life, and paid scant and sometimes awkward attention to *The Awakening*. The *Globe-Democrat* merely referred to it as a 'fascinating novel', and the *New Orleans Times-Democrat* identified *Bayou Folk* and *A Night in Acadie* as Chopin's major achievements, and dealt with *The Awakening* cautiously: 'This more sustained effort, while esteemed a success, did not overshadow the two preceding volumes, and it is still to the latter that the discriminating reader turns in a study of the best work of their author.' The writer for the *Boston Evening Transcript* agreed, noting that 'while [*The Awakening*] met approval, seemingly it did not bring forth the true talent of the author as had "Bayou Folk" and "A Night in Acadie"' (Toth, 394). Even the testimonials by two of Chopin's St Louis friends serve as reminders that women writers were judged as much by their personal as by their intellectual qualities. The conservative Alexander De Menil wrote in *The Hesperian* that Chopin had none of the 'manners, airs, affectations and eccentricities' of the 'blue stocking'. Rather than writing with 'serious purposes', Chopin was 'simply a bright, unaffected, warm-hearted, unpresuming and *womanly* woman'. The far more liberal William Reedy, in his *Mirror* article, twice called Chopin a 'genius', but even Reedy remarked that she managed to attain this stature 'without sacrificing the comradeship of her children'. And Reedy joined others in characterizing Chopin as 'a depictor of Creole life and character in the Sunny South' (Toth, 395). Thus, obituaries and memorial notices, like the assessments of contemporary critics, constructed a version of Chopin's place in literary history that would endure for more than 50 years.

Kate Chopin was buried in the family plot in Calvary Cemetery in St Louis on 24 August 1904. The grave marker bears only her name and the dates of her birth (wrongly identified as 1851) and death. *The Awakening* was reprinted in 1906, and then disappeared again until Per Seyersted edited *The Complete Works* for publication in 1969.

Notes

1. Peggy Skaggs, 'The Boy's Quest in Kate Chopin's "A Vocation and a Voice",' *Critical Essays on Kate Chopin*, ed. Alice Hall Petry. New York: G. K. Hall, 1996, pp. 129–33.
2. Barbara C. Ewell, *Kate Chopin*. New York: Ungar, 1986, p. 160.

Further Reading

Primary works

The Complete Works of Kate Chopin (CW). Ed. Per Seyersted. Baton Rouge: Louisiana State University Press, 1969. Includes nearly 100 of Chopin's short stories, 20 poems, several essays, and the texts of *At Fault* and *The Awakening*.

A Kate Chopin Miscellany (KCM). Eds Per Seyersted and Emily Toth. Natchitoches: Northwestern State University Press, 1979. Includes portions of several unfinished stories, 26 poems, the 1867–70 and 1894 diaries, assorted correspondence and essays, a chronological listing of all of Chopin's extant writings, and a chronological bibliography of secondary work, including reviews.

The Kate Chopin Companion (KCC). Ed. Thomas Bonner, Jr. New York: Greenwood Press, 1988. Includes Chopin's translations of French stories by Adrien Vely and Guy de Maupassant.

Kate Chopin's Private Papers (KCPP). Eds Emily Toth and Per Seyersted. Bloomington: Indiana University Press, 1998. In addition to previously published diaries and letters, includes Chopin's manuscript account books, several rediscovered short stories, some fragments of uncompleted stories, and a copy of Chopin's will.

The Awakening is available in several editions, including a Penguin Classics edition, a Norton Critical Edition, and a volume in the Case Studies in Comtemporary Criticism series from Bedford/St. Martin's.

Secondary works

(a) Bibliographies

Bonner, Thomas, Jr, 'Kate Chopin: an Annotated Bibliography', *Bulletin of Bibliography*, 32 (July–September 1975), pp. 101–5.

Inge, Tonette Bond. 'Kate Chopin'. In Maurice Duke, Jackson R. Bryer and M. Thomas Inge, eds, *American Women Writers:*

Bibliographical Essays. Westport, CT: Greenwood Press, 1983, pp. 47–69.

Springer, Marlene, *Edith Wharton and Kate Chopin: a Reference Guide*. Boston: G. K. Hall, 1976.

Springer, Marlene, 'Kate Chopin: a Reference Guide Updated'. *Resources for American Literary Study*, 11 (1981), pp. 25–42.

(b) Biographies

Rankin, Daniel S., *Kate Chopin and Her Creole Stories*. Philadelphia: University of Pennsylvania Press, 1932. The earliest biography, based in part on interviews with several of Chopin's children and some documents subsequently lost, Rankin's book perpetuated some myths about Chopin's life and career, and shows a decided preference for her 'local-color' stories.

Seyersted, Per, *Kate Chopin: a Critical Biography*. Baton Rouge: Louisiana State University Press, 1969. Written by the scholar largely responsible for the resurgence of interest in Chopin's work, the book presents Chopin as a 'long-neglected pioneer' in American fiction.

Toth, Emily, *Kate Chopin*. New York: William Morrow, 1990. The most comprehensive biography to date, Toth's study is extensively researched and corrects some misconceptions about her life and work.

Toth, Emily, *Unveiling Kate Chopin*. Jackson: University Press of Mississippi, 1999. Published to coincide with the centennial of the publication of *The Awakening*, this is a shorter, more informal biography that does not supercede Toth's 1990 biography.

(c) General studies and collections of essays

Ballenger, Grady *et al.*, eds, *Perspectives on Kate Chopin: Proceedings from the Kate Chopin International Conference*. Natchitoches: Northwestern State University Press, 1992.

Bloom, Harold, ed., *Kate Chopin*. New York: Chelsea House, 1987.

Boren, Lynda S. and Sara de Saussure Davis, eds, *Kate Chopin Reconsidered: Beyond the Bayou*. Baton Rouge: Louisiana State University Press, 1992.

Ewell, Barbara C., *Kate Chopin*. New York: Ungar, 1986.

Hoder-Salmon, Marilyn, *Kate Chopin's* The Awakening: *Screenplay as Interpretation*. Gainesville: University Press of Florida, 1992.

Koloski, Bernard J., ed., *Approaches to Teaching Kate Chopin's* The Awakening. New York: Modern Language Association of America, 1988.

Martin, Wendy, ed., *New Essays on* The Awakening. Cambridge: Cambridge University Press, 1988.

Petry, Alice Hall, ed., *Critical Essays on Kate Chopin*. New York: G. K. Hall, 1996.

Skaggs, Peggy, *Kate Chopin*. Boston: G. K. Hall, 1985.

Index